"So you think what happened tonight was pretty tame? What the hell do you do for excitement?"

Jake's darkened visage and outraged tone made me laugh. "You have a point. But I've been trying to make sense of this—"

"So you've been overthinking it," he finished for me. "It's simple, really. Either we're dealing with a real psychopath…or a real vampire."

I laughed again. "Yeah, right."

But he'd said it with a straight face. So Jake was either into black humor, or he was a little loony, I thought, wanting it to be the first one. Of course he had to be joking. Normally I would respond with a wisecrack rather than a laugh, but tonight I couldn't manage it. Whether or not I'd needed help, he'd really looked after me earlier.

I was grateful to him.

And strangely attracted

Dear Reader,

Like the fast-paced holiday season, Silhouette Bombshell is charged with energy, and we're thrilled to bring you an unforgettable December reading experience. Our strong, sexy, savvy women will have you cheering, gasping and turning pages to see what happens next!

Let *USA TODAY* bestselling author Lindsay McKenna sweep you away to Peru in *Sister of Fortune,* part of the SISTERS OF THE ARK miniseries. This military heroine must retrieve a sacred artifact from dangerous hands. The last thing she needs is a sexy man she can't trust—too bad she has to work with one!

Check out Debra Webb's *Justice,* the latest in the ATHENA FORCE continuity series. Police lieutenant Kayla Ryan will risk everything to find her murdered friend's long-lost child and bring down an enemy who is closer than she ever suspected....

In *Night Life,* by Katherine Garbera, a former spy turned mother and wife finds herself drawn back into clandestine games when her former agency calls her in to catch a rogue agent—her estranged husband.

And don't miss Patricia Rosemoor's *Hot Case,* the story of a detective who enters her twin sister's dark world of wannabe vampires—and maybe the real thing—to find out why dead bodies are disappearing almost before her eyes.

As an editor, I am often asked what I'm looking for in a Bombshell novel. Well, *I* want to know what *you're* looking for as a reader. Please send your comments to me, c/o Silhouette Books, 233 Broadway Suite 1001, New York, NY 10279.

Best wishes,

Natashya Wilson
Associate Senior Editor, Silhouette Bombshell

Please address questions and book requests to:
Silhouette Reader Service
U.S.: 3010 Walden Ave., P.O. Box 1325, Buffalo, NY 14269
Canadian: P.O. Box 609, Fort Erie, Ont. L2A 5X3

PATRICIA ROSEMOOR

HOT CASE

Silhouette®

BOMBSHELL™

Published by Silhouette Books

America's Publisher of Contemporary Romance

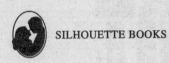 SILHOUETTE BOOKS

ISBN 0-373-51338-0

HOT CASE

Copyright © 2004 by Patricia Rosemoor

Printed in U.S.A.

PATRICIA ROSEMOOR

has been a bombshell for as long as she can remember. Whether dreaming or playing with other kids, she was always the hero of her own fantasies. She was the Lone Ranger and Robin Hood and Superman...rather, female versions of her childhood heroes. Now she gets to invent new female heroes. The writing life doesn't get much better than this. Drop her a line and tell her what you think—Patricia@PatriciaRosemoor.com. Or use snail mail—Patricia Rosemoor, P.O. Box 578297, Chicago, IL 60657-8297. You can visit her on the Web at www.PatriciaRosemoor.com.

Thanks to Tina Raffaele for everything Goth,
and to Officer Susan Heneghan for everything cop.

Also thanks to Sergeant David Case,
and an officer who wishes to remain anonymous,
for additional details about police procedure.

Prologue

Feathers of fog curled around the hood of my Camaro as I crossed the Chicago River on my way home. It was one of those weird spring nights when the downtown area looked ghostly, half-lit skyscrapers rising out of the mists like skeletons.

I was totally exhausted after a long workday and what had felt like a longer family get-together with my mom and sister. Stifling a yawn, I tried to ignore my cell phone when it trilled and politely informed me, "You have an incoming call.... You have an incoming call.... You have an incoming..."

I had a real love-hate relationship with technology.

I checked the caller ID and sighed wearily as I flipped open my phone. "It's after midnight. This had better be good, Junior." Junior Diaz was one of my most reliable informants and the only reason I'd bothered answering.

"Where you at?"

Nice opening. As if this was a social call or something. "I'm on my way home. What's up?"

"You gotta see for yourself, Detective."

"See what?"

"The body. This girl…she ain't got no blood left. It's all been drained outta her."

"And you know this how?"

"I saw…"

A muffled sound on the other end sounded like Junior heaving his guts.

"Where are you?"

It turned out he was maybe a half mile from my present location, west and north of the Loop.

"And don't you call for no backup," Junior gasped. "My deal's with you, no one else."

"I'll be right there. Alone," I promised. "Don't go anywhere."

In a little more than two minutes, I made the intersection in an area anchored to the expressway. Not really a neighborhood, just a couple of blocks of red bungalows and two-flats with little to recommend them. I turned down a side street, went a quarter of a block and turned again. Then I slammed on the brakes.

My headlights cut into the fog-shrouded alley. I flicked on the brights but still didn't see anything.

No Junior Diaz.

What was his game? I'd told him not to move.

Was he simply lying low until he was sure I was alone? I grabbed my cell and speed-dialed him.

"Hey," his recorded voice grunted. "Gimme reason to call you back."

Part of me really, really wanted to go home and forget he'd called at all. But another part of me—the cop who wouldn't let go of a lead—made me look hard enough to pierce the darkness and the blanket of fog.

Something lay in the middle of the alley. Junior or this girl supposedly with no blood?

Only one way to find out.

Cursing under my breath, I removed my weapon from its holster under my navy blazer, grabbed the combination lantern-flashlight from the floor in back and cautiously opened the door. This wasn't a particularly bad area, and I wasn't afraid, but it never paid to let down my guard.

"Junior?" I called out, turning and swinging the light around to make certain there were no nasty surprises waiting for me. "You there?"

No answer. My stomach knotting, I moved toward the lump in the middle of the alley. As if the fog decided to cooperate, it rolled off the body and framed it, giving me a picture I would never forget.

She was sprawled across the alley pavement, her skirt up around her waist, panties shredded, legs spread and bruised—she'd obviously been sexually assaulted. I moved closer, my eye caught by an intricate design high on her outer thigh—a winged gargoyle. A tattoo. Even in the dim light I could see how young she was. A teenager. Just a kid. Her jaw looked as if it had been dislocated, one of her eyes rolled partly out of its socket and an ear was half ripped off.

She'd fought her attacker like hell, I thought. She'd fought and lost.

Her caramel skin was ash-pale, and I knew a person's skin color came from the oxygen in the blood. Her body hadn't been oxygenated in a while. Even so, I set the lantern down next to her and felt for a pulse. Her flesh was icy against my fingertips. Nothing moved inside of her.

I looked for wounds and on the inside of her arm found a nasty slash that severed the median cubital vein—the primary site used to draw blood by medical personnel. Her arm was smeared with red and the gashed flesh lay open. If she were still alive, it would have been a gusher, but it wasn't bleeding because her heart wasn't beating and maintaining blood pressure. No other wounds that I could see. Only that gash, meaning she must have died of blood loss.

The problem was…where had all the blood gone?

I flashed the light around through the fog, but there were only a few splotches on the ground near her arm. The short hairs at the back of my neck rose, and I tried to tell myself that this wasn't the primary site. That she had been killed elsewhere and dumped here. Only it didn't look that way.

Junior had said he'd seen her being drained of blood….

Where the hell was he?

I looked all around me again, but the only thing I spotted was a book bag tumbled on its side as if it had been tossed in the struggle. Fog rolled over it and swallowed it whole.

I heard a muffled noise, maybe a garbage can hitting a garage door.

"Junior, are you here?"

No response. No nothing.

Continuing to call out for him would be futile, so as the fog drifted over the body once more, I checked for my cell phone but couldn't find it. I raced back to my car where I'd left it. Since I was off duty, I didn't have a radio to call in to dispatch, so I dialed 911.

"This is Detective Shelley Caldwell, Area 4 Violent Crimes Unit," I said, squeezing my ears against a sudden weird, high-pitched noise. What the hell was wrong with the damn cell phone? I'd never heard anything like this before. I raised my voice as I settled back into the seat. The fog was too thick to see anything anyway. "Call Dispatch. I have a body…"

Or I'd had a body.

By the time they arrived on scene a few minutes later—uniforms followed by a case supervisor and CSI—the fog had lifted, leaving me with a few bloodstains, a book bag and nothing else.

The dead girl's body had vanished.

Chapter 1

Three months later...

He was a hell of a lot bigger than me. Bigger and frickin' scary-looking.

With lightning speed, I grabbed his wrist and twisted, and before he could turn, I used my free arm—palm to forearm—to slam him hard in the back below the shoulder.

Bam! He went down.

As I pushed a knee in his back to keep him there, the room went up for grabs.

"Woo-hoo!"

"Sweet!"

"Yo, Jackson, I thought you was a tough guy," someone said with a snicker.

I climbed off him. "At ease!" I commanded. "You'll all get your turn."

An embarrassed Gary Jackson quickly rose from the floor without looking at me. I couldn't spare him a moment's pity. He wouldn't get any out on the street.

"That's what we call rolling the ball," I told the recruits who'd just reported to the gym. "If you do it right, it works, no matter how big the suspect."

That's why I'd picked Jackson—I might be tall and strong but he beat me on both counts, and I'd wanted to make a point and fast.

The regular gym instructor was out on sick leave, and because I was PSS certified—the Police Safety System, which combined moves from several different martial arts—and because I was a novice instructor at the training academy, I'd been pulled from my assignment with new detectives to teach control tactics to recruits.

I'd been one of them about nine years ago. That's when I'd joined the Chicago Police Department in hopes of following in my mother's footsteps.

But that's another story.

The story of the moment was that I was underwhelmed by the work I'd been doing for the past month. It took a certain talent and patience to be an instructor—traits that I didn't have. Just as it took a particular talent and yes, guts, to be a detective.

That was me—Detective Shelley Caldwell, formerly Violent Crimes Unit, Area 4. Now I was an instructor at the training academy, and the sucky situation wasn't one I could easily correct. If ever. I should have been hip-deep in investigations, identifying offenders and getting them off the streets of my city. That was what I was really best at—using my brains to solve crimes rather than brawn.

"All right, it's your turn," I said to the room of more than thirty kids in their early twenties, mostly fresh-faced and without a clue as to what they were getting into.

Most of them were just out of college, idealistic, and few of them knew the reality of the streets…or the hell they would be in for during training, courtesy of all the instructors. That was standard CPD practice—breaking them down like the army did to boot-camp soldiers and then building them up to be cops tough enough to survive the mean streets. They wouldn't all make it through the training.

I told the class, "Time to pair up and take turns being the offender and the uniform."

"You want us to do what you just did with Jackson?" one of them asked.

"To start," I said. And then demonstrated again, with another recruit, this time in slow motion, step by step. "Your turn." I picked up the stopwatch from a cord that hung from my neck and shouted, "You'll have thirty seconds to get your partner on the ground…starting…now!"

I kept an eagle eye on the pair-ups working on mats, mostly guys but a few young females with male partners, as well. They were dressed alike no matter their gender—navy shorts and gray T-shirts with their names on the back, so I could keep track of who was who.

Recruits fell like sacks of potatoes in half the time allotted. Good. A few more seconds and everyone who was supposed to be down was down.

But before I could blow my whistle, a female cry got my attention. I whipped around to see a slender brunette on the floor beneath the knee of her decidedly bigger partner, one Fred Guerro. She started sobbing and Guerro popped right up, his expression disconcerted.

"Sorry, I didn't mean to hurt you," he mumbled.

The name across the female recruit's back identified her as Lara Morris.

"What's the problem, Morris?" I asked.

She turned big blue eyes wet with tears toward me. "He was too rough! I think he bruised me."

I sighed. This one wanted to be a cop? Cops can't cry, not on the job. He bruised her? Guys on the street could do a lot worse to a woman who couldn't handle herself.

No pity, I reminded myself.

Pity could get her killed.

I gave Guerro an exaggerated disapproving expression and said, "Shame on you, Guerro! You hurt Morris. What's wrong with you?"

Then I turned to Morris, and for one heart-stopping moment she reminded me of my sister, Silke, all innocence and trust. But I wasn't looking at my twin. This was a wanna-be cop. A woman who had chosen a tough, sometimes unforgiving profession.

So, my voice sweet and solicitous, I said, "A gang

member would never hurt you, Morris. No, no. He'd just hold his gun to your head and blow out your frickin' brains!"

Lara Morris was the first recruit to quit.

After teaching a second morning class, I entered the cafeteria and filled my tray with more food than I could possibly eat. But it was moments like this that I ate to assuage that wretched feeling that told me I'd failed. Food took away the edge of disappointment, but then I had to run a couple of extra miles to work it off. A recruit quitting was not a big deal, but on the first day and because of me? I took it personally, as if it was another strike against me.

"So how's it hanging, baby?" Al Washington took a seat at my table.

Al and I had worked the street together way back when. He'd been hard on me, but he'd also been fair. One of the really good guys. His kinky hair had grayed, and his gaunt dark face had started to sag. He was getting close to that potential twenty-year retirement, which in my mind would be a big loss to the department if he took it. He was a good cop. A great cop. I'd respected him when we'd worked together and had even more respect for him as an instructor. He was one of those officers who had both the talent and patience to be an instructor, and I couldn't help wishing I were more like him.

"I'm surviving." I forced a smile.

"Such enthusiasm."

"I'll get into it."

"Sounds like you'd rather get into something different."

"Yeah, well..."

"No law against you asking to be sent back."

Go back. Could I really? I'd made detective nearly two years before and because of one case I'd lost my post. You would think my dedication would have been enough to earn some respect. Instead it had nearly ruined my career.

"I don't know, Al. I just have to get used to the change is all."

"Uh-huh."

"Really," I mumbled, stuffing my mouth with another forkful of food.

He knew me too well to believe me. Not that I was admitting to anything.

"I suppose you'll want to say hi to the district commander before she leaves."

"Mom?" My mother, District Commander Rena Caldwell, was one of the highest-ranking women in the department. I frowned and swallowed. "She's here?"

"In a meeting with Aniceto. I saw her go into his office a while ago."

Commander Maurice Aniceto was in charge of the training academy. Considering he was out of the crime loop, I wondered what business Mom had with him. Curiosity nagged at me all through lunch and the afternoon while I taught another session in the gym. Thankfully I got through that one without anyone quitting on me.

But the whole time, my instincts were on alert and

I couldn't help but wonder if my future was some-how involved. Mom had pushed me to make detec-tive. I knew she didn't like me working at the training academy. Not that it had been my choice. She and Aniceto were on the same level in the CPD hierarchy, and they undoubtedly did each other favors. That's the way the department rocked.

So, had she asked him for a favor today? Involv-ing *my* future?

I was showered and dressed and on my way out when I spotted Mom coming out of Aniceto's office. As usual, she was wearing her uniform rather than street clothes—her choice, not a mandate—and she'd scraped her lush chestnut hair, so like my own, back into a twist.

Pulse humming, I hurried to catch up to her. "Hey, Mom!"

When she turned, she didn't so much as smile at her own daughter. "Detective."

The way she said it was meant to remind me I that on CPD ground I was just another cop, not her daughter. "Can I speak to you for a moment, Com-mander?"

"Certainly. You can walk me out to my car."

I waited until we were out the door, then asked, "So what's the big deal? Why were you here all af-ternoon?"

"A meeting. I'm not sure I like your tone."

"Are you speaking to the detective or to your daughter?"

"Either one." Mom stopped and faced me. Her shoes had big chunky heels that put her on my five-foot-ten level. The skin around her gray eyes was furrowed. "Respect goes two ways."

I know, I know. If I wanted it, I not only had to earn it, but I also had to give it. How many times had I heard that? Only I gave respect where it was due. I swear. I respected the hell out of Mom. Dad died on the job, when Silke and I were seven. Afterward, Mom changed drastically. Suddenly becoming the head of the household, she had taken responsibility superseriously. She'd concentrated on working and making her way up in the ranks so she could give us everything we ever needed.

"Okay, let me rephrase that," I said. "I knew you were here and was wondering why you didn't stop to say hi."

"I wasn't here to see you. I also wasn't here to talk about you, if that's what you were thinking," she informed me. "Commander Aniceto and I had department business to discuss. There's been buzz about some cult activity in the area, and I was consulting with him."

Cult activity?

That made sense, I thought, my interest suddenly picking up at the word *cult*.

While the academy was its own district in the sense that it had its own commander, it sat in the middle of Mom's district. So of course she would take advantage of Aniceto's background. Several years before taking this job, he'd been a detective in the gang units with a specialty in cults.

But before I could prod Mom about this cult activity, she asked, "So how's the job?"

"I had a recruit quit on me today."

"Good."

"It doesn't feel good."

"Would it feel better if the recruit became a cop and then got hurt or killed in the line of duty? We can't make people into what they're not."

So why was she always trying to do that with me? I wondered. "You're right. She didn't have what it takes."

"She?" Mom nodded. "It's hard being a woman on the force."

Didn't I know that. It had to be even harder for Mom, considering she was one of the few women who'd made it big in a predominantly male field. Only she'd sacrificed something on the way to the top. She'd forgotten that Silke and I had needed a mom who would be there to tuck us in at night, someone who would soothe our hurts when we were kids.

"Have you spoken to your sister yet?" Mom asked.

Ah, so suddenly we were related. I knew she wanted me to counsel Silke, to see if I couldn't help my twin figure out a professional path that would make sense to our mother.

"Silke listens to you, Shelley. You're closer to her than anyone."

"I don't want to live her life for her."

For one brief second an unfamiliar expression crossed Mom's still beautiful face. She seemed unsettled...guilty...and then her expression cleared. Still, the fact that she might be affected hit home.

"All right, I'll talk to her," I said in a rush. "No guarantees, though."

Mom nodded, and I swore I heard relief in her "Good. You'll report back to me, then."

The last part ruined my generous mood—it sounded too much like her giving me an order. Not like my mom, but like my superior. I gave her a non-committal nod in return and we went our separate ways, me wondering once more what it would feel like to have a normal family life.

A spin in my red Camaro convertible chilled me out. Though I lived close enough to the academy that I could be home in ten minutes, I took the long way via the expressway and let the power of the engine hum through my veins. The sports car was my one vice and driving it made me feel better. I'd always wanted a Corvette, but even a used one had been too rich for my bank account, so I'd settled for a secondhand Camaro instead.

I was in better spirits by the time I got home to my cats. I opened cans of food for them and nuked a dinner for me. The open kitchen area was actually decent—nice wood cabinets and fairly new appliances—but unfortunately, I'd never learned to cook.

My one-bedroom conversion condo was a rental in a recently gentrified area. Some yuppie bought it as an investment, not to live in but to rent out. Fine by me. All my life, I'd lived in city apartments, and being able to afford a nice space like this one kept me from feeling deprived. Being a homeowner sounded like too much work anyway.

I ate my dinner while watching one of those reality programs about cold cases. Most of those solved were years or even decades old, and new technology like DNA testing got investigators evidence that had been lacking before. An unsolved murder was never officially closed, but if there were no clues, no witnesses, nothing to go on, it fell to the side in light of more productive cases.

I got a vicarious high from watching old murders being solved. This one was about a woman who'd supposedly died in a fire twenty years before. Her body had been found beneath the building's ruins, and she'd had a bullet in her head. The investigation had revealed the fire had been arson, intended to cover up the murder.

Every time I watched one of these programs, I thought of LaTonya Sanford—my last case as a working detective—and wished I could have put some closure to it. The girl's mother and little sisters deserved to know why she'd disappeared. Sometimes I even dreamed about nailing the killer. About seeing that justice was done. I'd suspected possible cult connections because of the bizarre way she had been killed, but no one had believed me. No one in the violent crimes squad had been able to wrap his or her mind around the concept of a young woman being completely drained of blood.

I could still see her poor, lifeless body sprawled across that alley. I still felt sick about letting her down. Unfortunately, Junior Diaz had disappeared, too, so I'd had no support.

As I had done so many times over the past months, I slipped a tattered folder out of a file drawer and threw it on the low table in front of the couch.

I considered the folder for a moment before opening it and spreading out the materials across the table. I shouldn't have this folder. I knew that. But I'd never taken the originals out of the murder book that I'd made up despite the fact that I was told there was no case. They were still safely back at the area office. What I had were copies of the official materials. Well, some of the stuff was. My reports, primarily. I had other things in here, too. Personal research, mostly on cults. I hadn't turned up anything shady on LaTonya herself, convincing me that she was a true victim.

I stared at a copy of her school ID blown up to life size. She stared back at me, her dark eyes accusing.

No body, no case, no one cared. No one but me.

My lieutenant had indulged me for several days after the incident, during which I'd become obsessed with finding an answer as to what had happened to her. But my co-workers had rolled their eyes at my continuing to investigate a murder without a corpse. Detectives weren't assigned partners. They were given case loads and the opportunity to mix it up themselves. I helped someone with his cases—he helped me with mine. Only no one would. They'd laughed at me instead.

And then the ax had fallen. I'd just begun researching cults when I'd been cut off at the knees. Not only had I been ordered not to pursue something that wasn't even a case, but I'd also been given administrative leave for the rest of the week and then had been ordered into psych evaluation.

While I'd been powerless, Junior's body had been

found in a garbage can a few alleys over from where
I'd gone to meet him. Mom had given me the
skinny—just about every bone in Junior's scrawny
little body had been broken. Speculation was he'd
been murdered because of the witness he'd given up
on a multiple homicide he'd helped me solve a few
months before the Sanford girl died.

I wasn't so sure that was true. I figured his death
was somehow connected to LaTonya Sanford's
death. But by then, my instincts meant nothing to the
department.

As a rubber-gun officer, I'd been assigned to the
callback center, answering phones and writing up
dozens of reports a day until, after weeks of probing
my mind, the therapist had declared me sane. His
professional opinion? I was a straight arrow and ded-
icated to the job, but I was also hard, tense and brit-
tle and had temporarily snapped from too much
stress. He'd also concluded that I would be no danger to myself or to the department...unless that kind
of stress built up in me again, of course.

Undoubtedly the reason I hadn't been allowed
back at Area 4. I'd been shoved into the training
academy, where—should I become delusional
again—at least I would be off the streets.

I hated it, but there was nothing I could do about
it.

And what about the victim?

LaTonya Sanford hadn't been considered a case at
all, at least not a homicide. She'd been deemed a
missing person, a teenage runaway, and since she was
seventeen, no official effort had been made to find her.

I knew she was dead, though, as cold a case as they came.

I replaced the research in the folder but left it on the table. Mostly I tried to forget about something over which I had no control, but the mention of cult activity earlier had stirred up my emotions. I shut off the television before the next segment started. I jumped into a hot shower in hopes the needles of water would beat the blues out of me. After pulling on pajamas, I climbed into bed. I wasn't used to the physical stuff I'd done earlier, not to mention that stress exhausted me.

No sooner were my eyes closed when I drifted off....

She sprawls across the alley, her skirt around her waist. The winged gargoyle high on her outer thigh grins at me. Her jaw is dislocated...ear ripped...eye rolled out of its socket onto her cheek.

"So young. Just a kid," I mourn.

Suddenly, she sits up and with her good eye stares at me accusingly. "Your fault," she whispers, the sound raw. "You left me...lost me...sealed my fate..."

I sat up with a gasp, my heart pounding. It took me a minute to get my bearings. I checked the clock—2:12 a.m.

Great.

The middle of the night and now I was awake.

I'd had all of three hours of sleep. I rarely slept through the night anymore.

Disturbing the cats, who'd snuggled down next to

me, I rose and paced off the vestiges of the nightmare. At this rate, I was going to wear out the carpet.

Wanting something to get my mind off bad things, I fetched a DVD I'd rented. I loved mysteries and suspense stories whether books or movies. My twin went for the woo-woo stuff like those *Evil Dead* movies she forced me to watch with her. A guy going after zombies with a chain saw…right…but I guess everyone deserves a guilty pleasure.

Mine would be watching a romantic suspense-thriller, maybe because it had been so long since I'd had a romantic experience myself. Dating had been difficult enough when I'd been in uniform. But once I'd made detective, my life had no longer been my own. And since then…well, who would want to hook up with a cop some considered a fruit loop?

While I was setting up the DVD, I got the first prickling along the back of my neck. The uneasy feeling had something to do with Silke, but I wasn't interested.

Silke and I were identical twins with a bizarre mental connection that she played on—one of those inexplicable twin things that used to freak me out. I knew a lot of people would love to have a psychic connection with someone. Not me. I'd rather focus on other realities, so now I just ignored it. When we were kids, we messed around with the connection sometimes. We also fooled people by trading places. But as we grew up, we grew apart. Matured.

Well, at least I had.

What could you say about a grown woman of

nearly thirty who colored her chestnut hair bloodred, whitened her pale complexion with makeup
and smudged her green eyes with enough dark
stuff to look like a raccoon? That's what my sister
had been doing lately between gigs on stage.
While I earned a degree in criminal justice, my
twin got one in theater and started using the name
Silke instead of Sylvie because it sounded more
theatrical. Though she got paying parts once in a
while, she mostly worked as a waitress, lately at a
Goth bar.

The prickling intensified.

Flashes of a couple kissing on screen got my interest and when Play was highlighted, I hit Enter to
start the movie. I flopped onto the couch and the cats
joined me. Sarge settled near my neck, his whiskers
tickling my ear as he purred into it, while Cadet
stood with two paws on my leg until I scooped her
into my side and got her to lie down, half on my leg.

The movie had just started with a couple in tongue
lock when my pulse shot up and it suddenly became
hard to take a breath. My physical reactions had
nothing to do with the on-screen kiss, though. What
I was experiencing wasn't romantic. It was fear
mixed with some other heart-palpitating emotion.

"Silke, what the hell?" I murmured as both Sarge
and Cadet, obviously sensing something weird was
going on, moved away from my body heat to stare
at me from a safe distance.

Normally, I was able to ignore Silke's signals, but
these were so strong they got my attention.

The phone rang and I snatched it up. "Silke?"

"Shell," she said, "something awful happened tonight."

"How awful?" I tried to keep my voice even when I was feeling anything but. This wasn't going to be good news, whatever it was. "What?"

"One of the Goth girls says she found Thora Nelson on the street under the tracks…dead!"

Chapter 2

Silke Caldwell parked her car in a well-lit area on Randolph Street in front of the building that housed Heart of Darkness, the bar where she worked, just as her sister had ordered. The bar was closed and the area was dark but for the streetlights.

So where was Shelley? she wondered, trying to zone in on her twin mentally. But, as usual, Shelley wasn't receiving. It took all Silke's energy to crack her sister's defenses and she simply didn't have it in her tonight.

They'd been closing up the bar when Raven had come crashing back inside and had pulled Silke aside with a wild story about Thora Nelson being dead. Raven had been too scared to call the police, and Silke had listened to the details that had left her dumbstruck. The devil was in those details, the reason she'd believed Raven. The reason she hadn't called 911 herself.

She checked the clock in the dash for maybe the tenth time. Twelve minutes and counting. The bar was closed now and she was out here alone.

Poor Thora—the popular Goth girl would never have to wait for anyone again.

Even as she thought it, Silke felt her stomach clench. What a shocker, and yet after the things Thora had told over her the past few weeks, why was she so surprised?

Only…who was next?

Her?

She slashed a hand across her eyes and came away with a smear of black makeup on the back of her hand.

How did Shelley do it? Silke wondered. Being a cop, coming in contact with violence and death on a regular basis? No identical twins were ever less alike. It had been obvious from the time they were kids and Shelley had beat up a boy who'd been torturing Silke that her twin took after their policewoman mother. Shelley had always been tough and could stomach anything without emotions getting in her way.

A knock at her car window made Silke jump. Heart pounding, she turned to see Shelley peering in at her. Opening the door, she flew out of the driver's seat. "Shell, I'm so glad to see you."

Shelley hugged her and rubbed her back the way she used to when they were little and their mother was working late at night and Silke was certain a monster lived in the basement. Shelley had always promised to protect her. It was only recently that Silke had begun exploring a different way to protect herself....

"So where's this Raven?" Shelley asked.

"I don't know. She wouldn't call the police, and while I was talking to you on the phone, she left without saying a word."

"But you know how to get in touch with her."

"Only if she comes into the bar. I mean, I know her, but we're not exactly friends."

Shelley had wanted her to call 911, and then, in exasperation, had said she would do it herself. But Silke had pleaded with her sister not to, insisted that it was imperative she come down here herself first. Then she could call whatever officer she saw fit.

"All right, let's see what we've got. Lock your car and get in mine." Shelley indicated the Camaro.

Silke quickly settled into the passenger seat.

"It's...*she's* over on the next block," Silke whispered. Thora wasn't an *it*. She was a person. Or she had been before someone had drained the blood from her. That's what Raven had said, the reason she'd wanted Shelley to come in person. Not that she'd told her sister that detail yet. She wanted Shelley to see for herself. "Make a right on Lake."

Lake Street was straddled by an elevated rapid transit structure for the Green Line that ran west into the suburbs. There weren't any stations close by— the old one at Halsted had been demolished. Now the Halsted/Randolph area was being gentrified, so the CTA was going to add a station sometime in the near future. But the fact that there was no station *now* meant there was little foot traffic in the area, especially late at night. Or early in the morning, depending on how one viewed it, she guessed. Bar-hoppers and restaurant-goers parked their cars along here if they didn't want to pay for valet parking. As did the car hikers themselves and employees of the local businesses.

Raven had been on her way to her car when she'd found Thora's body.

"Park anywhere." Silke pointed ahead and to the right. "Raven said she found Thora over there, by the overturned trash can."

The vehicle came to a stop at the curb and they both alighted, Shelley pulling her weapon and frowning as she scanned the area. "So where is she?"

Silke blinked and waited for her eyes to adjust and pierce the darkness.

"She's…gone!" Silke knew this was the right spot. The trash can had been knocked over in a struggle, just as Raven had said. "Another body gone!"

Silke's words blasted against my ears as I stared at an area littered with booze bottles and paper bags but no formerly animate objects.

"Yeah, she's gone," I agreed, thinking I'd wasted my time when I could have been catching some *z's.*

"She didn't have a pulse. I mean that's what Raven told me."

"Was Raven in her right mind?"

"You mean was she drunk?"

"Or on drugs."

"Could be. But the details…I believed her."

I was still looking over the site when something caught my eye—I stooped and snatched up a metal object. I held it up to the light. A small gargoyle glared back at me.

"That's her pin," Silke said excitedly. "Thora's!"

Okay, so this proved Thora had been here at least. And the clasp of the pin was torqued, as if messed up in a struggle of some sort. Sighing, I considered what might have happened. The Goth girl could have been dead drunk, sloshed on the contents of one of those empty bottles. Or she could have had some kind of seizure where she seemed dead. Or, she could have been *dead* dead.

Okay, I admit it was possible. But if so, what happened to the body? Did someone come along and scoop her up like so much garbage? My mental turn of phrase bothered me—this Thora really might be a true victim. I was trying to keep from thinking of LaTonya, but considering my nightmare, that was impossible.

"I really don't know what to tell you, Silke, other than to report the incident." I pocketed the pin. "But without a body or evidence of foul play…without knowing where to find this Raven to back you up…"

Cops had way too many in-their-face cases to get excited over a disappearing body and a story that couldn't be corroborated. Didn't I know that firsthand. They would take one look at Silke in her Goth gear before deciding she was too far out to take seriously.

Realizing my twin's attention was centered somewhere over my shoulder, I asked, "What?"

"Something moved. A shadow."

Instinct raised the short hairs on the back of my neck and had me going for my gun and being grateful I could legally carry it off duty. I raised the weapon into position as I turned, but I saw no one, moving or otherwise. "I think your imagination is playing you, Silke."

"I'm telling you I saw someone."

When I saw a dark figure slink suspiciously between the rapid-transit supports a few dozen yards away, I didn't wait for an answer. Reasonable suspicion was valid incentive for a seasoned cop to detain and question someone not acting right.

"Freeze!" I yelled. "Police! Come out where I can see you, hands up!"

Rather than complying, the shadow took off. And I ran after him. Rather, after a figure that could be male or female. It was dark and the person's clothing was darker—loose pants and a hoodie hiding what lay beneath.

"Stop or I'll shoot!" I bluffed.

It didn't matter if you were off or on the job, an officer was expected to respond—though I wasn't about to discharge my gun unless the suspect intended to use one on me. The paperwork involved was just not worth it.

I stumbled to a halt to catch my breath. He or she was climbing up the slats of the frickin' elevated support as if it were a slant board!

Great! I was chasing Spider-Man.

I holstered my weapon and did my best imitation of a Cirque du Soleil star.

The hair-raising climb up angled slats of steel gave me some time to think—maybe I should find a different occupation. This stuff was for rookies.

Like my first day on the job when Al and I had spotted a guy flying out of a convenience store with a wad of cash in one hand, a gun in the other. He'd taken one look at us and had run the other way. Al made me get out of the squad car and run after the guy, while he drove ahead and blocked him with the vehicle. The thief had turned on me and aimed his weapon, and my training, fueled by adrenaline, had kicked right in. It didn't matter that I was exhausted and winded. I'd dropped into the position low to the ground to make myself a smaller target. Luckily, I hadn't had to take him out. Al had left the squad car, gun drawn, and the thief had given up.

I'd been sick anyway, all over the sidewalk.

Over the years, I'd used my gun more than once, but I'd never actually had to shoot anyone and I wasn't in the market to break that particular record. I knew that even though I'd passed psych evaluation, I was still considered a personal-concern officer and would be until I'd proved otherwise. I couldn't afford to make any mistakes.

The screech of metal on metal alerted me to a train coming from downtown, jerking my gaze toward the glow of skyscrapers in the distance. I was distracted only for a second, but when I tried to pin the suspect, I was stunned. No prey. The shadow had disappeared.

I tried to hurry the rest of the way up. A mistake. My foot slipped, my body followed, and the next thing I knew I was dangling from one hand twenty or so feet above the street. My stomach clutched and my heart pounded as fast as the approaching train. I contemplated my fate and wondered if I had enough pluses in my favor to make up for the minuses before I got in front of those Pearly Gates.

Just in case.

They say when you're about to die, your whole life flashes before you. Well, nothing was flashing, so I figured I was going to be okay.

But Silke was directly below me, screaming, "Hold on, Shell!"

Pain shot through my arm as, with a grunt, I swung my body toward the steel structure. I found purchase for my free hand, but my fingers couldn't get a grip. It took a couple of breathtaking grabs to get hold of it. Then I hooked a foot on a steel slat and hesitated for a second to catch my breath and let my heartbeat steady.

Just then, the train clack-clacked overhead and rained soot down on me. I closed my eyes against the grit and tried not to breathe for a moment until the train was gone. Blinking and coughing, I finished my climb only to come up on the tracks to find them empty.

No body.

No suspect.

Saying that I was ticked was an understatement.

I escorted Silke back to her apartment. The possibility of another homicide being covered up had gotten to me, and I wanted some answers. I'd thought about making out an official report for about five seconds before deciding I wasn't about to call anyone.

No body, no case.

I didn't need another psych evaluation. Not that I could just forget about it.

I still couldn't figure out how I'd lost the suspect—if the person even was somehow connected to what had happened to Thora Nelson. So how had he or she disappeared into thin air? Silke had suggested the person hopped the train. But since there were no nearby stations, that sucker had been chugging hellbent for leather. So was it really possible that anyone could have leaped onto the side and held on?

I didn't see any other explanation.

I didn't know what to think about Thora.

I was uneasy, though. I felt raw and defensive. A too familiar feeling.

We entered Silke's apartment in an old courtyard building—a big, cheerful studio filled with lots of color and plants. She hadn't changed any of that when she'd gone Goth. Then again, she often changed who she was—the actress in her, I guessed—and Goth was simply her latest interest. I threw myself onto the sofa bed, thankful Silke had made it up that morning—she wasn't the neatest person in the world. She had a bunch of books tossed to one side. I glanced at them and shook my head.

Witchcraft. Wicca. Shamanism.

What was my sister into now?

Even though I wasn't sure of what this Raven had seen, I had a gut feeling the situation was a potential danger zone for Silke. I didn't want her going back to work at Heart of Darkness until the wee hours of the morning and then going home alone, but I doubted Silke would listen to reason.

"Want some tea?" Silke was already heading for the tiny kitchen off the main room.

"Okay. I didn't need sleep anyway."

"Tomorrow is Saturday. No work, remember. And you can crash here."

"Sure, why not," I said. "Since we're meeting Mom for an early lunch tomorrow anyway…" My mind was still on the missing body. That's what I wanted to talk about. "Whatever happened to Thora…I'm worried about *you*. If there *was* foul play…" Then Silke might become a target through her association with Raven. Not that I wanted to jump to conclusions, but my protective instincts were engaged, and my mind made those connections automatically. "Tell me about Thora."

"She was nice, but kind of a lost soul."

Exactly the kind of person Silke would be drawn to, I thought. "Lost how?"

"She didn't have anyone, not here in Chicago. Her family doesn't even know she came here. She was from a small town in southern Illinois, but she always said she didn't fit in."

"So Thora decided to become a Goth to fit in?" I asked. The notion of a Goth fitting in to anything was odd.

"I guess." Silke came into the living area and set down a teapot and two mugs on the coffee table. "It has to steep for a few minutes."

She'd made something with spice that smelled wonderful. Silke was more homey than I was. Despite the Goth phase, she liked brilliant colors, exotic foods—*she* learned to cook—and great-smelling stuff whether it was candles or shower gels or teas. My needs were less complicated.

"So, how well do you know Thora?"

Her face fell. "We hung together sometimes."

"So then you have her address and phone number, right?"

"We always met somewhere if we were going to do something together. All I know is that Thora was living in a communal situation with some other Goths who hang at the bar. They pool their resources to pay rent and stuff."

Sounding worse and worse, I decided. At least Silke still had her own apartment and was taking care of herself in some fashion. "Maybe you ought to think about getting away from that bar. You can find a better job downtown."

"The only better job I want is on a stage."

"Okay, how about a safer job?"

"Look, Shell, I know you're trying to be protective and all, but we're not kids anymore. I respect your choices, and I'd appreciate your respecting mine."

"I do. Really." I tried to be supportive, despite Mom's putting me in the middle. "I just want you to be safe is all."

"Quitting won't do it. They can find me if they want."

Her dramatic statement made my chest tighten.

"Who can find you?" I could feel her agitation. "What aren't you telling me, Silke?"

I recognized her tense expression. I'd seen it often enough looking into my own mirror. I gave her as good as I got. I was used to getting the truth out of offenders. And out of my sister. Finally, Silke sighed and I knew I had won.

"Okay, Thora was seeing this guy who's part of a bizarre crowd. She told me things…well, things you wouldn't like, Shell."

I was liking this less and less. "Things like what?"

"Things." Silke turned her attention to the teapot. She avoided looking at me for a moment and concentrated on filling the mugs. Then she handed one to me and met my gaze. "Thora told me about some really dangerous stuff…about people bleeding other people. I'm afraid that's maybe what happened to her. That she died from loss of blood."

"Loss of blood?" I echoed, suddenly feeling sick inside.

"That's why I wanted you to come and not call 911. It sounded so crazy. Raven said Thora was really white…that her body was cold like she didn't have any blood left in her at all. I mean, she didn't leave the bar that long before Raven found her. And Raven said the inside of Thora's arm was slashed open."

"Slashed?" I echoed. "Why didn't you tell me this right away?"

"I figured you wouldn't believe me unless you saw for yourself. And then, when her body wasn't there… Most Goths are chill, but some of them…

well, they can be scary. A vampire cult hangs at the bar, and Thora had a thing with the leader. That's who she was living with—the vampire cult. Only she was doing it because of Elvin Mowry, not because she wanted to trade blood. What if Thora knew more than she told me, but the murderer thinks I know everything?"

This would have sounded crazy to me if not for my own experience. A body seemingly drained of blood…a slash on the inside of her arm…a vampire cult.

Cult?

Just that afternoon, Mom had been talking to Commander Aniceto about cult activity in the area. This couldn't be a coincidence…so why hadn't she told me?

I took a deep breath and a long, hard look at my sister. Her smeary raccoon eyes looked larger than usual. Even so, I was reminded of the image I had of her, when the recruit Morris had been down on the mat bemoaning being hurt.

Silke could get hurt.

Silke could get dead.

The thought drove down into my core like a hot knife.

I was the sensible one. I saw the world in black and white, while Silke saw it in living color. She explored it, celebrated it. And took chances that could spell disaster for her.

Now here we went again.

I didn't want to believe this Thora had been drained of blood, or that Silke could be next for knowledge she didn't even own. But I had seen La-Tonya Sanford with my own eyes, and she'd been *dead*-dead, no matter what the department's official position was.

Who had killed her and why? How had her body disappeared so fast—so fast that she might have up and walked herself out of that alley?

My gut was making me wonder if maybe I could find some answers here. Maybe even clear up the idea that I'd had a fruit-loop moment. No more psych evaluations for me, thank you. Two months at the callback center had been nearly enough to make me lose my mind, so I tried to remain pragmatic.

"There could be an explanation about what happened to Thora."

"I want you to be right, Shell. I don't want her to be dead. Only I think she really is. I think they drained her blood. You could find out for sure. You *are* a detective."

"Not anymore I'm not. I'm a trainer at the academy," I reminded her, though in my heart of hearts…

"You just hit a bump in the road. If anyone can find the truth of what happened, you can. Detecting is what you were born to do."

Who knew me better than my twin?

I was pumped at the idea of getting back into an actual case—one possibly related to my biggest failure. My blood was already rushing through my body so fast I could feel my pulse. But I couldn't do this through the department. If I made an official report, I'd be headed for Psych City in no time.

I couldn't let that happen, not again.

Before I went public with this, I would have to make sure I had some kind of evidence that a crime had been committed. A witness who wouldn't do a disappearing act. Maybe even the murderer himself.

"I just have to get on the inside without anyone being suspicious of my motives."

"How?" Silke asked.

"We do what we did when we were kids. We fool everyone. We trade places."

Chapter 3

Trade places. Was I out of my mind? I winced at the reference and tried to convince myself not.

Pretending to be a cop, Silke would last...oh, about thirty seconds. On the other hand, I could probably get away with pretending to be her for a while.

If I decided to do it—how could I not...what would a night or two hurt?—I would see if anyone knew Thora's whereabouts, make sure she was missing. I'd already called Detective Stella Jacobek, a friend in the department, to get an official update. No Jane Doe found along Lake Street or anywhere nearby. No call to report Thora Nelson missing, either, which didn't surprise me since Silke had said the girl was from southern Illinois and didn't have anyone here.

No one but an Elvin Mowry, the head of this bizarre vampire cult.

Assuming Raven came back to the bar, I would talk to her myself. If she didn't, I would see if I could get an address on her. A phone number. A last name.

Equally important, I would get the lay of the land, see how dangerous this vampire cult seemed to be.

Cults. That was the reason I hadn't cancelled lunch with Mom. Could I get her to share what she knew without arousing her suspicions?

"Silke, must you wear so much makeup away from your job?" were the first words out of Mom's mouth.

"Hi, Mom, love you, too." Silke gave our mother a hug and a kiss on the cheek.

I didn't move to follow suit. Neither did Mom.

The criticism of my sister was uncalled for, especially since Silke had gone conservative to please Mom. Her hair was neatly coiled at the base of her neck, and she had a pale, languid, smudgy-eyed look, which was nothing like the Halloween mask she'd worn the night before. Mom, on the other hand, had let loose—well, for her—with lipstick and a hint of blush and hair out of its tight confinement.

Me, I went light on the makeup. My pale skin looked decent au natural, and my green eyes were large enough that a simple swipe of mascara brought them out. My chestnut hair was long and thick enough to look good in a ponytail. So I could stick my lipstick and wallet in my pocket and I'd be good to go. Not having a purse simplified life.

I'd picked up Silke and we'd met Mom at the

ritzy second-floor North Michigan Avenue restaurant. Our table overlooked the street. The food order settled, my mind drifted back to the Goth bar and vampire cult. "So, Mom, you never told me the results of your meeting with Aniceto."

She lifted an eyebrow. "He filled me in with the history of cult activity in Chicago. Homegrown religions. Satanic groups."

"Weird stuff, huh?" I asked, immediately pushing it. "Like sacrifices—have you heard about any kind of bloodletting?"

Silke gaped at me. I'm sure she was horrified that I might tell Mom about the night before.

Mom frowned at me. "You're not a detective anymore, so why the sudden interest?"

"I've always been interested in your work." Which was the truth. "Maybe you just never noticed."

"Hmm, seems to me there's more to it, Shelley. You're not happy at the academy, are you?"

Also true, but how had this suddenly become about me? It was supposed to be my interrogation. She did know something—I could read that much from her.

"Back to the cult discussion—"

"I knew being away from the action wouldn't suit you."

"You mean my doing something that landed me on the psych couch didn't suit *you*."

"Can we all get along just for one lunch?" Silke asked. "We should be supportive of each other."

Luckily the food arrived, cutting short the quibbling.

Not to mention my third-degree. Apparently Mom wasn't going to tell me anything. Maybe she thought if she did, I would screw things up…just like with the Sanford case.

Unfortunately, Silke and I had never lived up to our mother's professional standards, but Silke had the good sense to stay as far away from police work as she could. On the other hand, I had no sense. I'd stepped right into Mom's arena. I thought my becoming a detective would stir her maternal pride. Hah. I heard more praise from my lieutenant, and that wasn't saying much.

After being given the crappiest caseload in history for an entire year—mostly simple assault cases where threats never actually turned into violence or called for my investigation skills, but rather generated a lot of paperwork—I'd hooked on to a big multiple homicide as a subordinate to the very male detectives in charge, of course. And just when Norelli and Walker had been ready to blow off the case due to lack of anything to follow, I'd found a key witness through an informant. Thank you, Junior Diaz.

That little gift should have made me the toast of Area 4. Yeah, burned toast. Male coppers didn't like looking bad. Liked it even less when shown up by a woman. And they hung together. So I was on the outs in the office. Worse, Norelli and Walker got all the credit and media attention because it was Norelli's case. I could have done without the last, but at least I would have appreciated departmental recognition.

Losing a body had ended any hopes for my career as a detective. Silke was right that detecting was my life. Mom was right that I missed the action. I wanted to be right about something. I wanted a do-over. I wanted to find the creep who'd killed LaTonya Sanford so she would stop haunting me. I wanted to sleep at nights and not have to get up to watch reality TV.

I'd thought it through and I was ready to go back in and find a way to make things right.

After lunch, I insisted on going back to my place to go over everything in my mind.

Alone.

I needed to psych myself before going ahead with my plan.

LaTonya Sanford had gotten to me in the deepest way possible. Guilt. Though her body had disappeared, I knew in my gut the teenager had been murdered. The case had never been dead for me. I knew it would never be until I'd solved it. The similarity between LaTonya and Thora was simply too in-my-face to ignore.

Once inside my apartment, I made over the cats, fed them and put on a pot of coffee.

After which, I stared at the tattered folder still on the low table in front of the couch. I stared down at it for a moment and simply breathed, tried to get that catch out of my chest. I was wound up.

A cup of strong French roast cleared my head.

Feeling renewed, I parked myself on the couch and once more stared at the folder as one of the cats jumped up beside me. Sarge. I didn't have to look at him. I knew him by feel and sound. He purred noisily and settled next to my hip. A flurry of fur caught my eye as it landed delicately on the table next to the folder. Cadet. She always tried to get in my way when I was concentrating the hardest. Knowing they were starving for affection, I petted both cats before taking a long slug of coffee.

Then I opened the folder.

LaTonya Sanford stared out at me. She had been a beautiful girl. An innocent girl from all accounts.

A very dead girl.

I would swear to that on a stack of Bibles.

I went over everything in the folder for maybe the hundredth time. I especially concentrated on the cult research I'd done. I'd caught a feature about cults on one of those reality cop shows, and instinct had led me to investigate cults that required blood sacrifice.

Like vampire cults.

One of the stories was about a woman who was led into a room naked and made to lie down on a raised dais draped with bloodred velvet. A nude man poured the contents of a pitcher onto the woman…the mingled blood of the other cult members, who then licked every drop off her. The man who'd poured the blood then sank sharpened eyeteeth into the woman's neck and drank, after which he slit himself below his groin and made the woman drink from him.

There were other accounts, equally disturbing, combining blood sacrifice with sex.

Is that what had happened to LaTonya? And now to Thora?

The accounts of cult rituals I had gathered didn't include murder, but accidents happened.

I was as sure that LaTonya Sanford had been dead when I'd checked her vitals as I was of anything.

"What happened to you?" I asked her black-and-white photo.

I had to find out.

Though I was armed, that healthy tickle of fear kept me vigilant as I approached one of the remaining project high-rises in the complex where the Sanford family lived. No one was safe there. Not the residents. Not the police. When responding to a call, a cop I knew had been wounded by a sniper on the roof. Last year, some scum had even thought it fun to shoot at the school in the buildings' midst. Rather than being repaired as they fell apart, the buildings were being demolished, one at a time, and the residents dispersed to hopefully better living conditions throughout the city.

Ironically, though, LaTonya Sanford had survived the projects only to be killed halfway to the Lake Street area near the bar, in what was considered a safer area.

I'd called ahead to make certain her family hadn't been moved out, so I went right in. The building's hallway was dark, a single bare bulb lighting the way to the elevator. I knew that often elevators in these buildings weren't operational, that residents had to use the narrow, poorly lit stairways where gangbangers sometimes awaited them.

The elevator doors opened within seconds of my pressing the call button.

A few minutes later, I knocked at the apartment door.

Mrs. Sanford herself opened it. She was still a young woman in her early to midthirties, but I swear she'd aged a decade since we'd last met. Losing a child could do that to a person. I'd seen it happen too many times in this city.

"Detective Caldwell," she said in a soft, musical voice. She stepped back to let me in.

"Mrs. Sanford."

I inclined my head as I passed her. I couldn't say it was good to see her, not under the circumstances. I'd been here before, so I was already familiar with the painted concrete-block walls and the scattering of worn furniture. The family's poverty was evident, but so was the mother's pride. The room was neat and several plants bloomed in the window. She offered me an iced tea, which I accepted. When she brought two glasses back from the kitchen, we sat opposite each other, me in a chair, her on the couch.

I sipped at the tea. "Mmm, good." As much as I hated to do so, I had to ask. "You never heard from LaTonya, right?"

"You told me she was dead. You found her."

"But her body disappeared. You know the department considers her a runaway."

"Not my LaTonya. She'd let me know if she was alive."

"I understand. I had to ask."

"You got new evidence or something?"

"I'm afraid not. But your daughter haunts me, Mrs. Sanford. I wanted to take another look at the case."

"You so interested, how come you never answered my call? I left a message."

"I'm sorry, but I never got it. When was this?"

"A couple weeks after."

At which time I was under psychiatric evaluation. Of course they wouldn't have given me the time of day. Forget a message that might be important. "Your call—what was it about?"

"I got my baby's purse back."

"One she was using that night?"

Mrs. Sanford nodded. "Someone must of found it. Got delivered in the mail in a big envelope. No money. Someone had kindness to return it, though." Mrs. Sanford rose, saying, "It's right over here."

As the victim's mother crossed to some shelving, I thought about the implication. Someone had found the purse. A potential witness? But my elation deflated when she returned to the couch and handed me the purse, still in a big brown envelope.

No return address.

No note included.

No clue as to the sender.

But Mrs. Sanford watched me with an expectant expression, and I couldn't bear to let her down by saying what I was thinking, that getting the purse back might be of no help whatsoever. It was highly unlikely that there would even be viable fingerprints.

Instead of discouraging her, I fetched a couple of tissues—I didn't happen to have plastic gloves on me, of course—and handled the bag carefully so as not to smudge prints if there actually were any that might be identified. Opening it, I turned it upside down and let everything spill out on a table. My gaze quickly swept over the contents, then stalled out.

My pulse jumped and my mouth went dry as my gaze connected with a pack of matches.

The cover was black, the letters scarlet: Heart of Darkness.

My own heart was thudding. Hard.

I now had evidence of a connection between the two missing girls.

"Jeez, hold still," Silke said as she applied a second coat of white makeup over my face and shoulders.

It was early evening and we were back at her place and in the midst of some hocus-pocus that would let me pretend to be her tonight. But the longer it took, the harder it was for me not to squirm. This was torture.

"How do you go through this every day?" I asked, my throat still dry from inhaling the loose powder Silke had dusted me with in between makeup layers.

"It's a ritual that gives me pleasure. You know, time to think."

I knew it took her at least an hour to get Goth. And that was in addition to coloring her hair bloodred, which she'd already done to me. Luckily, I'd convinced her that I would strangle her with my bare hands if I couldn't easily get my hair back to normal, so on the way home, we'd picked up a product that washed out.

"Why don't you go over the important stuff while I do your eyes?" Silke ordered.

"Okay, okay." Trying to ignore the thick black pencil about to attack my eye, I concentrated on the people she'd told me about—the major players, so to speak. "Desiree Leath, owner of Heart of Darkness…tall, thin, pale, long blue-black hair. Hung Chung, head security guard of the whole alternative scene, both bar and shops…Asian, the sides of his head shaved. Jake DeAtley, bartender…classic dark and handsome good looks, a small scar on his cheek. Blaise Allcock, tattoo and piercing artist…fair and somewhat effeminate, his arms tattooed from shoulders to wrists. Elvin Mowry, head of the supposed vampire clan and Thora's squeeze…slender pretty boy with spiked purple hair. Thora Nelson, beautiful, black shoulder-length hair with red streaks. Wait a minute. What about Raven?"

"She looks like a little bird—fragile with short black hair that tufts out like ruffled feathers. She also has three eyebrow rings."

"Got it."

My plan was to work at the bar for a night or two and not only get the lay of the land, but to see what people knew about LaTonya and Thora. I'd never made the connection to the bar before, because that alley where I'd found LaTonya's body had been several blocks north, and the area that lay between was an old manufacturing district. But now I figured she could have been walking home from the bar. I hoped Raven would show because Silke didn't have a last name on her. If she didn't show, then I would try to get someone to tell me where I could find her.

"Your memory has always been right on," Silke said, switching the black pencil to my other eye. "But just in case, I'll tune in, make sure you stay on track."

Though having backup was always a good idea, Silke's poking around in my head wasn't. "If I get stuck, I can call you on my cell."

"We have different strengths, Shell. This one's mine, so let me do what I can do."

"You've done your part," I insisted, keeping my voice firm without raising it. "Leave the investigation to me."

Thankfully, Silke didn't argue.

When we'd first showed signs of being in synch, Mom had told us we should each be our own person and not draw attention to the fact that we were different or people would treat us…well, like we were different. Even as a kid, the connection had me freaked, and since I'd wanted to fit in, I'd tuned Silke out.

That was the thing about us. We had different strengths. Mine was logic and focus and fearlessness on the street. Silke, on the other hand, got into the woo-woo of life, a place I really didn't want to visit.

So when she said, "Um, Shell, there's something I didn't tell you," while outlining my lips with that same black pencil, my warning antenna went up.

"Mmph-umph," I muttered, not wanting that black line to go off and give me a weird smile.

"You know the vampire cult I told you about…" Her expression wary, she stopped the outlining and backed up. "Well, there's worse."

Though I had a feeling I wasn't going to like this, I said, "Go on."

"I've heard rumors that someone hanging at the bar is a—" she cleared her throat "—a real vampire."

My thudding heart steadied and I rolled my eyes. "Yeah, okay." Now she was going over the top.

"I'm not kidding."

"So I'll wear garlic."

"You shouldn't joke about it." Silke slapped down the pencil and picked up a pot of purple eye shadow. "You joke about anything that you can't see in black-and-white. That's why I didn't want to say anything. Close your eyes."

Silke dabbed a bit of color on my right lid and then on the left. But she didn't go on and on about this real-vampire business. Which made me wonder why she'd brought it up in the first place. I knew she was frustrated with me for not wanting to develop this mental pathway she was so into. I suspected she believed in lots of things I would find totally unbelievable.

"You can open."

I did and was startled by my own reflection. I'd shed my girl-next-door look for one that would make heads turn. I looked more like Silke than ever before. No one would be able to tell I wasn't her.

"Okay, Silke, show me how you walk in this getup…carry a tray…count your money."

I was leaving nothing to chance, and becoming a Silke clone didn't come naturally. So I spent the next half hour imitating her walk and gestures and getting down her expressions and patter. Good thing I was a quick study.

When we were done, Silke started sorting through the lipsticks on the makeup tray. "You aren't going to take any foolish chances, are you?"

"Hey, this is my kind of gig." And I would be wearing a weapon, which I could legally do off duty. "I'm going on a fact-finding mission, is all. What could go wrong?"

Famous last words.

Well, let's hope not.

But an hour or so later as I approached the building that held Heart of Darkness, I got that twist in my gut I always get when going undercover. I'd done this kind of thing dozens of times in my career, starting when I was a tactical officer working vice, and I knew all I had to do was breathe and get into my part and I would be okay. It was probably the same way Silke felt before going on stage. Then, once there in the spotlight, everything seemed real and the butterflies went away.

Only thing was, in an official capacity, I'd worked with a team, including someone to watch my back, even if from a distance. This time, I would have to remember the only backup I had was Silke via cell phone.

So basically, I was going it alone.

I thought about that all the way to the bar.

Though I could have parked somewhere west on Randolph, I wanted to check out what was going on under the el on Lake Street. Besides, it wouldn't do to let anyone who knew Silke's old beater see me getting out of something more upscale.

So I parked my car under the tracks and walked around to the main drag, all the while keeping an eye peeled for anything out of place. All I saw was a hiker getting out of a car and jogging back the way

he'd come. The area was still in an early stage of gen-
trification and not necessarily safe at night. Thora
should have known that, I thought, part of me hoping against hope that she would actually show at the
bar tonight and I could tell Silke all the fuss was for
nothing.

Only my gut told me that wasn't going to happen.
I was ninety-nine percent convinced that Thora Nelson had met the same fate as LaTonya Sanford.

A mile west of the Loop, Randolph Street had
once been part of the city's old market area, but now
it was a mix of upscale restaurants and businesses
and paper companies with a couple of those surviving meat and produce markets thrown in the mix.
Heart of Darkness was the main attraction in a converted building that held several other businesses:
Snazzy Trash, resale and sexy clothing mart; Taboo
Tattoo, tattoo and piercing parlor; Bad Hair Day,
cuts and coloring salon; and Garden Goths, fantas-
tical critters depot.

As I approached the door of the bar, I caught my
reflection in the plate glass. I still couldn't believe
how very Silke I looked wearing her long, ragged-
hemmed black skirt and red bustier. Thankfully, I'd
insisted on adding one of her capes. This one was
black and short enough not to get in my way. Not
only did the cape give me a little added modesty, but
it also hid my gun, which I had holstered behind me
at the waist.

The bustier was making me nuts, though, so I
sucked in my gut and pulled it up in front. Then, taking heart that even I couldn't tell the difference be-

tween Silke and me, I opened the door of the establishment and stepped inside to determine whether someone connected with the bar was a killer.

Jake DeAtley sensed a new arrival and turned from the drink he was mixing to see who had slipped in the door.

Silke Caldwell, late again.

Not that it really mattered since the place had yet to fill up. But the Goth waitress stopped just inside the door and looked around as if she was hesitant. But just for a moment. Then she gathered herself together and marched back to the small office where employees signed in.

Curious, Jake couldn't stop himself from watching her, which in itself was a curious event. While he thought Silke was pretty enough—as far as he could tell, that is, considering the war paint covering her fine features—he could take her or leave her. But tonight, there was something about her that piqued his interest.

Something he couldn't put a finger on.

"*Chéri,* the drink," Desiree said, her accent lightly French. "We keep the customers happy, yes?"

"Sure, boss, coming right up."

Getting back to work, Jake wondered how many drinks he would have to make before he was either satisfied or too bored to keep up the pretense.

As he served the waiting customer, Jake glanced at the bar owner, whose appearance was as steamy as her voice. Her waist-length hair was loose, a sheet of blue-black satin around naturally pale skin. She appeared to have been sewn into the midnight-blue dress that barely covered what passed for breasts. Desiree was so model thin, he swore any day she would melt to nothing and float away in the ether.

Not that he was interested in her personally, either.

He wasn't interested in anything but his mission.

The two non-Goth women sitting at the end of the bar closest to the door had ordered a couple of Bloody Cosmopolitans, the red being a big dose of cranberry juice. He was always mystified by the "normal" people who hung around the bar for a free show. Locals mostly, but the bar's reputation had been spreading. Heart of Darkness had become a hip hangout.

A new group of customers entered, both sexes looking appropriately pale and dressed in black, purple or bloodred. He'd seen some of them before, but several new faces clustered around the one who called himself Elvin Mowry. As if being above all others was his due, the purple-haired prince of freaks ascended the half-dozen stairs to the raised deck of the bar. One by one, his troupe followed.

Jake delivered the Bloody Cosmopolitans to the two young women who were watching Elvin Mowry and his sycophants.

Then his attention was drawn back to Silke when she appeared to take their orders. Jake was aware of the action around her—a newbie with electric-blue streaks in his long black hair eyed Silke with a lecherous grin.

And as the waitress moved closer to the guy, Jake

tensed. His gut told him the guy was going to pull something, and Hung Chung was nowhere around to break it up. Though he usually spent most of his time hanging around the bar, the security guard must be doing a round of the other businesses in the building. Ready for an altercation he would have to deal with himself—and he would enjoy every minute of it, because Mowry and his minions irritated the hell out of him—Jake focused his attention on the newbie.

"Hey, sweet cheeks. You and me. Let's grind hips together later," he heard the guy say while sliding his hand up the back of the waitress's skirts.

About to leap over the bar, Jake froze when she grabbed the guy's hand and bent it back so fast it looked practiced. The pressure took the creep out of the chair and onto his knees on the floor. And still she didn't let go.

"Don't ever try that again or you'll be sorry," she said, her voice soft but threatening. "You know how many bones there are in a hand? You will if I break them all." She let go, saying, "Now, can I take your order?"

The moron slid back into his chair and cradled the wounded hand to his chest. "Beer. A red beer," he said, refusing to look at her until her back was turned. Then he shot a vile glare of hatred at her.

As if nothing had happened, Silke continued taking orders, leaving Jake to wonder what in the hell he'd just witnessed.

Chapter 4

I couldn't believe my luck. First night playing waitress—no, first order—and I was assaulted by some loser with roaming hands.

How did Silke deal with this kind of crap? I wondered, stalking toward the bar to hand over my order. She wasn't a fighter. Oh, she knew the moves. If she remembered them, that was. I'd made her take a self-defense workshop, but that had been years ago. She'd said it had been to appease me, but I figured she'd thought it might come in handy if she ever had to be part of a stage fight.

I felt that prickling, got a vague feeling that told me my twin was tuning in. I ignored not only her but also the music assaulting my ears—Gothic keyboards, dense guitars and mournful vocals going on about bloody kisses.

Arriving at the bar, I handed the order to the bartender. "A red beer and a bottle of Shiraz."

"You okay?" asked the guy who I knew to be Jake DeAtley. The fine scar in the beard stubble gave him away.

"I'm okay," I told him, visibly shivering the way I'd seen Silke do when she didn't like something.

Eyebrow slashing upward, he asked, "So how many bones does the human hand have?"

"Twenty-six."

How had he heard my threat? The place was pretty big—not terribly wide, perhaps, but long. And Mowry and his crew were on the raised level in back, which put them even farther away. The acoustics in this place must be something, I thought as Jake opened a bottle of red beer. When I tried to tune in on Mowry and company, I got nothing but music. Maybe there'd been a break between tunes, I thought.

"That was some fancy move," Jake said, pulling me out of my musings. "Where did you learn it?"

"Cable television has something for everyone."

Though he didn't respond to my tart remark, Jake gave me a piercing look that made me nervous. I took it to mean that he hadn't thought that I—rather Silke—was capable of an effective defensive move. Or that Silke would be so acerbic. Uh-oh, I didn't want to arouse suspicions.

So I said, "Sorry, I'm still a little uptight. Actually, my sister got me to take a self-defense workshop. You know, one of those one-day wonders that give you a couple of moves to protect yourself. She doesn't like me working in this neighborhood at night."

"Any neighborhood can be dangerous at night." Jake set the beer on the tray in front of me.

"Yeah, but I've heard stuff that creeps me out."

"Stuff?"

"Like last night, Raven was all worried about Thora. She was certain something bad happened to her." Considering Raven had spoken only to Silke, Jake wouldn't know what was said, and I didn't elaborate. "You haven't seen Thora tonight, have you?"

"Thora…no, can't say as I have."

"What about Raven?"

"Sorry."

"Hey, did you ever catch Raven's last name?"

He shook his head.

I watched Jake open the bottle of red wine, his expression suddenly closed. Could he possibly know something? I wondered. While he was busy, I gave him an intense once-over.

Six feet tall, athletic build, dark hair and smoldering good looks played up by a black collarless shirt. His skin was pale. I might think he was a Goth, but he wore no makeup at all, and only had a single piercing. The stud in his right ear looked like a black diamond. The pale scar slashing through the beard stubble on his left cheek was window dressing as far as I was concerned. I had a few scars of my own. It simply made me think he was rugged, a man's man, and made me curious as to whether or not he had any additional scars on that pumped body.

"Here you go." He cut into my musings by pushing the tray toward me.

The way he was studying me—as if he was trying to read my mind or something—made me back off. I was getting vibes a whole lot stranger than the ones I got off Silke. Only these I didn't understand.

I took the tray and almost dropped it. "Nerves," I said, purposely doing a Silke twitch. "I guess that guy really got to me."

Before Jake could respond, I moved through the poorly lit bar, looking for Thora as I had been doing since I'd arrived. I'd asked several people about her now, with no results. I'd been looking for Raven, as well, but as far as I could tell, she hadn't shown, either.

Great. I was getting nowhere fast.

I tried to imagine who might know LaTonya Sanford in this place. She'd been underage, but that didn't mean anything. Lots of these customers might be using fake IDs. As a cop, I knew it wouldn't be hard to get one. Not that I had ever found evidence of one in the Sanford case. But there had been those matches. If she hadn't been in here herself, she'd known someone who had.

LaTonya's purse had presented me with a conundrum. What to do with it? I'd been reluctant to accept potential evidence on a case I was not actively working for the Chicago Police Department. And what I had found hadn't been enough alone to take it in and make the investigation official. In the end, after returning the contents into the purse—including those matches—I'd regretfully left it in Mrs. Sanford's care. Temporarily, I reminded myself.

The bar had enough atmosphere to attract a growing number of customers, enough that I had to dance around a few to get to the stairs. Deep purple walls, black ceiling, wood floor stained a dark red, no mirrors, and lamps that looked like and gave off as much light as candles. Cigarettes rather than candles filled the air with a nasty cloud of smoke.

I headed to deliver the drinks to Elvin Mowry and what I figured were the other vampire cult members. I put a beer in front of the creep whose hand I'd wanted to break. He sucked on his cigarette and immediately looked away.

Then I set wine glasses down before Mowry and his companions.

"I shall taste before you pour, my dear," Mowry said. "And please forgive Ronald for his poor judgment earlier. He's new," he said, as if that explained away the little creep's transgression.

I smiled into Mowry's pretty face and poured a splash of the ruby-red wine in his glass. Then I watched as he lifted it with ring-covered fingers—a wolf, a bat, a gargoyle, all in pewter. He held the drink up to a light fixture overhead and licked his lips in anticipation. I was certain he'd chosen this vintage because he thought it looked like blood, and the action creeped me out. Unless he actually had something to do with draining women of their blood, he'd probably never seen the real stuff in any quantity. If he worked homicide, his romance with vampirism would fade fast. Nothing like a blood-splattered wall to kill one's appetite for red wine.

"Wonderful. Pour," Mowry commanded. When I began filling glasses, he said, "You are a lovely and complex woman, Silke."

The name reminded me to give him a subtle Silke

smile and soften my voice as I set down the bottle and asked, "Would that be a compliment?"

"Definitely. Your unexpected vigor tonight adds a spiciness that I appreciate to our relationship."

Relationship? Silke thought Mowry was nothing but creepy. But I smiled again and said, "I always aim to please."

"You would pleasure me greatly if you would join me when the bar closes."

Great. Was this going to be grope number two?

"Thanks, but no thanks."

"I am a gentleman, Silke—"

"Sorry. I don't fraternize with customers. It's kind of a rule of mine."

I tried to keep that smile pasted to my lips as I flicked my gaze over the purple spiked hair and settled it on Mowry's pretty-boy face.

Ironically, the song blasting through the bar was "Love You to Death." How many young women had been? I wondered. And did Mowry see me as the next victim? Did the creeps who took enough blood from a woman to kill her do it while having sex with her? Was that what had happened to Thora? And La-Tonya Sanford?

The mystery eating at me as it had been all these months, I said, "Besides, Elvin, I thought you and Thora had a thing going on. Where is she, anyway?"

I caught a fleeting expression chase Mowry's features before he shuttered them and said, "I have no idea of where she might be. Thora can be amusing, but she is not anyone I would consider…well, permanent."

The way he said it made my blood pressure come knocking at my arteries.

Had Elvin Mowry just admitted to killing Thora Nelson?

"Everything's okay, right?" Silke asked anxiously when I finally took a break to call her.

"So far."

In addition to packing my weapon, I'd of course brought my cell phone. I'd told Jake I needed some air, so I was outside the bar where my conversation wouldn't be overheard. I'd needed a break, a few minutes of being out of a crowd that had tripled since I'd arrived…of being away from the haze of smoke that threatened to choke me…of not having to worry about every word coming out of my mouth.

"Mowry didn't seem broken up over Thora's absence," I told her. "He said she was amusing but not permanent."

"Jerk!"

In my opinion, that was the general consensus about men. Until they got blindsided by the love bug, they were casual with the women in their lives, thinking there was always another one around the corner. And usually there was.

And speaking of men…

"What about Jake DeAtley? How well do you know him?"

"Uh-oh," Silke said. "Do your hormones kick in when you look at him?"

I suddenly felt annoyed. "Do *yours?*"

"What is it you're really asking?"

I'd felt this tension humming off the bartender more than once, but I hadn't wanted to define it. "It's probably nothing. Just the way he was looking at me…"

"Hey, if you can get his attention, I say go for it."

"He was assessing me," I told her, "but it wasn't attraction. It was like he was trying to see inside me."

"He does get weird sometimes. One minute he can be smiling and charming and the next minute he's a completely different person."

I digested that assessment and wondered what Jake really was all about.

"Did Raven show?" Silke asked.

"I haven't seen her, either. Listen, I need to get back inside before someone gets suspicious."

I'd barely made it past the security guy stationed at the door to check IDs when, seemingly out of no-where, the owner appeared in front of me and gave me a good start.

"Hey, Desiree." My breath caught as I wondered if she saw through my disguise.

Her eyes narrowing, Desiree leaned toward me and, through the curtain of blue-black hair that slid along her face, said, "*Chérie,* I do not pay for you to chat on the phone while my customers thirst."

Her tone was as mild as her French accent, her lips were curved, and yet I knew from the glitter in her dark eyes that she was truly irritated with me.

"I'm on it."

Before I could say anything to arouse her suspi-cions, I quickly made myself scarce. Then I realized she'd known I'd been on my cell. Had she been spying on me through the window?

I glanced back, and caught sight of her at the far end of the bar. How had she gotten there through the crowd so fast? I wondered. Her attention was centered on another pretty boy, this one with long blond hair. Blaise Allcock, I presumed from the description Silke had given me. They were sequestered away from other people, apparently arguing about something.

I would have given my eyeteeth—whichever ones those were—to know what they were arguing about. Too bad I'd never gotten around to taking a course in lip-reading.

I arrived at the table of newcomers, non-Goths who were gazing around, sending up smoke signals with their cigarettes and whispering to each other. I took their order and rushed back to the bar, where Jake got right on it.

"Air fresh enough for you?" he asked.

"As fresh as city air gets. Better than the smog in here."

A dark eyebrow shot up, and Jake's gaze flicked from the drink order to me. He didn't say anything, but I was getting weird vibes off him again. I couldn't wait until the order was filled so I could get out of his space.

What was his story? I wondered, remembering to handle the tray as Silke had showed me. For some reason, I couldn't get a read on Jake, and I was pretty good at reading people.

As I served drinks, I looked over the crowd for the

hundredth time, but I didn't see anyone who fit either Thora's or Raven's description.

With the bar filled with bodies, most of them with a cigarette in hand, the atmosphere was thick enough to cut. I would be wearing the smoke until I jumped out of my evening's costume and into the shower. And I couldn't wait for that. In an era where women were allowed to be comfortable, why did anyone want to dress like this? I was wary of bending over, both because then I could hardly breathe and because I feared falling out of my bodice.

Even so, I had to admit there was something seductive about walking among a whole group of people in disguise, me included. I felt anonymous, as if I could disappear into myself and no one knew who I really was. Which they didn't. Maybe that was the attraction. That and the theatrical atmosphere of the bar itself, which drew as many neighborhood regulars as it did Goths.

I swung through the crowd, taking orders while keeping an eye out for either of the Goth girls. As Jake filled an order for me, a commotion got my attention. A couple of guys trying to get into the bar were making threatening noises. The man blocking their way was solid looking—Hung Chung himself. The head security guard grabbed the two guys by their collars and shoved them out the door with him following.

"Huh, what's going on there?" I muttered to myself as I turned to see if the drinks were ready.

"You know Chung likes to assert his authority. Scares the pants off underage kids."

"I wonder what scares him." He was being unnecessarily rough, and I'd never had a fondness for bullies.

"Not much probably. What scares you?"

The unexpected question threw me. And the way Jake was staring at me. Speculation licked his features, and I wondered what conclusions he was drawing about me.

"You want to know what scares me?" I asked, looking around at the young women in the bar and seeing them as potential victims.

"Just making conversation."

"What scares me is that some people are so damn trusting they don't recognize evil when they face it."

Jake's expression altered subtly, but I didn't miss it. I'd managed to surprise him.

He said, "I'd like to continue the conversation. After work?"

"I need to get these drinks to my customers." I picked up the tray, but my mouth went dry.

What exactly was he suggesting?

"I find your perspective fascinating, Silke. So what about it? Breakfast, I mean."

"At four in the morning?"

Heart of Darkness had a late license on the weekends. One of its draws, I knew.

"Why not? You could use a meal. I could use company."

Was that all? I wondered suspiciously.

What I could use was information. About Thora. About Elvin Mowry and his vampire cult. About

Raven and LaTonya. Silke had told me Jake was okay so maybe this was a way to get what I needed.

"All right. Breakfast."

By the time the bar closed and all the patrons left and we got things in order for the next day, it was nearly four-thirty. Thankfully, the next day was Sunday and I could sleep in. I wasn't used to the hours.

"Ready?" Jake asked.

"As I'll ever be."

We exited the bar, Chung locking the door behind us, me thinking the security guard was staring hard enough to see right through my disguise.

"I'm parked over this way." Jake indicated west on Randolph.

"I'm over on Lake Street. We can take both cars and meet at the diner."

Though it was far from dawn, the streetlights on Randolph allowed me to see Jake's visage tighten.

"Lake Street's dicey after dark," he said. "You really should stay away from there. I'll drive and bring you back to your car."

Get in a vehicle with a man about whom I know nothing when someone—him?—may be killing young women?

Not hardly.

"I'm perfectly capable of driving myself." I was already backing away. "See you in ten."

Before he could object, I was on my way. The all-night diner was a short drive west and north on Ashland. It wouldn't take long to rendezvous. As I rounded the corner, I glanced over my shoulder to catch Jake staring after me. Feeling thrown a bit, I waved him off. He turned and jogged west, while I headed for the elevated structure.

The area was deserted and middle-of-the-night quiet. So quiet I could hear my own breath.

Was this what it had been like last night when Thora had left the bar?

A quick shiver shot through me, and I pulled the light cape closer. How odd. Summer evenings in Chicago were fairly comfortable, and not usually cool enough to give me a chill.

Then I realized the chill came from deep inside me, as did the prickling along the back of my neck. This was no message from Silke, but the kind of prickling that came from gut instinct.

From the certainty that something was amiss.

Approaching Lake Street, I slipped my hand behind me and unfastened my holster so I could get to my weapon quickly if necessary. My eyes never stopped moving, my head never stopped turning, my ears never stopped straining.

Nothing, nothing, nothing.

Nothing but this sense of unease, of something about to happen.

I spotted my Camaro, so I should have been relieved, but my stomach was knotted. Then a skittering sound sent my pulse shooting skyward, but I couldn't place the direction. I kept moving toward my car but danced around in a circle to search the shadows for Elvin Mowry or one of his so-called vampires.

But I saw no one. Heard not another sound until

my key was in my car door lock. Then a high-pitched whine—familiar somehow—made me whip around and go for my gun.

A flurry of material and wildly flashing limbs seemingly dropped down on me from above. I flew back and threw out my weaponless hands against the car to catch myself. In the dim haze of streetlight, I could see my attacker was a woman. As she came at me, a sweet, cloying smell enveloped my senses and yards of velvet material surrounded my body.

What the hell!

I felt her wet breath and a pinprick on my neck even as I shoved her off.

"Hey, get away from me!"

I was really strong. She was smaller but stronger. It took everything I had to keep her off me. No way could I get hold of her, either. I would rather not have hurt her, but I had to defend myself, and the simpler control tactics I knew weren't going to work here.

I hit her, elbowed her, kicked her, all with little results.

The streetlight caught her eyes and they seemed to glow strangely against the dark, as if the irises were on fire. She made a mewling sound and licked her lips before coming at me with a fury. Somehow, I kept her from getting too close. Our movements were jerky, as if we were engaged in a bizarre dance.

"What the hell do you want?" I grunted.

She gave me no answer. Her expression vacuous, she seemed not to hear me, as if she were completely focused on some internal need. Or she was drugged.

She was also determined to get to me, but for what purpose?

I put some distance between us and tried a round-house kick. My leg was halfway to her when she caught my foot and twisted hard and fast. My other foot went flying and so did I. My body did a three-sixty. I landed on the sidewalk with an explosion of breath. She was coming for me once more, her face eerily illuminated by streetlight, her eyes still having that spooky glow. I lashed out with my foot and she jerked back, then came for me again.

Another high-pitched whine suddenly assaulted my head, and I squeezed my inner ears to protect them, but the pain didn't diminish. I couldn't help myself—I put my hands to my head and covered both ears.

My attacker stopped and stood still, as if enthralled by the blast of pain. And then, as if against her own will, she backed away from me.

Meaning to go after her, to stop her, to get some explanation about what was going on, I let go of my ears and jumped up to my feet just as the high-pitched whine stopped. I pulled my weapon and ran after her. She was too fast for me. I couldn't catch up. Then she slid around a corner, and by the time I got to the cross street, she was gone.

"Damn!" I stood there, breathing hard.

Wondering what the hell had just happened.

Chapter 5

Jake melded with the shadows even after he'd convinced the new one to give up her attack despite her need to feed. What had thrown him was that Silke had covered her ears as if she were able to hear the high-pitched command.

How was that possible?

And was it equally possible that this was not Silke Caldwell?

He watched her now as, weapon held out in a two-handed grip, she peered around into the dark, but Jake didn't think she was ready to see the real danger. Few people were.

She managed to get her car door open without letting down her guard. Gun still in hand, she slid into the driver's seat and slammed the door shut. Listening intently, he caught the click that told him she'd locked herself in.

Whoever she might be.

All night, he'd felt something off…something different about this Silke. Like when she'd floored Mowry's follower—not the sweet-natured Silke he was used to, certainly, not unless she'd been play-acting all along and had showed her true colors only tonight.

A woman with a weapon…

Waiting until her car was headed west under the elevated track, Jake left the shadows and headed for his own vehicle, wondering how he was going to deal with the armed and dangerous woman.

I was still shaking inside as I headed down Ashland Avenue toward All Night Long, the diner where I would meet Jake.

One of the recruits in my gym class had asked me if I was ever afraid being a cop. Hell, yes, and I never wanted to stop being afraid. It was the overconfident cops who got themselves hurt or killed.

You never knew what you were getting into when it came to a street altercation. And I still didn't know what I'd just run into.

That sound that had stopped me cold was familiar. And now I knew why. I remembered the night I found LaTonya. When I'd called for backup, I'd heard that very sound, though not as loud; I'd thought it was my cell phone gone bonkers. I'd been wrong. So what *had* I heard?

Whoever had attacked me seemed out of her mind

on drugs. And she probably had been trying to get up close and personal to get money off me to feed her habit.

As to those weirdly glowing eyes...

I reminded myself they had some pretty fancy contact lenses these days. Ones that made a person's eyes look like those of a cat or a lizard or other animal. And crazy ones for Halloween. Ones that looked like fire. That had to be it—the only thing that made sense.

So why was the skin at the back of my neck crawling as I remembered feeling her wet breath on it?

What had *that* been about?

Too up close for my comfort.

I saw the neon diner sign ahead and started looking for a place to park. Even at night, parking was at a premium. But for once Lady Luck was smiling at me. I got a spot practically right in front of the door.

But then when I walked into the diner, I changed my mind and thought maybe Lady Luck was having a good laugh at my expense.

No Jake.

Considering how long I'd been held up by the woman attacking me, Jake should have been here a while ago. Okay, so had he stood me up or what?

I was still charged, pumped, the adrenaline queen. No way was I going to sleep anytime soon. I might as well give Jake a shot at showing.

No sooner had I claimed a table than the outside door opened and Jake himself strolled in. This was the first I'd seen him in good light. Candlelight—even the fake kind like that at Heart of Darkness—

romanticized everything, especially a person's appearance. But in Jake's case, I was sure he could stand up under bright sunlight.

He spotted me and immediately headed for my table.

"You showed," I said. "I was beginning to wonder."

He glanced at the table empty of anything but salt and pepper shakers and a napkin holder. "Looks like you just got here yourself."

"I had some trouble getting into my car. What happened to you?"

"Had to stop for gas."

Gas, huh? Now, where in the world would he find a station open in this area at this early hour?

Jake took the seat opposite me. His lips were slightly curved as if he was amused about something, and his teeth shone white under the fluorescent light. I could hardly take my gaze off his mouth. And as I stared, I swore his incisors seemed slightly longer than normal. Then I blinked and realized my imagination was playing tricks on me.

The waitress came around and asked if we wanted coffee. Call me nuts, but I did. The adrenaline was pouring out of me now and I needed that caffeine jolt to clear my brain cells if I was going to get any worthwhile information out of Jake DeAtley.

He had coffee, too.

Before the waitress could get away, we each ordered the manager's special: three eggs, three pancakes, three slices of bacon, three sausages and hash browns.

"A woman who eats," he mused.

"Most women eat, just not in public." Thinking to myself that, despite her exotic beauty, the bar owner probably starved herself to stay so thin, I said, "Not every woman is a Desiree Leath."

"I would hope not."

I could hardly miss the irony in Jake's tone. Well, he for sure knew more about the woman than I did. How much more?

"You and Desiree seem pretty friendly."

"Strictly business."

"And what a business, right?"

"It keeps life interesting."

"How interesting?" I pressed. "What's the weirdest thing you've seen go on in the bar?"

"I think it's pretty weird that non-Goths come to be entertained by a group shunned by most of society. Even weirder when a non-Goth tries to pass as one."

He was staring at me so hard I thought he could look right inside me when he said it.

"People like to pretend they're someone they're not once in a while," I said. "Sometimes a costume is necessary."

One of his eyebrows shot up, a dark slash over oddly pale irises. "You know, I really do admire a woman who can handle herself."

I was not immune. The short hairs on my forearms stood at attention. "So you said earlier."

He leaned back in his chair and watched me through slitted lids. "And you said something interesting about evil. About people not recognizing it."

"Ted Bundy." I was unable to think of a better or

more appropriate example. "He used his charm on twenty-eight young women to get them in situations where he could rape and murder them. Twenty-eight that we know of. His victims could actually number more than a hundred."

"There are other kinds of evil in this world," Jake said. "Evil that can't be fought in traditional ways."

A curious sensation slid through my stomach. "Examples?"

"Evil that's seductive, that will make a normal person rethink his or her values to get what they most desire."

"Which would be?"

"Power. Wealth. Immortality."

My stomach twisted, but I told myself the smell from the grill was getting to me. Jake could be weird, all right. And serious. He wasn't so much as cracking a smile.

"About that creep with roaming hands," I said, hoping to get his take on the vampire cult. "Do you know anything about him?"

Jake shook his head. "I've never noticed him with Mowry before. *Have you?*"

"Uh, no." That was the truth since I'd never even been in the bar before. "He's probably one of Mowry's cult members."

"Cult?"

"You know, the vampire cult."

Jake snorted. "Pretentious little pissants. They wouldn't know a vampire if one bit them."

I raised my eyebrows. "If there really were vampires, you mean."

"How do you know there *aren't?*"

I gave him a look. Of course he was joking, but I played along with him anyway. "I'm a rational woman."

"Not everything in life is rational."

"No, murder isn't, for example," I said. "Nor draining women of their blood. I really have heard rumors about the vampire cult doing such a thing. Actually, Thora pretty much confirmed them." Even though it had been to my twin rather than to me. "I just hope Mowry doesn't know she was talking to me about it. Or to anyone else."

"You sound worried."

"I am. It doesn't help that Thora didn't show to-night, either." I eyed him to see his reaction when I said "It makes me wonder what happened to her."

"So call her and find out."

"Are you kidding? She can't afford a cell." Or so Silke had told me. "And I don't know where she lives, either. Well, I do know she's living with Mowry. I just don't know where that might be. You wouldn't know, would you?"

"Sorry."

Was he? Rather than sounding concerned, Jake seemed aloof. His eyes were hooded and trained on me. I shifted in my chair and tried to think of a new tactic.

"For someone who has been at the bar awhile, you don't seem too connected. I thought bartenders knew everything about their customers."

"One could say the same about waitresses."

Here we were at an old-fashioned standoff, and me without a tiebreaker line.

Then Jake said, "I haven't been working for Desiree all that long, remember."

Of course I didn't remember. And Silke hadn't told me how long anyone had been there, something I hadn't thought to ask. I didn't know how to respond.

Luckily for me, the waitress arrived with our breakfasts. She set an oversize plate in front of each of us. For the next few minutes, food was the center of interest and conversation fell to the side. I hadn't realized how hungry I was. Or maybe I hadn't been hungry until after expending the unexpected energy of fending off an attack.

"So tell me about yourself," Jake said when half his plate was empty.

"What's to tell? You know I'm an out-of-work actress. Out of theater work," I amended, not liking the topic. I didn't want to talk about Silke. "What about you?" I asked, turning the question back on him. "What's your excuse for bartending?"

"Paying the rent. Buying you breakfast."

That he was being as evasive as I came across to me loud and clear. But why? And after working with Silke, why had he chosen this particular time to try to hook up with her?

Not that any actual hooking up would be going on, I thought, not in the literal sense. As I pierced a whole sausage with my fork and nibbled off the end, I suddenly realized Jake was staring at my mouth. I shoved the rest of the sausage in and grasped at a way to get our conversation back on track.

But all I could think of was, "You don't seem like the bartender type."

"What type am I?"

"Someone who should be in charge."

"I am in charge. Of myself, anyway. The rest of the world has to take responsibility for itself."

I was getting vibes off him again, as if I'd hit too close to home about something he didn't want to discuss.

Jake gave me an appraising look. "Why did you accept my invitation to breakfast this time?"

This time? Silke hadn't mentioned any other invitations.

So I echoed his "This time?" My nerves fluttered as I hedged, "You mean the only time."

"Uh-uh. A couple of weeks back I asked if you wanted to meet me for coffee."

"No, you didn't," I said, wondering if it was true. I simply didn't believe it. Silke knew what was at stake here, so she wouldn't hold out. Even so, my senses were all at alert as I tried to remain casual, because I couldn't figure out why he was testing me. "You're confusing me with someone else."

"Mmm. The Silke I know would get flustered rather than get rough with some guy who came on to her. She doesn't have a sharp retort in her repertoire. She wouldn't answer a question with a question."

I pretended to go along with him. "It sounds like you know this Silke of yours pretty well."

His gaze sharpened. "She's not mine, but you... well, that's an interesting proposition."

A provocative statement from a potentially dangerous man, I decided. He *had* made me. Not that I would admit it. What reason did he have for playing games with me? My fluttering pulse shot into overdrive. I forced a laugh and made another Silke expression.

"I'm tired." Of playing games with him, though I didn't finish my statement, either. "Thanks for breakfast. It's been…well, unusual if entertaining." Unfortunately, I hadn't gotten what I'd hoped for. Instead, I was simply suspicious of Jake. "But as much fun as I'm having, I guess I'd better head for home. A girl needs her sleep, and it's late."

"Almost dawn," Jake added glancing toward the windows, where the first streaks lightened the sky. "Let me take care of the check and I'll walk you to your car. City streets can be dangerous. You never know what might be waiting for you out there."

If only he knew how true that statement was.

Or did he?

With her good eye, she stares at me. The other rolls along her cheek. "It's about time."

"I never gave up."

"Words don't mean anything."

"I'm on it, I swear. I'll find your murderer if it's the last thing I ever do."

"Until you do, I can never rest…."

I awoke to an annoying racket. I pulled the pillow over my head, but I could still hear it. The telephone had no pity. At least it had pulled me out of another unwelcome dream. Groaning, I rolled over, and after eyeing the clock, which told me I'd had little more than four hours of sleep, I picked up the receiver.

"This had better be important," I groused.

"Don't you check your messages or answer them?" Silke asked. "I've been worried about you."

"I got home too late."

"Well, don't scare me like that again, okay?"

Wanting to clarify things Jake had said, I told her about having breakfast with him and how he'd suggested that he'd asked her out before.

"He was lying," Silke said. "But why?"

"He was testing me. And I don't know why. But he guessed the truth, that I wasn't you. He thinks he knows anyway. Not that I admitted to anything."

"Well that's that, then," Silke said. "It's over."

"No, it's not. I'm going back to the bar tonight."

"You were just supposed to go for one night, to see what you could find out."

"I barely got started with that cast of characters."

"But if Jake—"

"What? You think he'll tell everyone?"

"He's not like that. He minds his own business. Well, usually. But what if he's not on the up and up?"

A thought I had entertained. Not only had I not gotten anything on Thora or Raven, but also I hadn't gotten anything on him. He'd been as evasive as I.

Almost as if he'd extended the breakfast invitation so that he could interrogate me…

"I can handle him," I said with more confidence than I was feeling. "I can beat him at his own game."

"That's important to you, isn't it? Winning, I mean."

"There's nothing to win here. Just a mystery to solve." Maybe a murderer to put behind bars.

"But you didn't get anything off Jake."

"You're right." Nothing other than raised suspicion. "But earlier, someone attacked me on the way to my car—a Goth girl, probably on drugs. That makes me wonder if the murderer is really a man."

"Omigod!"

"Don't worry, I'm fine. But I'm going back to the bar tonight."

Silke tried to talk me out of it, insisted it was too dangerous, apologized for getting me into this mess in the first place. As far as I was concerned, no apology was necessary. After being attacked by a woman who apparently had been drugged out, I was sure something dark and dangerous was continuing to go on in the area. And I was going to get to the heart of the matter.

I was going to put LaTonya to rest.

After assuring Silke I would be at her place with some kind of take-out dinner so that she could do my makeup again, I cut our conversation short.

I dressed, then sat down in front of my computer. Part of me thought I should be investigating Jake DeAtley, as well as the other key players who hung around the bar—Desiree, Blaise, Chung, Mowry.

I started with Jake.

I Googled him. No links. 411-ed him. No phone. Searched the white pages. No address.

I tried the others. My frustration continued.

I wanted to check them all through the CPD system, but I didn't have a squad with a computer, so I would have to report in to an office or to the academy and log in. Unfortunately that meant that I would leave a record of my search that could be traced back to me. Not good. Not in my circumstances.

And if I leaned on Stella too much, I would raise her suspicions. I was supposed to be teaching rather than detecting, after all. So approaching her could wait one more day until I had more to go on.

I tried another search engine with the same results. Nada. I could hardly believe it.

You couldn't find everyone on the net, but nearly everyone. But not these five. Not one of them. Strange that they all had that in common.

If I hadn't seen them all with my own eyes, I would think that not one of them existed.

Chapter 6

I took a long nap before heading for Heart of Darkness—I had to report to the training academy the next morning, and I wouldn't get off until after midnight. Sunday was an early night at the bar. Luckily, the bad dreams stayed at bay.

I entered the bar with a sizzle that had nothing to do with Jake DeAtley, no matter how he stared at me when I swung by the bar, done up in Silke's finery—a black velvet dress with loose elbow-length sleeves and a plunging neckline revealing the lace edging on a red French-cut bra. The biggest problem with this outfit other than its making me highly uncomfortable—who had ever decided bras needed wires, anyway?—was hiding my gun. I'd had to holster it under the full skirts of the dress and open the seam of a pocket so I could get to it if necessary.

Since Raven hadn't shown up, I decided to concentrate on LaTonya. Who'd known her, whom she hung with, and whom she might have been with that night three months before. My first several attempts were met with shrugged shoulders and grunted denials.

Then I handed a drink to a fuchsia-haired Goth who called herself Sheena and asked, "Do you by any chance know a girl named LaTonya who used to hang here?"

Sheena's brow furrowed. "LaTonya?"

"Fair-skinned African American, really tall? She's not a Goth. At least I don't think so. But apparently she likes the atmosphere here."

"Oh, yeah. Toni. She came in a few times…not lately, though."

A thrill shot through me, but I tried to appear surprised. "Oh, really? Well, do you know anything about her?"

Sheena blinked and her expression turned curious. "Who wants to know?"

"One of my customers wants an intro. He said he'd make it worth my while if I could hook them up. Normally, I don't do that kind of stuff, but I've got rent to pay."

"Yeah, tough," Sheena said. "So ask Elvin. He was into her."

Elvin Mowry, leader of the vampire cult. Great. He'd been into Thora, as well.

Another of those vampire-cult references I'd found in my research flashed through my mind.

A young woman had decided she was ready to

"feed" and the leader cut an area below his wrist as he was having sex with her. She sucked his blood as they came together. She slept a while, then needed more blood, and went after another of the members to satisfy her. After that, she swore the only thing that stopped her hunger was more blood while having sex.

I shuddered inside and said, "So Elvin was interested, huh?" I hoped that outwardly I didn't show what I was thinking. "Anyone else?"

Sheena shrugged. "I saw her wandering around the shops. Maybe one of the owners has info on her."

"Good thought. Thanks."

I moved on and took my next order. It wouldn't do to press Sheena for information too hard. I didn't want her getting suspicious and passing on the word that I was asking too many questions at once.

The tattoo on LaTonya's thigh…could she have gotten it at Taboo Tattoo?

I'd noticed tattoos on most of the Goth customers, male and female, and suddenly it occurred to me there might be some significance to the type of tattoo. I also wondered if Thora'd had one. Maybe Silke would know.

I glanced over to where Mowry sat, the centerpiece to his minions, as I liked to call them. I wondered if there was a way to get him alone without giving him ideas. Blaise would probably be the better place to start. Or so I hoped.

Now, how to get to Blaise. I checked my watch. Taboo Tattoo would only be open for another hour. Either I had to go into the shop on my break and possibly tick off Desiree for doing another disappearing act, or I had to take the chance that he would come straight into the bar for an after-work drink as Silke told me he often did.

I saw my opportunity a quarter of an hour later, when Blaise Allcock walked in the door and sat himself at the bar.

"I ought to change my hours on Sunday," I heard him grouse to Jake. "The number of customers hardly makes it worth my while to open up at all."

"Must have something to do with church day," Jake agreed, setting a goblet of red wine down in front of the tattoo and piercing artist.

"Avoidance or something."

Blaise was an odd one, I thought, taking a better look at him than I had the night before.

His bleached hair was shoulder length, his skin had a natural pallor. He did wear makeup, if far more subtle than the Goths—his gray eyes were lined and lids colored with shades of gray from dove to charcoal. And the faint blush across his lips wasn't natural, either. His nails were long for a man and polished with a transparent silver. He wore tight black pants, which I swore held a cup to enhance his sexuality. But his poet's shirt trimmed with ribbons and lace and showing off his hairless chest was definitely feminine. I didn't think he was gay, merely sexually ambiguous—just like the name Blaise.

Perhaps his taste in sex partners was all-inclusive. I simply couldn't read him more directly than that. The question was how to be subtle yet get what I needed.

I slid up to the bar and gave Jake my order. "Two glasses of Shiraz and a Bloody Cosmo." Then I smiled at Blaise. "What's new at Tattoo?"

"Awesome chandelier earrings."

He swung his hair over one shoulder and my gaze immediately shot to his ear, but all he wore was a sparkly stud.

"My favorites are the bloodred crystals," he told me.

"How much?"

"A steal at thirty-five."

"Hmm. Sounds like."

"They would look beautiful against your long throat," he said, his voice low, his lids lowering as he considered it. "Just like drops of blood."

Blaise was certainly dramatic. Or perhaps I ought to say affected. Purposely. He sold himself as part of his product.

"I'll think about it." I glanced Jake's way. The order was about filled, so I got to the point with Blaise. "Say, did Toni ever get that tattoo she wanted?"

"Toni?"

"Tall girl, African American. Not a Goth." I bluffed. "She wanted one of those great winged gargoyles on her thigh."

"Doesn't ring a bell," Blaise said, just as Jake set the drinks on her tray. "Not that my memory is the best, what with thousands of customers over the years."

"Thousands?" I echoed, disappointed that he didn't seem to have any memory of LaTonya.

"Tens of thousands."

"You must be older than you look, then." Which now that I got up close and personal, I surmised to be fortyish.

He tilted his head and looked at me through eyelashes thick enough to inspire envy in any woman. "You might be surprised."

I would swear Blaise was flirting with me. And from behind the bar, Jake was scowling. What? He couldn't take listening to a little banter?

I pulled the tray toward me, intending to take off. "Customers. In the dozens," I added jokingly. "I can't remember them all, either."

"Hey, come see those earrings tomorrow," Blaise said. "And maybe I can talk you into one of my very special tattoos."

"The earrings sound like a possible. But needles?" My stomach clenched and I shivered visibly. "Those I can do without."

I felt his eyes follow me through the crowd.

Only later did I wonder if I'd made a mistake about the needle thing. Silke had never told me about getting a tattoo, but for all I knew she could have several in places that I hadn't seen in a while. I'd have to remember to ask her, and if necessary, do damage control.

Not that I would actually get a tattoo.

Needles really did give me the willies. My avoidance went all the way back to my childhood, when a series of bronchial infections had made me feel like a human pincushion. Silke'd had to get me drunk before I got my ears pierced. No way would I ever consider getting a tattoo.

What felt like a heavy gaze followed me and I glanced back, expecting to see Blaise looking after me. Or Jake. But both were busy. But the feeling didn't let up, so I craned farther and found that I had Desiree's interest.

I was the first to look away.

I was too busy for a while serving drinks to think about the real reason I was here. As the crowd thinned, LaTonya and Thora and the attack on me filled my mind.

I didn't know anything about Thora Nelson, and I didn't think my sister was much better informed. She didn't even have Thora's phone number or address, so how close could they have been? But what I knew about LaTonya told me she was too level-headed to get into the weird cult stuff and go off the deep end.

Unless someone had pushed her…

My attacker the night before had definitely been out of it. There were plenty of drugs that could send someone off the deep end.

Sheena had said to ask Elvin Mowry about Toni/LaTonya. I glanced at the upper deck, where he held court, a Goth girl I didn't know seated across his lap. Suddenly he reached up and pulled her head down toward his. It looked as if he was nuzzling at her neck. Her expression was thoroughly sexual, and I wondered if they would abandon all propriety and have at it right there in front of everyone.

I felt a surge of disgust and yet I couldn't look away, kind of like when you see a multicar pile-up on the expressway. The cult leader seemed to have a grip on her neck and wasn't letting go, as though he was sucking the life's blood out of her....

My heartbeat quickened and my instincts went on alert.

Focusing on them alone, I casually moved toward the stairs as her lids lowered and her features went slack. What did he think he was doing? And what could I do? I couldn't break cover just when I was getting somewhere. I looked toward Jake. Busy.

By the time I climbed the stairs, the girl had slumped over, eyes closed. And when Mowry raised his head, he quickly licked his lips.

Was that blood on them?

Then Mowry's companion sat up and moaned.

"Oh, can we do that again, Elvie, but someplace more private?"

I stared and she eyed *me* with distaste. Nice.

"Another round?" I asked, trying not to sound out of breath.

"Nah, not tonight," Mowry said, giving me a look that said I could have been the one receiving his personal attention. "We have more delicious treats on the menu."

Goth Girl stood and flicked her hair. Her neck was red where Mowry had been sucking on her, but as far as I could tell, no blood had been exchanged.

Chagrined, I let the wanna-be vampires pass by me and then faced the table filled with discarded bottles and glasses and ashtrays filled with half-smoked cigarettes.

As I cleared the table, I became aware of the rumble of voices, words smothered by the ever present thump-thump of music. At first I tuned them out somewhat as I tuned out Silke. But then I realized the voices were raised in argument…or worse, a struggle of some sort. And one of the voices was that of a young woman.

I looked around. Nothing. Where was the argument coming from?

When I heard a muffled "Don't!" from the woman, followed by what sounded like a body being tossed, I left the table half-cleared and went to investigate. The muted noises drew me around the end of the bar and to the door that connected the bar to the inside of the shopping mall.

Without thinking about the possible consequences, I opened the door and raced out into the mall. It was after hours so all the stores were closed and the mall was completely dark. But I heard a physical struggle to my left and saw Hung Chung pressed up against a shopfront window, his meaty arm pinning a fragile-looking woman with dark hair in tufts around her face and three earrings in one eyebrow.

Raven!

Her top was torn and Chung was groping her chest with his free hand. She was pushing at him and trying to free herself to no avail. Her expression was frightened and tears smudged her eye makeup into drippy dark pools.

"Get out!" Chung ordered me.

"I don't think so. Raven doesn't look like she's enjoying your company."

"What she wants is none of your business."

"It is if you're forcing yourself on her."

"If you know what's good for you—"

"Raven, talk to me."

I knew from my time as a patrol cop that some women liked rough sex and if you tried to interfere, they made it rough on you. But this was clearly not a two-way affair.

"I—I just want to go," she whispered.

My gut tightened. He *was* messing with her against her will. "You heard Raven. Let go of her, or—"

"Or what? You think you can take me, Silke?"

"Try me," I said.

Chung turned his back on me and ground his mouth into Raven's. I cursed him under my breath, then grabbed the fleshy part of his underarm and twisted. He came away from the girl with an explosion of sound and movement. I was lucky to get out of his way without being hit by one of his ham-sized fists.

"Go now!" I told Raven.

She didn't hesitate, and as she flew by me, she croaked, "Thank you."

"Call the police!"

She didn't answer.

I didn't take my eyes off Chung, who was focused and deadly-looking. Suddenly, he came at me in a frontal attack. I sidestepped, tugged at his arm to spin him around and then elbowed him in the back. He went down hard but rolled and struck out with powerful legs. I took a blow that knocked me off my feet. I landed hard on my hip, but conditioning didn't allow me to cry out. I was so pumped, I barely felt it anyway.

Silke was freaking, though. I felt it not only in my head, but all through my body. Busy determining the security guard's next move, I shut her out without another thought.

Chung got to his feet and I did the same, quickly reorienting myself to the bar door. I was no fool to stay in this fight any longer than necessary. It wasn't like I could arrest the pervert without blowing my cover. I just wanted to dissuade him from further criminal behavior.

"Is this all you know how to do?" I asked. "Physically assault women?"

"You mean bitches like you?"

He came for me again and I waited until he was just close enough. I snapped out my leg and caught him at the side of the knee with my foot. His big body torqued and I followed up with a flat-handed strike to the side of his head.

He went down hard.

I knew that I'd scrambled his brains a bit and that he would be disoriented for a short while.

Enough time to get out.

I didn't make the mistake of turning my back on Chung, though. I kept my eye on him until I was actually inside the bar. I took a moment to breathe, to let my adrenaline level even out. Then, looking for Raven, I wondered if Chung was simply a bully…a potential rapist…or a murderer.

Chapter 7

I could feel that I was the focus of attention. Jake's. He was staring at me, and I got the weirdest feeling that he knew what had just gone on in the mall.

Which was impossible, of course.

And yet, he asked, "Are you all right?"

"I'm fine." My hip was now refuting that statement, but I would live. I looked around. "Did Raven leave?"

"I saw her run into the women's bathroom."

I immediately headed that way, wondering if Chung's attack on her was related to Thora's death in any way. He was both violent and a sexual predator—both traits of LaTonya's murderer. I wanted to know if Thora had been sexually assaulted, as well.

Inside the rest room, I heard muffled sniffling and

realized Raven was in a stall. She'd left the door
open. Her back was pressed to the stall and she was
shaking. When she saw me she let out a sob.

"Hey, are you all right?" I asked.

She nodded. "H-he didn't hurt you, did he?"

"I'm okay. Did you call anyone for help?"

"N-no." She sobbed again. "I—I'm sorry. I should
have told J-Jake."

Truth be told, I was glad she hadn't. He could suspect all he wanted, but he hadn't seen what had gone
on in that mall between Chung and me.

"You shouldn't let Chung get away with molest-
ing you." I was ticked that I couldn't arrest him myself without putting an end to my investigation from
the inside. "You could have him arrested."

"Thanks for helping me out, Silke, but he won't
try that again."

He would—if not with her, then with some other
young woman—but I didn't want to argue. I wanted
to get information from her. "Listen, about the other
night—"

Raven's eyes went wide and she looked around
wildly as she lowered her voice. "Forget the other
night!"

"How? Thora's dead. You found her." I assumed
she had no clue that the body had disappeared.

"Well, maybe she wasn't dead…I was, um, a little high. I could have imagined some of it."

No shocker there. Yet I thought she was using
drugs as an excuse, so she didn't have to face what
she'd actually seen. "What *do* you remember?"

Raven shrugged and had trouble meeting my gaze. She was scared, probably doubly so after being attacked tonight. That added to a good dose of guilt in my regard. Had Chung convinced her to forget what she'd seen?

"You don't really want to forget Thora, do you?" I prodded. I could tell she was torn. Most of a detective's work was talking to people, wearing them down until you got to the truth. "You have to remember something about how Thora looked when you found her."

Raven shook her head.

"I know I wouldn't forget if I saw something like that. It would haunt my dreams." I knew I shouldn't lead her, but I was getting desperate to make another positive connection with the first murder. "Did Thora look like she was sexually molested or anything?"

"Okay, yes…her skirt…it was up." Raven's voice low and frantic, pleaded, "Can we drop it now?"

Her skirt was up—the same as with LaTonya.

"You need to tell the cops what you know," I said in Silke's most persuasive voice.

"I—I can't."

"It'll happen again. You know that. You don't want to see anyone else hurt or killed."

I could see Raven's mind working—*she* could be that *anyone else*. She was staring down at her hands, which were knotted together. Fear leached off her in waves.

"Raven, please. You might have seen something that could lead to the murderer."

"Or lead the murderer to me."

"The police can help you." I would see to it. I would help her myself if I had to. "They can keep you safe."

"I—I don't know."

She was weakening. I could feel it. "Don't let this happen to another girl," I pleaded.

"I'll think about it."

Was she serious or brushing me off? I pulled a sheet of paper from my order pad and tore it in half. I scribbled the number to my cell and handed it to her, then gave her the other half and the pen.

"Can I least have your number? I'll call you later, after the bar closes."

Raven hesitated, then gave in. I wanted to tell her to give me her last name and address, but I was afraid of pushing too hard. I just prayed the number she was giving me was real. If it was, I could do a reverse directory and get her name and address from it.

"Okay, Silke," Raven said, handing me the paper. "I'll think about it. I'll think about everything. I—I promise. Thanks for being a good friend."

We headed back into the bar and had barely gotten inside when Chung entered. Having recovered faster than some would from a blow to the head, he quickly zeroed in on me and Raven and didn't let go. I meshed gazes with him, wanting more than anything to lock him up personally...but I couldn't.

So I was the one to look away first.

Raven quickly put herself between two of her friends, so I got back to work with a feeling of satisfaction. I thought I'd gotten to her. I would have to call her later, when she was away from the bar, and talk to her again. If I could cinch a witness willing to tell what she saw, I would make the investigation official. Then I would have the full resources of the department at my disposal. And a better shot at nailing the killer.

I was trying to think of a way to convince Raven when Desiree caught my eye and waved me over. I approached her warily. Had the security guard complained to her already?

Her dark eyes looked almost black in the low light as she gave me a piercing look. "You and Hung Chung. You don't play together nice."

That was certainly putting a spin on things. So did everyone in the bar know about our altercation? It happened in the mall, so I didn't see how. Undoubtedly, she'd sensed the tension between Chung and me when he'd come back into the bar.

"He was forcing himself on someone. So I just tried to stop him. That's it."

Desiree slid a glance to the bar and I followed. Even though he was still on duty, Chung was nursing his wounded pride with a beer.

"A man of his nature has no control," Desiree said. "He could have hurt you."

"Sometimes fear isn't a good enough reason *not* to do something." I swore that made Desiree look at me with respect. "Does Chung have any kinky tricks other than force?"

Desiree's expression turned inscrutable. "His tricks will prove ineffective."

"Does that mean you're going to do something

about him?" Wondering if I was making a mistake in trusting the bar owner simply because she was a woman, I pushed her a little further. "I've been hearing weird stuff lately, like someone here at the bar has a taste for blood."

Desiree went ashen, if that were possible. I swear her already pale skin lightened.

"Rumors," she said. "Considering our customers, this is no surprise. But you, Silke, you prove to be quite a surprise."

Was that a compliment? Or simply an observation that should tell me I had now raised her suspicions where I—rather, Silke—was concerned? She certainly hadn't liked the question, and she'd brushed it off rather than really answer it.

"I don't like seeing women get hurt," I told her. "Especially ones I know."

Desiree nodded as if she agreed. "Don't worry, I shall take care of Chung," she promised. "He won't bother anyone here again. That includes you."

And indeed, a short while later, I saw the bar owner in conference with the security guard. Hot anger radiated off Chung. Desiree was coldly angry.

And I got a little nervous about the whole incident. What if Chung gave Desiree a load of crap about me and she believed it? Then I would be out of here, and my investigation would be ended.

But a few minutes later, Desiree passed me with a distracted smile. So far so good. Too bad she'd avoided telling me anything of value about Chung.

Did she know something about him that she wasn't telling?

* * *

Silke continued to worry long after Shelley had shut her out. What the heck had happened?

She hated this whole identity switch. Hated being shut out when her sister was in danger. Hated that she'd been the one to pull Shelley into this mess.

What had she been thinking?

No matter what Raven had wanted after finding Thora's body, Silke knew she should have called 911 instead of her sister. She'd simply thought Shelley should be in on this, so she could clear her name. If only Shelley would relax and accept their psychic connection, Silke thought, picking up a book on casting spells.

She'd always been attuned to her sixth sense, something Shelley had denied ever since the time she'd gotten her signals crossed and had mistakenly roughed up a guy Silke had been flirting with. Puberty had done weird stuff to them both, but she'd gotten past it. Shelley hadn't. That incident had been it for her. Shelley had blamed their twin mind-meld, as she used to call it, for her hurting someone who was innocent. So while Silke learned to expand her mind and her personal power, Shelley had closed down and had never trusted that particular instinct again.

But why couldn't her twin open up now, when her life could depend on it? Silke wondered, worry eating at her.

She set down the book and called the bar and when Jake answered, affected one of the accents she'd used on stage.

"Silke Caldwell, please," she said, her voice ripely Southern and a little breathless.

"Who is this?"

Not a polite "Who can I tell her is calling?" but a demand that made Silke crash the receiver into its cradle. Great. Now what?

Glancing at the clock, she realized it was almost midnight. Heart of Darkness was about to close. It wouldn't take her more than ten minutes to get there at this hour. Part of her wanted to march down to the bar to see that Shelley was all right for herself. But doing so would blow Shelley's cover and put her in even more danger.

Calling Shelley's cell or home phone would probably be as futile as it had been the night before when her sister hadn't bothered with her voice mail.

There was only one thing for it. She went to her key depository—a fancy bowl on a bookshelf—and pulled out the ones to Shelley's apartment. She would go to her sister's place and wait for her there.

I was exhausted when I left the bar, relieved to find parking across the street from my building. Before getting out of the car, I checked my surroundings to make certain there were no nasty surprises awaiting me. All I saw were a couple of guys out with their dogs for a late-night stroll.

I hurried to my building. Tension I hadn't even realized I was holding drained from me as I hurried up the stairs to my second-floor apartment. By the time I got to the landing, I was relaxed.

Which lasted all of a moment until I saw who had

a shoulder wedged against the jamb of my apartment door. My pulse pushed against my veins like a locomotive picking up speed. I stopped dead in my tracks.

"What are you doing here, Jake? How do you even know where I live?"

"I followed you. Unless you were trained to spot a tail—and you're not, are you?—you wouldn't have seen me."

Which was why he'd beat me to my door, right? I narrowed my gaze on him and thought maybe I ought to get my hand on my weapon.

Mouth dry, I asked, "Okay, how did you know which apartment is mine?"

"The number on your mailbox."

Right. My mailbox said S. Caldwell.

Jake said, "Hung Chung is no one to mess with."

He'd followed me out of concern? "I wasn't messing with him."

I hadn't been. I'd seriously meant to discourage Chung from his aberrant behavior. But how had Jake known what had gone down between us? Remembering his knowing look earlier, I wondered if he could possibly have heard the altercation or if he'd put two and two together and come up with four simply by seeing a disheveled Raven, then me, then a furious Chung come into the bar.

"You've made a dangerous enemy," Jake said.

"I can take care of myself." I moved toward my door and him.

"How badly did he hurt you? You cover pretty well, but you're limping."

Hearing what sounded like real concern in his voice, I asked, "What's it to you?"

"I wouldn't like to see anything happen to you."

"I can take care of myself."

"Can you? Some people are so damn trusting they don't recognize evil when they face it."

I started. He'd basically turned my own statement about fear back on me. But I was one of the least trusting people on earth. "What evil?"

"It's all around you. And if you're not careful, it will eat you alive…whoever you are."

Whoever…

He was challenging me on more than one level. My identity. My ability to see what was right in front of me. I felt my blood humming.

"And you see this evil?"

"Clearly."

"Then tell me about it."

Jake didn't answer, but even in the dim light I could see that his features had gone taut. I had the crazy notion that he wanted to tell me…but wouldn't. He kept those fathomless eyes glued to me. Did he know something I should know? The identity of a murderer, perhaps? Or was he conning me? One thing was for certain: he had his own agenda.

Not knowing what to think, not sure I could trust him, I pushed by Jake and inserted my keys in the dead bolt.

"Hung Chung," he said. "You should have called for help."

I turned to face him. "You?"

"Don't underestimate me."

"Don't underestimate me, either."

We were in the midst of a glaring match when a warning buzz assaulted me. With my senses sharpened, I immediately knew Silke was agitated. Though I was frustrated at her timing, I didn't close her out. I concentrated on letting her feel my rising irritation. But once I opened that gate, Silke took full advantage. I felt her grab on with every psychic vibe she could muster, and I suddenly knew she was in my apartment.

"I think we'd better call it a night," I said, fearing Silke might open the door and then Jake would see us both.

Jake's gaze intensified, and for a moment I felt weird, almost as if he were trying to force his will on me. Strangely enough, for a moment I felt as if he could make me do anything he wanted if he tried hard enough. Then, with a sigh, he disconnected, leaving me irritated and wondering what that had been about.

"I'll go," he agreed, "as long as you promise me to stay put."

"Where do you imagine I would go at this time of night?"

"Don't go anywhere." He started down the hall. "I wouldn't want yours to be the next body found drained of blood."

The statement was like a whack to my solar plexus. My heart kicked into overdrive, and it had nothing to do with attraction.

"What the hell do you know about it?" I demanded.

He whipped around to face me. "You first."

I realized he'd just tricked me into admitting I did know. But it was an even trade, because now I knew that *he* knew. Where exactly did that get us?

"I'm not the one who brought it up, Jake." My mind was whirling with questions about his stake in this. "And I can't believe you're being so protective because of a rumor."

"Then it's time for some straight talk," he said. "Heart of Darkness holds dangerous secrets—"

I interrupted with a breathless "You've seen a body?"

He hesitated just a second too long before saying, "Near the bar? No."

Something about that statement was off. "Then what makes you think the rumors aren't just that?"

"I have my sources."

Sources? As in an informant? Someone like Junior Diaz? If so, that would make his interest official.

"So what are you doing about it, Jake?" I asked. "Running your own investigation?"

"Something like that."

"Why?" I wanted to ask whom he worked for, but I thought the situation would be best handled with a little more finesse. "Is this a full-time preoccupation or a hobby?"

"What is it for you?"

We would have done well on that game show that makes the contestants come up with a question as answer.

"Enough. Good night."

As much as I wanted to keep after Jake for the truth, I suspected I wouldn't get a straight answer out of him. I suspected Silke had her ear pressed to the wood panel so she wouldn't miss a word of our dialogue and worried that if we kept this up long enough, Jake would hear her move around.

I unlocked the door, then made sure Jake wasn't close enough to see inside before opening the door. The moment I closed it, Silke slid into view.

"Shell, what were you thinking taking on Hung Chung? I wasn't tuning in, but when your adrenaline surges it turns up the frequency. Chung is dangerous!"

"So is my job."

I made my way into the bedroom, planning on getting ready for bed. From the chest of drawers, I pulled a pair of soft cotton pajama bottoms and matching crop top. I turned around and practically ran over Silke. I threw the pjs on the bed and started stripping.

"You're not doing this for your job," Silke said from the doorway. "You're doing it because of me. I don't want to be the cause of your getting hurt. You need backup. Other cops. You need to make this official."

"Not yet."

"When, then?"

"When I have something tangible to bring to the table. Hopefully, Raven." I pulled out her number from a pocket. "I'm going to call her right now."

But all I got was her voice mail. I left a message, asking her to call me. Rather, I asked her to call Silke, but I left my number.

Silke looked as disappointed as I felt.

"At least Raven gave me her real number," I said. "I can work with that. But until I get her to agree to tell what she saw, what am I supposed to say—that there's been another dead girl who then disappeared but again I have no proof?"

I see dead people….

Maybe this time the psych evaluation would be done in a rubber room.

Silke didn't say anything until I was climbing into my pajamas. "Hey, those are some bruises."

I glanced down at the back of my thigh and knew this was just the start of the pretty discolored pattern that would settle there. Icing it would help keep down the swelling and bruising, so I headed for the kitchen with Silke following.

Silke was right behind me. "Shell, I want you to stop."

"No, you don't," I countered, grabbing a plastic bag and opening the freezer door.

"I do. You can't keep doing this alone. It's my fault, and I'm admitting it. Take this to Mom, let her know what's going on. She'll know what to do."

"Mom? Not hardly. You just want me to be safe. Believe me, Silke, I'm on my guard."

"That's not good enough, Shell. I didn't know you would go this far. I just wanted you to be the one to make the report on Thora, because I thought it might help you clear your name. I didn't want you to put yourself in danger. Either you talk to Mom or—"

"What?" I interrupted. "You're going to tell on me? Like you said to me, we're not kids anymore."

Silke didn't continue the argument. Instead, she settled into a quiet mode I didn't like. I filled the bag with ice and secured it.

"Look, Silke, I've got to get some sleep. I have a training class to teach first thing in the morning. Don't go, though. I'd rather you bunked in here for the night."

I didn't want my twin running around taking chances any more than she did me. At least I was experienced in protecting myself. On the streets, anyway.

But when it came to men...

I couldn't believe I was attracted to a man with an agenda. Was Jake DeAtley on some kind of citizen-vigilante quest? Was he a media type looking for a story? Or was he official, another cop?

Now I would have to figure out how to take advantage of the connection with Jake. Whatever he knew, I wanted it. The problem was, how would I get him to give it to me?

The creature of the night could sense the *thump-thump* of her heartbeat as she moved along the street. She wasn't really necessary—no reason to hunt for several days, at least—but she was easy pickings.

Besides, she smelled so good—not just her blood, but her heightened emotions as she threw a glance behind her as if she thought someone might be following.

You're looking in the wrong direction.

But then, they usually did.

The fear radiating from her was an aphrodisiac,

tempting and promising an ecstasy that proved as potent as a drug.

She scooted along, her short hair ruffling around her face like little wings. Too bad she didn't have any. Then maybe she could fly away.

Thump-thump…thump-thump…thump-thump…

The sound of her racing heart was too tempting to ignore.

Her instincts warned her, but there was nothing she could do to protect herself. So she ran.

That's it. Faster, faster.

The blood lust surged with the chase.

Too quickly the chase was over…and the little bird screeched for the last time.

Chapter 8

"Commander Aniceto asked me to give this to you," one of the rookies in my second class of the morning said.

"Thanks."

I checked my watch. Three minutes to class. Enough time to read the note that wasn't from my commander but from my mother.

Detective Shelley Caldwell:
Report to me at the district office after your last class of the day.
District Commander Rena Caldwell

Considering the way she was pulling me in—an order—my antennae went up. What was going on?

I stuffed the missive in my shorts pocket and tried not to worry.

Something was up.

I wasn't in the mood for a confrontation after what I'd dealt with the day before. At least I'd had the sense to sleep with an ice pack all night—that and some ibuprofen had done wonders for my physical well-being. My nerves were on edge, though. I'd tried Raven's number a couple more times. She hadn't answered.

Not good.

I got through the class without thinking about why Mom wanted to see me, but by the time I got to the lunchroom, my brain was circling.

"Hey, baby, late night?"

"Really late," I said, sitting across from Al.

I was fully aware that I looked as if I'd been through the mill. I'd awakened too late for a decent breakfast, so I'd picked up a coffee and croissant on the way in to work. The smell of the gloppy, stewy stuff on my plate wafted to my nose, and my stomach growled in appreciation.

"You look like hell. Can't be because of a man. When you gonna find you a real one?"

Swallowing a mouthful of stew, I got a brief flash of Jake. "I already found one. *You.*"

"Yeah, but Rosalee would kill me if I so much as looked at another woman."

"See—all the good ones are taken."

Joking with Al put me in a better mood, and I began to wolf down my lunch. We ate in companionable silence for a moment before I said, "My mother sent me an order to appear in her office when I leave the academy this afternoon. Why couldn't she just call me like a daughter and say she wanted to talk?"

"Why do you think?"

"Because she likes to give orders."

"Maybe."

"Hey, you're not saying it's my fault?"

"It takes two to tango…and two to fight."

Rather than answering, I practically inhaled the rest of my lunch. But for the rest of the afternoon, I couldn't help thinking about the intimation that I might be partly responsible for the uneasy relations between Mom and me.

Fearing that might be true, I decided I would do my best to assuage whatever gripe she had this time. I would be the model daughter.

That vow didn't last very long.

The moment I stepped into her office—a cold regulation CPD space warmed by a few personal touches like an area rug and a couple of framed prints on the walls—she gave me a look that could freeze a runner in her tracks. I pushed through the negative and gave her what passed for a smile.

"Reporting as ordered."

No answering smile softened her expression. "Please sit, Shelley."

Shelley. She called me by name rather than by title, so this was a mother-daughter thing, after all. I sat and wisely kept my mouth shut. Let her take the initiative.

But when she leaned forward, elbows on her neatly organized desk, and asked, "Are you out of your mind?" all that tension I'd released earlier came flooding back. "I always gave you credit for being smarter than most of the population."

I bit my tongue so I wouldn't say anything.

Mom went on. "But what you're doing…I just don't understand it. What were you thinking, putting yourself at risk?"

My mouth dropped open. She couldn't possibly know.

But I realized she *could* know, *did* know, when she said, "It's against CPD policy to act alone without calling for backup."

"Silke told you?"

"Don't sound so horrified. I'm the one who has a right to be horrified. Pretending to be Silke, going undercover to seek out a potential murderer—"

"Do you know about the connection to LaTonya Sanford, too?" When Mom didn't even blink, I shook my head. "Silke's been a regular Chatty Cathy."

"Your sister is worried about you, Shelley. She says she's sorry she involved you. She wanted you to make an official report or at least to come to me yourself, but apparently you wouldn't listen to her."

I didn't care that Silke had tried to stop me and then to warn me. I hadn't believed she would actually go behind my back to let Mom know what I was up to.

"I didn't have anything to come to you with. Not anything you would believe any more than you did the last time."

"I did believe you, Shelley. I just couldn't do anything to change what happened."

"They said I was crazy! You didn't stand up for me." And, currently, that was the crux of the problem between us.

"How would that have looked? I respect procedure. And in the end, the system worked the way it should. You were okayed for duty."

"No thanks to you. And I didn't get reinstated as a detective. The powers that be don't trust me on the streets with a black mark on my record. It's nice that you respect procedure. I only wish you would respect me."

"Of course I respect you."

"I asked you directly about cult activity at lunch." This wasn't me the daughter talking, but me the cop. "You told me nothing, and there's no department regulation saying you can't discuss a crime being investigated with another officer. That was your choice. I figured whatever information you were getting from Commander Aniceto was related to what happened to Silke's friend Thora. Maybe he saw this kind of thing on his watch when he was heading up that gang unit. Will you *please* tell me now?"

Mom sighed and her shoulders lost their sharpness as she sagged back against her chair. "No, it wasn't exactly the same," she said, switching from Mom to cop. "I went to him the other day because we have a homeless man a couple of quarts low stashed in the morgue."

I blinked at her, trying to take in the implication. "How much blood loss?"

"Enough to do the job."

"And you still have the body?"

"We have two, actually," Mom said, watching me closely, as if for my reaction. "Late last night three jocks partying a couple of blocks from Heart of Darkness were on the way to their car when they found a young woman unconscious. Unfortunately, she died before the paramedics got there. They couldn't revive her because of the severe blood loss. One of the young men said he thought he saw her attacker slinking away in the shadows. He took chase, but unfortunately, he wasn't fast enough to get a good look at the person."

"What does the victim look like?"

"Early twenties, short spiked dark hair, Goth makeup and clothing, three earrings in her eyebrow, tattoo of a black bird on her upper arm."

The description took away my breath, and I choked out, "Raven!"

"You know her?"

"She's the one who told Silke about Thora's body."

I had saved Raven from sexual assault only to have her fall to a much worse fate. My stomach knotted and my chest felt hollow, and though cops weren't supposed to cry, I wanted to. This victim wasn't some unknown person to me. I should have broken cover and had Chung arrested. Then Raven would have been questioned, maybe escorted home in a patrol car. She wouldn't have been in the wrong place at the wrong time. And if Chung was the murderer, he would have been locked up.

"Can you tell me more about this Raven?"

Stunned, I shook my head. "I didn't even know

her real name." I hadn't asked her. "Raven was her Goth name. Maybe Silke…"

"I'll talk to her about it. You seem very upset."

"Of course I'm upset! I agreed to go undercover to stop anything like this from happening again!"

Mom nodded, and I would swear her voice grew gentler when she said, "Then you're not going to like the rest. The girl's body has already been examined and there's evidence of rape."

"Semen?" I asked, automatically thinking if Chung had gotten his hands on her again, we could run his DNA.

"No semen. But bruising and tearing."

I took a big breath and tried to let it go. It felt as if it took forever to get rid of the extra air, and even when I did, I couldn't breathe normally.

"There's even more," I said, and told Mom about the scenario on the stairwell that I'd interrupted.

To her credit, Mom listened without judgment. And if she already knew, if Silke had already told her about my fight with the security guard, she didn't say so.

She merely said, "So this Hung Chung could be the one."

"He's definitely a suspect."

And if I found out he had raped and killed Raven…

I realized my hands were balled into fists so tight my fingers began to hurt. I wanted to rip him apart with my bare hands. Taking several more deep breaths, I got my anger under control.

"So the medical examiner has already done his report. What about the missing blood?" I wondered if Chung could be part of Mowry's vampire cult. "How was it taken?"

"Through a slash on the inside of the arm."

"Like LaTonya Sanford and Thora Nelson."

"But not like the man—his blood was drained through holes in his neck. As to this Raven, the M.E. thinks the blood was being removed during the sex act."

The visual I got on that one made me wish I could have done something more. I could hardly believe the girl I'd saved last night was dead this morning. I should have tried harder to get her to press charges—maybe then she would still be alive. "How has the press not gotten hold of this?"

"They missed the John Doe. Or maybe they simply weren't interested in him. And we're keeping a low profile now. No need for a public panic."

"Still, I'm surprised some reporter didn't pick it up on a scanner."

"It didn't go out over the air. The beat cops were informed that if they found another one, they were to call for backup in code."

The pieces of the puzzle were mounting, but they didn't exactly fit together perfectly.

LaTonya Sanford, Thora Nelson, Raven and the homeless John Doe…someone really was taking their blood, if not in the same way. The women had been bled from wounds in their arms, the man from puncture holes in his neck.

So now Mom believed me.

Another person I knew believed a bloodsucker was hanging around the bar.

Jake DeAtley.

Again, I wondered if his interest in the subject was official. "You don't by any chance already have an undercover officer working Heart of Darkness?"

Mom's surprise seemed genuine. "No. And as far as I know, neither does anyone else. Why?"

I told her about Jake DeAtley. "He admitted he was investigating but wouldn't say why."

"And you couldn't get more out of him?"

"Maybe I could…if I get closer."

Mom's expression registered her understanding. "That's not an option."

"Right."

Not an option procedure-wise, perhaps, but definitely an option I couldn't help considering personally. Not that I would prostitute myself for a lead. But I could work Jake for more information.

"I need to check DeAtley out through the system for priors or arrests," I said, telling her how I'd already run him and others linked to the bar on the Internet for information and coming up with nothing on any of them. I had to admit I was hoping Jake would come up clean, but something was going on with him. "I wonder if DeAtley could have some connection to one of the victims."

"If he does, we'll find that out, too." Mom's brow furrowed. "Shelley, the case went to Detective Norelli, and he's working with Walker."

"Great. Give the case to the very guy who laughed in my face in the first place. He'll probably bury the case so no one will evaluate *him.*"

"Not hardly. Not when we have two bodies in

the morgue. I'll get you transferred back to Area 4 immediately."

That had been my goal, but the idea of having to work under Norelli didn't sit well with me.

"I'm already undercover and I'm working this alone."

"Not anymore you're not. You'll work the case as part of the team or you won't work it at all."

I knew she meant business. This wasn't my mom anymore; this was a cop with a lot of clout, clout that she could use for me or against me.

"I'm not handing this investigation over to anyone."

"That's not your decision."

"I can go on furlough," I warned her.

"It won't be approved."

"Then I'll get the blue flu."

Blue flu being the operative phrase when cops thought to go on strike without actually going on strike, which they couldn't do by law.

"Detective, be reasonable."

"I am reasonable, Commander. I'm on the inside—they're not. It's my lead. I won't have Norelli messing up this case. It's *my* case. It has been since I laid eyes on LaTonya Sanford in that alley."

"All right. I'll see what I can do."

Mom made the calls necessary to get me cleared and assigned back to Area 4. She filled in the Area 4 commander about my undercover activities and said she was certain that Detectives Norelli and Walker would bow to my greater knowledge of the case. I watched her work in awe.

After hanging up, she said, "It's still their case technically, but you're in charge of the undercover operation. You'll run it the way you want."

Reluctant partners. This wouldn't make any of us happy, but it would have to do. Compromise. Mom admitted to having done it. I guess I could, too.

Her pulling strings put extra pressure on me. I had to get it right, to prove to my mother that her faith in me wasn't wasted. I had to get justice for LaTonya and Thora and Raven, and yes, the homeless guy, too.

I would make the best of working with detectives who gave me no respect.

I would succeed in putting the murderer away despite them.

Returning to the Area 4 office before donning my Goth gear for the evening was one of the hardest things I'd ever done. I wasn't expecting a grand reunion—not from the detectives who'd held me in so little regard—but I was hoping for a truce.

Detective Mike Norelli looked up from his work when I walked into the pasty green-walled bull pen and nodded. "Caldwell" was all he said before going back to whatever report he was perusing.

"Norelli," I muttered, my lips stiff. Most of the other detectives working the phones or filling out the endless paperwork didn't so much as glance my way. The only other woman in the room, Detective Stella Jacobek, gave me a thumbs-up. I waved and put my things on my old desk, which I'd been told was still free. I nodded to the man who usually teamed up with Norelli. "Walker."

The other half of the violent-crimes tag team gave me a wide-toothed grin. "I knew you couldn't stay away from us for long."

As far as I was concerned, forever wouldn't have been long enough.

Detectives Mike Norelli and Jamal Walker were as different as night and day. Middle-aged and beefy, Norelli wore a blah dark suit, white shirt and forced smile. His tie usually held some clue as to what he'd had for lunch. Younger and fitter, Walker had more interest in being a snappy dresser. Today he wore a canary-yellow suit jacket that made his coffee skin appear darker.

"So apparently you've been playing loosey-goosey with the system," Norelli said.

I clenched my jaw and turned the grimace into a smile. "Go to hell."

"So what you got?" Walker leaned back in his chair and hooked his hands behind his head as if preparing himself for a good story.

Well, I could give him one if I gave it all up. But I wasn't there yet.

So I said, "Another missing body and a couple that aren't." Which reminded me to turn in the gargoyle pin to the lab to check for fingerprints. "Suspects? A sexual predator and some wanna-be vampires."

"Vampires!" Norelli snorted into his paperwork.

"Watch it, Norelli, or I'll let one of them feed on you."

Walker snorted. "Hey, Norelli, that sounded like a threat."

"Jealous I didn't include you, Walker?" I asked in an innocent voice. "Oh, I know I make you laugh, but that's not intentional. And now it seems that I have the last laugh, since I was right about LaTonya Sanford, after all."

"Hey, come on," Norelli growled, "lighten up."

Norelli didn't like to be wrong. Being told he was wrong put him in a bad mood. Or maybe just knowing he had to work with me had been enough to twist his boxers into a knot.

The two detectives exchanged glances. And while I waited to see what road they were going to take, tension sucked the life out of me. I felt trapped with no way out.

So when Walker said, "Look, about the Sanford case...you gotta admit it didn't look good or they wouldn't have shrunk you," I breathed a little easier.

That was probably the closest I could expect to an apology.

He added, "The important thing is we stop this killer or killers before someone else dies."

"Well, something we can agree on at last," I said. "I need to see what you've got."

"Not much there," Norelli growled as he handed me the murder book.

I spent the next half hour reading the reports that started with the discovery of the homeless man found dead and drained of blood. Not much activity there. While they'd done some interviews, they truly hadn't canvassed the neighborhood. They'd kept a low profile on the case, as Mom had said. But how long could this be kept out of the media?

I continued reading. Only when they'd found Raven early this morning had the investigation stepped up.

Norelli and Walker had even been to Heart of Darkness late this afternoon and had interviewed Desiree Leath, who had seemed truly shocked by the news of Raven's death. They hadn't told her how the girl had died, of course, and they hadn't mentioned the homeless man.

They'd questioned Jake, as well, which reminded me that I wanted as much information on him as I could get. Starting the process myself, I found no priors and no arrests, a fact that relieved me. When I tried looking him up in the DMV, I could find no records of a driver's license or plates. I hadn't gotten a look at his car, so I supposed he could have out-of-state plates. And an out-of-state license. Or a fake name.

I needed to get home and get ready for tonight, so I asked a support officer to keep digging for me. I wanted anything she could find on him. Anything. I told her to broaden the search if she had to. Our system was connected to nationwide data banks. She assured me that the results would be ready for me first thing in the morning. I also gave her Thora's gargoyle pin and asked her to get it to the lab.

Then, turning my attention back to the murder book, I said, "Norelli, you missed something here."

"What?" he growled.

"LaTonya Sanford. I don't see anything in this report about her. She was the first victim."

"But she wasn't a case."

"Good thing I put together a murder book for her anyway. You might want to loosen up and use it."

Before he could comment, I dived back into his notes, hoping to find a pattern. But other than both victims being a couple of quarts low, as Mom had put it, and both being found in the vicinity of Heart of Darkness—within a quarter of a mile—the murders might have been committed by two different people. The man had been drained through two puncture holes in his neck, while Raven had been drained on the inside of her arm, near the elbow. The other difference being that Raven had been raped, while there was no evidence of sexual assault with the homeless man.

I glanced up to check out my partners-in-solving-crime. Norelli was still at his paperwork and Walker was on the phone, no doubt trying to track down information of some kind.

I closed the book and walked it back to Norelli.

"We need to talk about tonight," I said, swinging into take-charge mode. "I need four people, two plants—one in the bar, the other wandering the stores in the mall until they close—and two in a car outside."

Since they'd done the interview with Desiree and Jake, the only way Norelli and Walker could be players in the undercover scenario was if they took the car duty—boring, boring, boring. So there was an upside to the situation, after all.

"Can you get me what I need?" I asked.

The middle-aged detective saluted me. "Yes, ma'am!"

"C'mon, Norelli," Walker said. Then he turned to me. "You gonna wear a wire?"

"A wire's not necessary, at least not at this stage."

"What if you get in trouble?" Norelli asked.

"Then I'll whistle real loud."

"Still a smart-ass," he grumbled.

Maybe I was, but after what I'd gone through with these guys, who could blame me? "Can you get me the men or not?"

Walker said, "We'll get 'em. We're working in the spirit of cooperation, right, Norelli?"

"Yeah, right," the other detective growled back.

Yeah, right.

"Cracking this case is gonna look good on my résumé," Walker went on. "I see a promotion in my future."

Dream on.

It would be me who would see that justice was done and that LaTonya Sanford could rest in peace at last.

Chapter 9

Jake kept an eye on the woman calling herself Silke all night. Of course now he knew her name was Shelley Caldwell and that she was Silke's sister.

The night before, he'd been aware of Silke being inside the apartment—he'd heard her moving around—and he'd feigned leaving so he could eavesdrop and learn what he needed to know. Unfortunately, a couple had entered the building and had given him a hard stare before he'd heard more than her name and the fact that the two women were sisters. He'd left before there'd been an incident. He didn't yet have all the pieces of Shelley Caldwell, but he would.

Since her shift had begun, Shelley had been flippant with him as usual.

The more he saw her, spoke to her, argued with
her, the more she piqued his interest.

She looked in his general direction without meeting his gaze and said, "I need a couple of Bloody
Cosmopolitans and a red wine."

"Is that it?"

"That's all the customers asked for."

"What about you? What do you need?"

As if unable to help herself, she looked directly
at him. "A break."

Thump-thump…thump-thump…thump-thump…

He was in tune with her heartbeat. Her scent tan-
talized him. His skin grew sensitive; even the cal-
lused pads on his fingertips sizzled as if electrified.
And when he really looked at her, Shelley took on
an unearthly glow.

He filled the order and set it on the counter.

If she noticed anything untoward, she didn't react
to it. Then she simply turned away from him, tray
and drinks in hand.

He watched her make her way up the stairs and
to the table next to Mowry's. The wanna-be vamp
watched her with hungry eyes, too, but Jake knew
she wouldn't be sucked in by him. She had her
own agenda.

So who was she really, beyond her name? And
what was her investment in playing detective?

One way to find out. He'd stick to her like glue.

With or without her permission.

Jake's watching me all night was unnerving. I
didn't need that extra burden of knowing I was already being watched.

At first I hadn't spotted the undercover officer, which in my book was a case of good news–bad news since I was still conflicted about going official with the investigation. Eventually, I spotted Hanson at the bar nursing a beer. I hardly recognized him in a black T-shirt and his hair pasted up with gel.

The officers in the unmarked car were parked outside a few doors down—a male and a female officer who were putting on a lovey-dovey performance. Well, hopefully it was a performance. Not that I wanted them here at all, but since I was ordered to cooperate, I wanted the best outcome, which meant they needed to focus on something other than their libidos.

Between the meeting with Mom and having to report in to the Area 4 office, I hadn't gotten any down-time before I'd had to do my transformation and get to the bar. Silke had been as devastated as I about Raven. To her credit, Mom had actually told Silke about the poor girl's death, so I hadn't had to go over the details.

For some reason, Chung seemed to be absent tonight. I still wanted to rip him apart with my bare hands, only I didn't have the energy. Luckily, my adrenaline kicked in on high, keeping me going, and now, as I approached the owner's office in hopes of getting some information out of her, my adrenaline level felt as if it was about to skyrocket.

"Desiree, do you have a few minutes?"

She turned to me, her pale, gaunt features glowing softly in the dim light. "What is it, Silke?"

Her calling me by that name was a reminder that

I had to play it as my twin would. "I need to talk to you about something."

Sitting behind her desk, her long blue-black hair surrounding her shoulders like a luxurious cape, Desiree extended her hand. "Sit."

I took the seat across from her in a ladylike manner as Silke would. The walls and ceiling of her office were painted the deepest blue as if to complement her. Curlicues of metal supported the thick sheet of glass that was her desk. Myriad pillows of dark hues enriched the black leather of the chairs and couch.

Before I could say anything, she did. "I assured you I would take care of Hung Chung."

"I…it's Raven," I said in Silke's soft voice, making it quake a little, speaking as if I didn't know Desiree had already been questioned about the murder. I wanted to read her for myself. "She was raped and killed and someone t-took her blood." I twisted my hands together and did my best to blink tears into my eyes when I murmured, "S-so shocking."

Desiree's eyes widened slightly—as if she were shocked that *I* knew—but other than that, she didn't react. "The luck was not with this girl."

"What about Hung Chung?" I asked, notching up my nervous demeanor a bit. "What if he finished what he started? Wh-what if he comes after me next?"

"Chung was not responsible for this tragedy."

"You don't really know that."

"Oh, but yes," Desiree said, meeting my gaze. "Last night, Chung was with me."

My heart began to thud. "With *you?*"

"Until dawn."

At which time, Raven had already been dead.

I was still staring. I wanted to make sure I got this right. "Chung didn't force himself on you?" If so, I would do my best to get her to make an official complaint.

When Desiree said, "No man would dare try," her smile was confident.

I could hardly believe it. She'd actually chosen to be with a would-be rapist. She'd said she would take care of him, and rather than castigating him, she'd rewarded him with herself? What kind of a woman was she? One who gave me the creeps, that was for certain.

I forced out a Silke smile. "I guess I was mistaken." I paused only a second before asking, "You wouldn't have any idea of who…?" I let the question dangle.

"Such a pretty girl? Anyone," Desiree said, as if being pretty equated with being a killer's target.

I nodded and rose. "Well, if you think of anyone else…"

Desiree caught me with her gaze, and I froze where I stood. For a moment, I felt as if my mind were wrapped in cotton.

"I do not need trouble here, Silke. You understand this, yes? There is no reason for the authorities to think the killer is someone who frequents my establishment."

"No," I found myself agreeing.

"So you will not be making trouble for me by telling others of Raven's death or your theories."

"No, of course not."

I left the office half-convinced to give it up, as if Desiree had somehow taken hold of my mind. But the loud music and smokey smell of the bar shocked me back to myself, and I realized Desiree had seemed more worried about the police than about Raven's death. Was there something she didn't want them to discover? Or did she simply fear the bad press as I knew she would?

Even functioning at a low level, I couldn't stop my mind from going over what I knew. If Hung Chung couldn't be the murderer... My gaze strayed to Elvin Mowry.

As if the pretty boy knew I was staring at him, he turned and smiled. And waved me over.

I asked, "What can I get you?"

"Away from here."

"You want me to call you a taxi?"

"I wish you to leave with me tonight. I have been watching you, Silke. You are the most fascinating woman here. I shall have a gathering at my place when the bar closes. I promise you shan't be bored."

"Not this time," I said, forcing a smile. "I didn't get enough sleep last night. A girl needs her beauty rest."

"Or enough makeup so it doesn't matter," piped up one of Mowry's followers.

"I shall give you a rain check, then," the cult leader said. "But do not keep me waiting too long."

Was that a threat? I gave him a quick smile and moved off to another customer waving me down.

So Elvin Mowry was having a gathering. Something involving bloodletting?

Energy coming back in a rush, I knew I had to find out.

Mowry and his band—two other guys and a young woman—were the last customers to leave Heart of Darkness. I hadn't seen the girl with them before tonight, and she wasn't dressed like a Goth. I wondered if she was a new convert. She also looked as if she'd had too much to drink, which would impair her judgment.

Since I'd already done the required setup for the next day, I exited the bar. I looked around for the backup team, but they'd already dispersed, so I was on my own. I'd told my lieutenant that I wouldn't be back at Area 4 until I had some sleep, so no one was expecting me.

The night held a chill that got to me. The temperature had dropped and the winds had picked up, all in preparation for a cold front and summer thunderstorm predicted for the early-morning hours. I wrapped Silke's cape tighter around my shoulders and tucked my chin into my chest as I hurried after Mowry. The vampire cult members were traveling on foot. At Lake Street, they crossed under the el tracks and continued north. Either they'd parked way off the beat or were within walking distance from their "nest."

I wondered where the nest idea had come from. I guess it had something to do with vampires that supposedly turned into bats, but I wasn't really certain.

Did bats have nests? I thought they hung around and watched the world from their topsy-turvy perch. Nests reminded me of birds, which reminded me of Raven, which reminded me that I might be dealing with one or more murderers.

I had no intention of putting myself in danger. I was merely on a fact-finding mission. I wanted an address on Mowry, and I hadn't been able to do it the conventional way. I figured he must be using an alias. He and all the others I'd tried to check out. Including Jake. I wondered what kind of vitals we would get on him using the CPD system. By morning, I would know everything there was to know about Jake DeAtley.

The night was dark, especially away from the main drag. Ahead, there were only a few streetlights and some of those were out. Through the clouds, the moon shed an eerie blue glow along the open space. An old manufacturing building was boarded up, its square-block-sized parking lot deserted.

That's where Mowry and company were headed.

Another chill shot through me as I quickly decided to fetch my car, which was parked a short distance away on Lake Street, as usual. Though I blamed the wind, the chill went deeper than bone and I reluctantly recognized it as fear.

Fear was healthy, I reminded myself, a cop's best friend. Fear kept you alert. Hopefully alive.

I wanted to know where Mowry lived or at least where he and his minions congregated for the gathering he was hosting tonight— I slid into the driver's seat of my car and quickly hit the lock. I started the engine and backed the car into the intersection. I didn't switch on my lights, which would warn the pseudo-vampires that they were being followed. I turned north to do just that.

For the next few minutes, I concentrated on not losing Mowry and not being spotted and not driving the car straight into one of the bigger holes on the pockmarked street. After crossing the open expanse, the cult leader made his way under a railroad viaduct and rounded the corner going west.

A few moments later, I did the same.

This was a neighborhood of sorts, old houses and two-flats mixed in with some businesses across from the railroad. The slope down from the tracks was a concrete wall that had been muralized by young urban artists.

The street itself was deserted. No Mowry. No cult members.

I thought about calling in, but to say what? That I'd followed Mowry and lost him?

I parked the car, got out and looked around, checking between each building as I moved down the street. Footsteps again. I whirled around to find Jake right behind me.

"What the hell! Why are you after Mowry?"

"I'm not. I'm after watching your back," he added.

I didn't disbelieve him, but I was disconcerted. For a few seconds the moonlight tricked me into believing his eyes glowed, and his teeth, revealed by an amused-with-me smile, seemed extra white and long. Then I blinked and vanquished the illusion.

What if Jake were the danger? How did I know he wasn't the one draining young women of their blood? I *didn't* know that. However, I also wasn't afraid of him. Not in the physical ow-you-hurt-me sense. He'd had a couple of opportunities to take advantage of me when we'd been alone and he'd passed on them.

Jake was standing very still, swiveling only his head as if it were a finely tuned antenna. At the same time, he held up his finger to his lips, indicating I shouldn't say anything. What was he listening to? I didn't hear a sound except the light traffic on the nearby expressway.

But suddenly he said, "This way," and crossed the street.

Following, I asked, "Where?"

What had he heard? Did he mean to climb the concrete incline to the railroad tracks? But as we drew closer, I saw it—the outline of a door set into the mural itself.

How in the world had he seen that from a distance and in the dark?

I didn't have time to ask questions, because Jake was already opening the door. No doubt any sound would carry through the tunnel beneath the railroad tracks.

He entered first.

The cavernous area was dark and musty smelling. I listened hard but the only sound I heard was a nearby scrabbling, like claws on metal.

Rats? I shivered. I hated rats.

Choking back my distaste, I whispered, "Which way?"

Jake murmured ahead, "Follow the voices."

"What voices?"

Was Jake kidding or had he really heard something? I stumbled through the dark after him, hoping I wasn't making a big mistake.

Gradually, the darkness lifted like a veil being raised a bit at a time, and a soft pool of light ahead acted as a beacon. My eyes adjusted and I could see furniture: upholstered chairs and couches, carpets and small tables, all heavily worn but still functional. The area was set up like a big rumpus room minus the electronic equipment. The light itself came from kerosene lamps, the kind people used when they went camping.

"Wh-what's happening?" a soft female voice asked.

"I just gave you a little something to make you feel better."

"Mowry," I whispered.

"But *I* wasn't feeling bad!" the young woman protested.

"But *I* was. You have something I need, my pretty. And you did say you wanted to be one of us."

She whimpered and cried out.

I could see her now, the new one, the non-Goth. She was sprawled in a chair, two of Mowry's minions pinning her shoulders so she couldn't get up. Mowry straightened; he was holding a thin-bladed knife. Dark red fluid coated the tip, and I could see that he'd cut the inside of her arm. Blood spilled over her pale flesh.

Blood rushed and echoed through my head at the discovery. Was this it, then? Was he the one draining young women of their blood? I couldn't let him do it, not even if I had to blow my cover.

I unsnapped my holster and rushed forward. "Leave her alone!" My hand hovered in back of me near my gun. I didn't want to pull it unless they gave me no other choice.

Mowry said, "Well, well, look who we have here."

His followers forgot about the girl and closed rank around him. In addition to the two guys who'd come from the bar with him, there were two more. And two young women in a state of half dress. It was obvious to me that these girls hadn't been coerced into anything. They watched the scenario with eager gazes and moist lips.

I recognized blood lust when I saw it.

"Let the girl be," I said quietly, sensing Jake right behind me. "Let her go."

I knew I was good, but as the cult members got closer, I wondered if I could possibly fight them all off and free the girl.

"You're not the one to give orders here," Mowry said.

One of the half-dressed young women moved forward and curled herself around the leader's back. "You tell her, Elvie."

Before I had to see exactly how good I was, Jake slid beside me and wrapped an arm around my middle, as if to remind me that I wasn't alone. I couldn't explain why I trusted him at this moment, but my instincts told me he was on my side and to play along.

"Silke told me you were having people tonight," he said in a party voice. "We thought we'd join you."

I hadn't told him any such thing. His hands were all over me. Then he bent over and nuzzled my neck. I flushed at the touch of his lips against my flesh, and for a moment, lost my concentration. Then I snapped to and fought the sensations going through my head. Having all my faculties was critical.

And yet, when I glanced at Mowry and company, they had all relaxed their stances. Mowry himself seemed to be enjoying my position, and something told me he wanted some of that for himself.

Instinct drove me to wrap my arms around Jake's middle. I felt his hand on my back. He slid it down to my waist, paused there when he encountered the holster, and then moved the hand around to my side. He couldn't have missed my piece, but he didn't react.

"This doesn't seem like my kind of party, after all," I said, making myself sound bored. "Not hers, either." I looked directly at the new girl in the chair. She couldn't hide her fright. "You want to leave, right?"

She nodded. "Yes, please."

"Come on, then," Jake said, holding out his hand.

I could tell that though he was looking straight at her, he somehow had his eyes on every person in the room. Tension was palpable and I prepared myself for trouble.

The girl stumbled out of the chair over to us.

Amazingly, Mowry and his boys didn't try to stop her. Maybe we would get out of this without casualty, after all, I thought gratefully, as Jake put his free arm around the girl to steady her.

"See you tomorrow night," he told Mowry as he started backing us all away.

Mowry seemed to grow taller and his men closed ranks around him. Whatever Mowry had planned, I knew I wasn't going to like it. My pulse tick-tick-ticked more and more rapidly, and my senses all heightened.

"Little Annie can go," Mowry said. "But I need someone to take her place."

I glanced at the other two girls. I was assuming he wouldn't kill them, but I couldn't take that chance with Annie. Not even if it meant destroying my cover.

"You have a couple of willing women to choose from."

"But it's fresh blood I'm after."

No doubt in my mind that he meant me.

"Not tonight, and definitely not Silke here," Jake said, keeping up the pretense though I was certain by now he knew that I wasn't Silke.

We were almost to the door. I knew that because it was becoming impossible to see again. The dark folded around us like a shroud. And I heard that scrabbling sound again.

"Let's get out of here," Jake murmured as he let go of me.

"You'll get no argument here," I said, every one of my senses at the alert.

Still, I hesitated, giving him a minute to get Annie out of there. If necessary, I would be the diversion. And it seemed as if I would get that very opportunity.

Bodies swirled around me even as I heard the outside door click open and Jake say, "Get out of here, Annie…now!"

I turned to follow and ran straight into the cult leader himself.

Wind blew in from the open door, and a combination of moon- and streetlight penetrated, too, enough that I could see Mowry's face. His pretty features were twisted in anger and something else that looked amazingly like lust.

But what kind of lust? Blood lust or the simple old-fashioned kind?

Whichever, I wasn't open for business.

But before I could get out of his way, he grabbed on to my arm.

I swung out to deter him, and the flesh of my other arm met a sharp blade for my trouble. I couldn't help the cry that escaped my throat.

"What happened?" Jake demanded.

"Cut!" I gasped, not wanting to let down my guard for an instant.

The two girls moved closer, bringing with them the kerosene lamps. Apparently, they thought they were missing out on the fun. Mowry's men were between me and Jake, whose eyes glittered with anger. The blood oozing from my flesh had me royally pissed. I feinted and got Mowry off guard, then moved in and smashed one of Silke's thick-soled Doc Martens into the side of his knee.

Mowry was ready for me and the blow glanced off his leg as he moved fast. At most, he missed a beat.

"You'll have to do better than that," he said, laughing, the sound echoing through the tunnel.

"Oh, I think I can manage," I said as I felt a fresh rush of adrenaline pump through me.

The problem was, not counting the women, there were five of them to one of me. I was good, but I didn't know if I was good enough to take on so many and be able to make it out of there in one piece. Of course there was Jake on my side, as well, but he was an unknown quantity. If nothing else, he could serve as a distraction.

As a last resort, I reminded myself, there was always my weapon. A gun tended to even things up when the numbers were skewed.

I let Mowry come for me. When he got close enough, I elbowed him in the sternum. He paused with a gasp and I danced around him and got a few feet closer to the outside door.

Then all hell broke loose. I was aware of Mowry's men attacking Jake. I would have helped him out, but I had the leader himself on my back. Literally. And his steely arm was around my throat. I couldn't breathe. I began to see stars. Pressure built in my chest and head even as I stepped back and slammed my heel down hard on his foot. He muffled his curse but loosened his grip. I gasped for air, filled my deprived lungs and brain with it.

Silke's distress distracted me for a second. This time I pushed her away before she got me hurt.

Then I felt Mowry's free hand slide between my

thighs. I saw red. I dug into the flesh of his under-arm and twisted—one of my favorite defense moves, crude but effective. This time his curse filled the cavernous space as he let go. I whipped around and grabbed *him* between the thighs and twisted there, too. He howled and went down to his knees.

"Elvie!" one of the females shrieked.

I registered a serious scuffle a few yards away and realized Jake was still fighting off the other four. I thought to help him, but Mowry was staggering to his feet, and I realized he was about to throw himself at me. I whirled and kicked out, planning to put him out of commission, but he somehow managed to grab my leg. I flipped and went down hard.

The other hip this time.

When Mowry descended on me, I rolled fast and he landed on the ground, facedown. I kicked out, smacking him in the side of the head—one of my all-time favorite offensive moves—and bounded to my feet.

"You bitch!"

The vamp girl came for me, clawed fingers going for my face. Not really wanting to hurt her—she might be idiot enough to be with Mowry, but she probably wasn't lethal—I grabbed her arm and threw my weight down against her body so she lost her footing and collapsed on top of her beloved leader.

"Get off me!" he howled.

Catching my breath, I turned to help Jake in time to see him pick up one of Mowry's minions and throw him against the other three. And I gaped when they all went down like so many bowling pins. Good grief, he was strong!

"Let's go!" he said, holding out his hand.

He didn't have to say it twice. I jumped over the sprawled bodies and grabbed on to his hand, and we burst into the night together.

I quickly looked around. The street was deserted.

"Annie…where is she? I didn't think she'd get too far drugged."

Jake was concentrating—doing his human-antenna act just as he had before we'd gone into the nest.

"Gone. She was a little woozy but she wasn't totally out of it. The night air probably sobered her fast."

"And the fear," I said, checking to make sure members of the vampire cult hadn't followed us out to the street. "Fear can do that to you."

"You know that bears some discussion, but not here. Car keys." Jake held out his hand.

"I can drive," I insisted, limping to my vehicle.

"You're bleeding."

So I was. The cut had been aggravated by the fight. I bent my elbow at the arm and raised my hand so the wound was above my heart in hopes that would stop the bleeding. What it did was dangle my keys directly in front of Jake's face. He snatched them from my hand, unlocked the Camaro and held open the passenger door.

"Get in."

I'd had enough conflict for one day. I did as he ordered, telling myself I could better tend to the cut if I wasn't driving. I buckled up and put pressure below the wound in hopes it would stop bleeding.

At the same time, I kept an eye on the door in the concrete wall. Nothing. No movement. They were probably too busy licking their wounds. Or so I hoped. Whatever, I breathed easier.

"Let's drive around—we need to find Annie. I want to make sure she's all right."

"And maybe take her to a cop shop and make a report?" Jake suggested.

Annie had gone willingly with Mowry. He'd scared her, had even cut her, but not badly. Supposing what he might have done, had Jake and I not shown up, wouldn't hold diddly weight with the state's attorney. We didn't have much of a case. And without Annie, we had nothing.

The other problem was arresting Mowry at this point in the murder investigation—he was a murder suspect, but we had no proof that he'd killed anyone. Taking Mowry in at this time could be a big mistake, one his lawyer could potentially use against us if we did get something on him later. I didn't want the murderer slipping through our fingers on some technicality.

After riding around in circles for several minutes, Jake said, "Okay, it's official. We're not going to find Annie tonight."

"Damn! I guess not."

"All right, then." Jake had barely aimed the Camaro out of that neighborhood before saying, "So, who are you really, sister to Silke? A private investigator? A cop?"

I thought about backpedaling, but the pretense of

being Silke with him was over. So I took the offensive once more.

"How about you, Jake? Trading secrets?"

"A little gratitude would be in order here, considering I saved your pretty butt."

"I fought my own fight."

"With one man instead of more. Though you were pretty impressive, I admit. You didn't learn to kick *other* people's butts like that watching an action movie."

He wasn't going to let it alone this time. No more playing games. He was angry. I could hear it in his voice, see it in the tension drawing his hands into fists around the steering wheel. While he hadn't actually saved me, he certainly had contributed to the good fight. Impressively, as well. And he'd seemed to be looking out for me all along. He'd warned me away from both Hung Chung and Elvin Mowry. For some reason, he seemed to be looking out for me.

I decided Jake deserved some answers. I needed someone I could trust who would watch my back. And no matter how we'd danced around each other the past few days, no matter that I still didn't know his intentions, I decided I did trust him, especially after what had just gone down.

I finally said, "Cop, and I need to call this in."

I pulled out my cell and called Norelli, who'd been sound asleep. To say that he was thrilled would be a gross exaggeration. I couldn't help but savor that. I quickly filled him in on what had gone down and not only asked him to get the patrol officers keeping an eye out for Annie, but I suggested he put a stake out on Mowry's nest. To my surprise, Norelli agreed and said he would make certain Mowry himself developed an extra shadow 24/7.

As I finished the call, I realized we were headed away from, rather than toward, Heart of Darkness. Jake must not have driven to work. Then I realized the street we were on was only vaguely familiar.

"Jake, where are you taking me?"

"Home."

Right. Only it didn't happen to be mine.

Chapter 10

When I protested going to his place, Jake said, "That cut on your arm needs some attention, so you have a choice—the E.R. or my place," and I could tell he meant it.

Since I didn't want to spend hours in some over-crowded emergency room, and I wanted to know more about Jake himself, I went along with his plan. He'd just put himself on the line for me. He could have been hurt, at the very least. In my book, his backing me up counted for a lot. At his place, he could fix me up and I could peel him open and find out what he was all about.

Jake lived in a gray-stone two-flat on the west side not far from the bar, but beyond the gentrified area. No name on the mailboxes, either. When he led me up to the second-floor apartment, I noted the hallway was clean and the faint scent of lemon oil lingered on the wood trim. The stairwell led into the middle of the apartment where there were no windows.

The central pieces of the room were a ceramic-faced fireplace with a carved wooden mantel and a sofa whose deep red suede-looking material glowed mellowly in the dimly lit room. Not exactly a guy color, I thought, making me wonder if someone else had picked it out.

"Do you live here alone?"

"I do," he said. "Can I get you something? Wine?"

"Sure, I could use something to help me relax." Truth be told, my adrenaline had been at an all-time high earlier, and I was still pumped from the action.

His back to me, Jake said, "So you're a cop."

"Detective Shelley Caldwell."

"Silke's twin sister, if I'm not mistaken." He turned from the cart, two stemmed goblets in hand. "Your looks are similar, but you're not really alike. That's why I knew you weren't Silke."

"No one else seemed to notice." At least I hoped not.

"I assume your going undercover has to do with the deaths in the area."

I didn't feel obligated to confirm the obvious, but how did he know there had been more than one death? I was pretty sure Norelli and Walker had only been questioning people about Raven.

Jake handed me one of the glasses of wine. The red was dense, reminding me of blood. I thought to check my arm.

"Let me see."

He set down his glass and gently pulled my arm toward him. At first touch, my breath caught in my throat.

"It's fine."

The blood had begun coagulating—I'd done a pretty good job of stopping the flow in the car—but dried blood stained my makeup-whitened skin and the cut itself looked pretty nasty. It was just now making itself known by throbbing sharply, as if in warning.

Jake seemed fascinated by it. He traced his finger along my flesh parallel to the still oozing wound. "You'll have a scar."

The comment drew my gaze to his scar, half-camouflaged by his beard stubble. I wondered how he'd gotten it. I hadn't thought on it much. I guess I'd assumed he'd had an accident. But after seeing him fighting, I wasn't so sure.

I shrugged and joked, "New addition. It'll go with the others."

He raised an eyebrow and met my gaze. "I'd like to see the collection."

"I just bet you would."

"In the meantime, let me take care of you."

He left the room for a moment, but his mere absence didn't settle my nerves. I sipped the wine and paced the space, inspecting it thoroughly. Not that the light from that single lamp showed me much. It did set a mood, though, and it was enough to get a feel for the place. On the cart where he'd gotten the wine rested a small framed portrait of a young and beautiful woman with dark hair and eyes. The one who'd picked out the sofa fabric? I wondered. I kept wandering and stopped before a photographic display spread on the wall behind the sofa. There were more than a dozen framed photos of cities—American, European, Asian—all taken after dark.

Jake came back into the room, hands filled with first-aid items.

"Great photos," I told him. "Yours?"

"Yeah, you could call it a hobby."

"You've traveled all over the world."

"Actually, I've lived in all those places."

I was feeling a warm glow from the inside out, not only from the wine but also from the rush of the battle. And, truthfully, from being alone with Jake. I blamed the adrenaline. I still hadn't come all the way down from my high.

"Sit," Jake said, indicating the sofa.

He set the medical supplies on the table next to it. I set my arm directly under the lamp so he could better see what he was doing. Hydrogen peroxide came first. I gritted my teeth so I wouldn't yelp at the pain. Then I noticed how focused he was as the mixture of peroxide and blood bubbled up red and spilled over my flesh. Again, he seemed fascinated…and then he tore his gaze away from the cut and looked directly into my eyes.

I got a jolt. Not more adrenaline exactly, but something even stronger.

Before I could analyze, Jake asked, "So what were you doing going after a bunch of wanna-be vampires on your own tonight? Where was your backup?" He gently cleaned the flesh around the cut.

"I looked for my backup, but they'd already left. Sometimes I act on impulse."

I wanted to tell him everything, starting with La-Tonya, but I still didn't know who or what Jake was, and until I did, I couldn't fully trust him with information that was being withheld from the press. For all I knew, he could be a reporter himself, a plant. That would go with his having traveled around the world so much. Perhaps it had been on assignment, to get unusual stories. Only, if he was a reporter, how had he been put on this particular story? As far as I knew, he'd been working at Heart of Darkness for some time.

Jake had finished securing two butterfly bandages across the cut to keep it closed. Now he covered it with a light coating of antibiotic cream and patted off the excess with a gauze pad. Quite a neat-looking, professional job.

I said, "I'm hoping to bring this case home before anyone else gets hurt."

"You mean dies."

"That, too. It's hard to know what to believe about Raven's murder, whether or not she was meant to die. Tonight, Mowry gave Annie a drug and cut her, but he didn't kill her. And I don't think he meant to. It looked more like an initiation. And from what I've read about vampire cults, a pretty tame initiation at that."

"So you think what happened to us after we got Annie away from them was pretty tame? What the hell do you do for excitement?"

His darkened visage made me laugh. "You have

a point. But I've been trying to make sense of this—"

"So you've been overthinking it," he finished for me. "It's simple, really. Either we're dealing with a real psychopath…or a real vampire."

I laughed again. "Yeah, right."

But he'd said it with a straight face. So Jake was either into black humor, or he was a little loony, I thought, wanting it to be the first one. Of course he had to be joking. And I was in a fine mood. Normally, I would respond with a wisecrack rather than a laugh, but tonight I couldn't manage it. Whether or not I'd needed help, he'd really looked after me earlier.

I was grateful to him.

And attracted.

"You're trying to simplify things, make what you know fit in some neat package," Jake was saying. He reached out and brushed a stray lock of hair back from my face. "You're going to have to start thinking outside of the box."

Vampires? Not likely. I shook my head. "Pretty far out for me. So what's your part in what happened tonight, Jake? Why involve yourself?"

Was he a reporter or a cop or what?

"I need to see justice done," he said simply.

A concept that needed no explanation. I could relate. "To whom?"

"To the person responsible for a lot of things—" he glanced back at the portrait on the liquor cart "—including my mother's death."

The breath caught in my throat. "That's your mother? She was killed like Raven?"

"She was burned to death."

"Oh, Jake, I'm so sorry...."

A fire. How horrible. Not knowing what else to say, I put a hand on his arm. A hand that he patted, as if feeling the need to comfort me. For some reason, the back of my throat grew thick with emotion. His pale eyes were filled with sadness when his gaze met mine. The woman in the portrait was so young. He might have lost her when he was a child.

"I've been searching for the truth for a lot of years," he said. "There are just some things you never can put behind you."

"I understand more than you know." I might not be related to LaTonya Sanford, but she haunted me all the same. "I'm assuming you don't know who—"

"Not yet. But I'm in the right place at the right time. And I will find the guilty one."

"So you think whoever killed Raven killed your mother? Why? What's the connection?"

"The way the blood was taken."

"But you said she burned—"

"That, too."

The cop in me said, "If you beat me to figuring it out, you'll tell me, right?"

He didn't answer, and I didn't press him. I didn't have all the facts yet, but I would get them. Just not right now. He'd finally reached out to me, and I didn't want to spoil it. Plus, I didn't want to ruin whatever it was we had going here.

In one night, everything had changed between us. Jake had backed me up. He hadn't laughed at me or questioned my reasoning; he'd just gone along with me and then had acted. He could have been killed, but he hadn't hesitated. Then he'd taken care of my wound and had shared his deepest secret, one that formed an unlikely bond between us.

Before me stood a man who might actually understand and appreciate me. And he seemed to be someone I could count on.

Jake gathered the medical supplies in a pile on the table and stood, but before he could pick them up and escape the room, I pushed up from the couch and provided a human blockade. He seemed surprised… and yet, not. If he was thinking about leaving the room, he didn't so much as twitch.

"So why did you bring me here, Jake?"

"I knew you would be safe here."

"My place is safe."

"But judging by last night, we might not be alone at your place."

Seconds ticked by as we stared at each other. I had that feeling again, as if he were inside me, trying to read me. Try as I might, I couldn't deny the connection. It felt familiar…and not. Like my connection with Silke, only different.

I remembered feeling that I might do anything he wanted. That he had some kind of mind control over me. Impossible. And yet…

My breath went shallow and my sense of expectancy—of something about to happen—increased. The rush of the night and heightened adrenaline continued, swept over me until my body went taut on the outside, soft on the inside.

I don't know who did what first, but the next thing I knew, we were locked together, body and lips. I felt I was drowning in his kiss, a kiss like no other I'd ever experienced. My head buzzed with it. And my body…well, my body seemed to unfurl and open to him.

We stayed in lip lock for I don't know how long. Somehow in that time and space, we managed to eliminate the barrier to getting closer. I worked on him and he worked on me—hands touching, exploring, exciting—and the next thing I knew our clothing and my holstered weapon were scattered around us on the floor.

And still we were kissing.

Suddenly, he gripped my hips and pushed me away and took a long, lingering look at my body that made me blush from the toes up. His expression was intense. And he was looking at me, for heaven's sake, like I was beautiful or something.

Then it was my turn to look at him. No avoiding it. The lights might be dim, but they were still on.

The first thing I noticed was that he was erect. Wetness pooled between my thighs as I considered straddling him and sliding down him until my flesh covered his.

My body overheated and my face felt flushed as I raised my eyes to his. Our gazes locked. My imagination was playing with me again. I swore his eyes glowed in the semidark. I saw him reaching into the table where the medical supplies were and pick up a condom wrapped in gold foil.

He held out his hand. I took it. Something live and

electric beat through me. He tugged and I stepped closer. And he placed my hand where my eyes had feasted. I spread the condom from his tip around and down him. Then I pushed him back until his legs hit the sofa.

He smiled that smile. That sharp-toothed smile I had noticed earlier.

I gave him another shove and he fell back lengthwise, taking me with him. I wasn't letting go, not yet. I crawled up over him and I rocked my hips as inch by inch he disappeared inside me.

My breath came in small gasps, and he growled deep in his throat in what I knew was a sound of satisfaction.

I fell forward, my weight on my arms and hands, one on either side of his face. I was open to him and he took advantage, licking my skin, every inch of it—neck, shoulder, arms—all except for the area that had been cut. Then he concentrated on my breasts, nipping the full flesh with sharp teeth and sucking my nipples into long, hard points.

I tried to control myself as I moved up and down his length. But try as I might to remove myself a step so that I could make this last, I was swept up in a rush of passion that made my ears ring and my inner flesh spasm.

I gave myself over to sensation and came in long, hard pulses.

"Sorry, I couldn't hang on," I gasped as I collapsed against him. "Give me a minute and it's your turn."

"No rush. We have hours until dawn."

Right. Hours. As if he could last that long. The thought certainly was titillating, and I wondered how long we could last. It seemed no matter what I did, I couldn't bring Jake over the edge. He made me come a second time and a third. And each time he became more inventive.

We were on the floor, then, and he was in back with me on my knees, my thighs opened to let him in. I tilted my hips and pushed at the same time he did. Once more he filled all of me. Surely he was ready....

His hands slipped around my hips, one going to my breasts, the other to my center. I was wet, so wet that we made soft, nerve-shattering sounds as he slipped in and out of me. He leaned over my body and nuzzled the soft flesh near my shoulder. He moved his head around, his lips dancing along my neck. I imagined he found my pulse with his tongue, then sucked down, gently at first, then with increasing pressure.

I felt a tension enter his body that hadn't been there before. He moaned and increased the pressure on my neck, exciting me beyond control.

"That's it," I whispered, unable to hold on any longer. "Faster. Let go."

I felt the pulsing start deep inside me, but this time he was the one. I let go, too. We came together.

I'd never had a night like this. I felt so weak I couldn't move.

As if he sensed that, he cocooned me with his body and pulled me down to the carpet.

I lay there panting, thinking it was over. That we

were both spent. But I was wrong. I could still feel him inside me, and if he'd reduced in size or hardness, I certainly couldn't tell.

I tried to move away, but he caught me to him and whispered in my ear, "Don't be in such a hurry. We're just getting started."

Enough to put fear in the heart of a woman who'd basically gone without for longer than she wanted to admit.

"I don't understand. How can you—?"

"Don't try to understand. Just enjoy the ride."

With that, he rolled over so he was on his back and I was mounted on him again, but this time I wasn't facing him. His hands curled around my hips and moved them so I rose and lowered on him.

The pressure began building once more.

I definitely enjoyed the ride.

This time when we floated down together, it was to collapse, to hold each other, to sleep. Dreamless.

When I awoke, I realized that Jake had put a pillow from the couch under our heads, and from somewhere, he'd gotten a throw.

As much as I hated to leave the cocoon, I knew I had to. I needed to report to the area office in a matter of hours. I needed to shower, to scrub the fake red color out of my hair, to set my thoughts straight.

I dressed quickly and quietly, not wanting to waken Jake. Now that my lust had subsided, I was seriously questioning my own actions. It wasn't like me to be so impulsive.

I glanced over at Jake. He still looked gorgeous and inviting, spread out on the floor with little of him covered. He snored softly and turned as if seeking something.

Me?

But he quickly settled down and so did I.

I was trying to solve a crime, not hook up with a man. The connection I'd felt with Jake in the dark seemed weaker in the cold light of morning.

So I quietly let myself out of his place, looking back only once.

No worry…

Jake slept the sleep of the dead.

Dawn was fast approaching. The creature cried out softly, calling to the initiate in a high-pitched demand. Time to take shelter.

No response.

A bit more searching found her feeding on a piece of human trash. The idea was repulsive. The food was unwashed, unclean. The victim's garments were soiled and the smell…

But of course the homeless were such easy pickings, even a rank beginner could hunt one. That was the problem. Too many homeless people in this city. The other had fed on one, too, with bad results.

A hard tug brought the new one upright. An expression of ecstasy hovered around her features, which were now smeared with a viscous red.

"Dawn approaches. Go…now!"

She mewled in protest and disappointment distorted her features, making her look like a spoiled child whose toy had been confiscated.

The next command was inaudible to the human ear.

But she was no longer human.

And she got the message. Giving her unfinished meal one more look of longing, she scurried away toward shelter.

Now, what to do with the body? This one needed to be hidden or the authorities would come after them with burning torches. No need to go through that again.

The hunger was driving this one to be careless. It couldn't go on. But how to drive the point home to her when she hadn't settled yet?

A vehicle turned the corner and inched down the street.

Time to blend with the shadows, up and out of sight…

The vehicle stopped directly below, and a rack of blue lights suddenly lit the darkened street.

Police! Damn!

Now there was no helping it. Now there would be trouble. Not that this was a new thing. It was the reason for moving from city to city, country to country. But choosing the right companion was sometimes difficult. Unfortunately, all weren't created equal.

But why did this have to happen now? Why so soon? The city had barely begun to give up its treasures.

He'd kill the new one if she wasn't dead already….

Chapter 11

I rolled into the office on all of four hours of sleep and a half pot of coffee. I'd barely signed in and checked to see if there had been any luck in picking up Annie—not—when I was told that Commander Caldwell had been looking for me and was in the break room.

When I found Mom there pouring a cup of coffee, the first thing she said to me was "We have another body."

"What? Who?"

"Another homeless man. Patrol officers found him just before dawn. Same MO as with the other homeless guy."

I sighed and threw myself into a chair. That was a mistake. My hip was sore from the fight the night before. "Has the M.E. seen him?"

"Autopsy's in progress. Your commander is starting to wonder if he has a serial killer on his hands."

Which made me wonder how long it would take
before he started talking about calling in the FBI.

"Looks like we have more than one killer," I
mused, "though they may be working together."

Before I could get too uptight about the FBI horn-
ing in, Mom changed the subject. "How did last
night go at the bar?"

"Chung went missing."

"No explanations?"

"Something weird is going on with the bar owner.
Desiree told me she would take care of him, and I
guess she did. She took care of him good enough to
give him an alibi for the night Raven was murdered."

"You believe her?"

"Unfortunately." She wasn't going to like the next
part. "And then after hours, I tracked Mowry and his
vampire cult members back to where they're holed
up."

"Shelley—"

"They had an innocent, someone who wasn't a
wanna-be vampire. They cut her to bleed her. We got
her out of there before anything worse happened,
then tried to find Annie. She was gone. Patrol hasn't
found her, either, and likely they won't."

"And you can't do anything about Mowry, not at
this point in the murder investigation," Mom said, apparently in tune with me. "Wait a minute. You said
we. Who's the other part of that we?"

"Jake DeAtley." I noted how fast Mom's expression soured and my stomach clenched. *Uh-oh.* I

didn't remind her that I told her I would take care of checking Jake out myself…not that I'd had time to finish the task personally. "What did you find out about him?"

"Nothing."

"Then what's the problem? He doesn't have priors or arrests." Or a driver's license or plates. "I checked."

"When I say nothing, I mean nothing. Nothing on him at all. As far as the world is concerned, Jake DeAtley doesn't exist."

"Jake works at the bar," I reminded her. "He has to have a social security number."

"Wrong. No social. No driver's license. No credit. Nothing. He's simply not who he says he is."

Remembering what he'd told me, that he was after the person responsible for his mother's death, I saw that he might want to use a false identity if he was planning to act against the law. Not that the idea sat well with me. The whole hidden-identity thing worried me, even if I was in the same position. I knew my reasons. I wanted to believe his, but Jake's pretending to be someone he wasn't added another layer of deceit to the investigation.

Yet I didn't want to nail him simply for lack of an identity we could verify. "Let's not crucify him yet."

"You're giving him the benefit of the doubt? Why?"

"Last night, he fought by my side to get the girl out of that rat hole."

"Fought? You had a physical altercation?"

"Okay, yes. I didn't have a choice. But as you can see, I'm fine."

We both fell silent and stared at each other.

I spoke first. "Look, I haven't been acting recklessly." At least not with the investigation. Jake was another matter, one I needed to sort out in private. "So I ran into some trouble while working the case. That happens. You know that."

"What about backup?"

"They left before I did. The trouble was unexpected. And I *had* backup in Jake." Not that I'd asked for his help. But I had taken what was offered. I wanted to think I would never have gone into the cult's hideaway if I'd been alone...but I wasn't sure that was true. "I was simply following the suspect to get a location."

"Apparently, you entered that location."

I told her about the supposed vampire's nest under the railroad tracks. "I just wanted to scope the place out. The only reason there was a confrontation was because I heard Annie cry out and I realized what they were doing to her. Should I have left her to them?"

Mom shifted uncomfortably. "I suppose not."

"After, I called Norelli and gave him the lowdown. He said he'd arrange a stakeout on the place and put a tail on Mowry himself. You know I couldn't arrest him without chancing blowing the murder case against him."

Mom nodded. "You made the right call. About the reason I'm here. I stopped by to leave you a stack of files. I got them from Commander Aniceto. They're on your desk. Maybe they'll help you figure out who's getting their kicks out of playing vampire before another person dies."

I started when the *V*-word spilled from her lips. But of course she wasn't referring to the real thing the way Jake had. And Aniceto must have turned over his cult-research files from when he'd worked the gang unit.

"Thanks, Commander. It's good to feel like we're in synch."

Mom nodded and took her leave. I walked her as far as my desk, where a two-foot pile of teetering folders awaited me. Before I went through them, I found the report on Jake. Unfortunately, it shed no light on the subject. If records were the test, Jake DeAtley didn't exist.

So I'd been with a ghost the night before? How spooky was that?

The lab results on Thora's gargoyle pin were equally frustrating. Yes, there were fingerprints from two different people—undoubtedly Thora and possibly her killer—neither of which were in the data bank. At least I knew that if I had a solid suspect, I could try to match them later.

I turned to the folders from Aniceto. I spent the next hour going through every notation in the first file, searching for something new and helpful in the case. I couldn't find anything useful in the articles about some of the well-known cults that had resulted in mass suicide.

When Norelli and Walker sauntered in, I said, "Hey, look at this loot. All kinds of info on cults. I'm willing to share."

"You need busywork," Norelli said. "So it's all yours."

I was glaring needles at Norelli's back when Walker said, "I can spare maybe an hour after I make some calls."

"Thanks. I'll count on you, then."

That Norelli left it to me was no surprise. Contrary to the way television depicted detectives, we really had individual caseloads. Rather than a single case at a time, detectives had lots of cases to work at once. I hadn't been assigned a load yet, maybe because the Area 4 commander wanted me to prove myself again. When Norelli got on the phone, I knew he was playing catch-up with his load. Leaving this case to me? That would suit me just fine.

I'd gotten through that first file when Walker took a few from the stack. Opening the one on top, he mumbled, "Psychiatric evaluations of former cult members," as he went back to his desk.

I opened another file, which gave me information on psychological manipulation and abuse, brainwashing and mind control, authoritarian groups, alternative and mainstream religions. More information than I could possibly process in one sitting.

So I decided to check the contents of each file to see if one stood above the others in the way of being helpful in this case. I found it halfway through the pile—articles about vampire cults across the country.

Four teenagers from Indiana involved in a vampire cult stabbed one of the girl's parents to death. According to the sheriff's office, all four teens claimed to be vampires. They admitted to human-blood-drinking rituals—they cut their arms and sucked each other's blood.

In another incident, a college student murdered a young woman, cut out her heart and drank her blood because he thought it would make him immortal.

In a Georgia case, a mother was beaten to death by a vampire cult. A friend said the cult's sire performed a blood-drinking ritual in a cemetery to induct, or cross over, the daughter as a fellow vampire. "The one crossed over is subject to the sire," a witness said in a deposition. "The sire has dominance over that person." A *V,* surrounded by a number of the same symbol obviously fashioned by different hands, was carved into the woman's body—signs of the vampire clan.

Another cult member said his friend had been intent on opening the gates to Hell, which meant he would have to kill a large number of people in order to consume their souls.

I wondered if Elvin Mowry had any such notions.

I skimmed other articles, found like stories. More indications that cults used particular symbology to represent them. A pentacle. A Celtic cross. An ankh.

I read this article in full. According to the author, the symbols went back not decades, but centuries, and had shown up in various places in the world, on dead people who'd been drained of blood.

I began to wonder about gargoyles. I'd only seen the blackbird on Raven, of course. But LaTonya's tattoo had been a winged gargoyle. And Thora'd had the gargoyle pendant.

I got online and searched gargoyles. Gargoyles and grotesques of various sorts dated back four thousand years to ancient Egypt and represented the struggle between good and evil. Some believed they came alive at night. Wings allowed many of them to fly above the populace. Oddly, they were considered a symbol of protection. The word *gargoyle,* from the Latin *gurgulio,* had double meaning: both throat and the gurgling sound that water made as it passed through a gargoyle.

Or the gurgling of blood?

Had the women been marked as victims? I wondered, considering Raven's blackbird might qualify to be included. Had someone been trying to protect them? Or were the gargoyles sheer coincidence, simply a Goth fascination?

I searched gargoyle and vampire together. The first several pages were mostly references to products and Vampire: the Masquerade, an increasingly popular role-playing game. Just when I was about to give up, I found a reference to an article in the *London Times.* I clicked on the link and read about killings of women relieved of blood through a slash in the inside of their arms. Several of those women had been tattooed with a gargoyle. The cases stretched over a period of decades and multiple countries. There was even a reference to a century-old cold case.

I printed the article, wondering what exactly it was that I had run into.

I got home ready to fall into bed for a couple hours of well-earned sleep before doing double duty. Silke was waiting for me, poking around in my fridge. I'd asked her to leave me a couple of outfits and makeup, but hadn't expected her to be hanging around.

Part of me was still ticked at her for going over my head. But another part knew she'd done it out of concern, so I was going to give her a pass this once.

I asked, "Hey, what's up?"

Straightening, she shut the refrigerator door. "I decided to wait for you. Do you know you're out of, well, everything?"

Non-news. Since my favorite food was anything take-out, I was nearly always out of everything other than leftovers.

Except for cat food.

I stooped to give Sarge and Cadet the attention they seemed to want at my presence, but the moment I touched them, they both sauntered off, tails straight in the air. They were obviously annoyed with me for being gone so much the past few days, and they were taking this opportunity to show it.

I left the kitchen and joined her. "Thanks for bringing the gear, Silke, but you didn't have to wait."

"I didn't just bring the things you asked for."

Nerves were evident in her voice, which meant she didn't think I was going to like whatever it was she'd added to the list. "Out with it."

"I respect your thinking like a cop, Shelley, but in this case, I think you're being incredibly naive."

"Me...naive?" Wasn't that the pot calling the kettle black? I loosened the ties on my boots and kicked them off.

"You're living in this world where things are normal, just the way you think they should be. Only maybe they aren't."

"So you say."

"You might, too, if you hadn't closed off yourself from other possibilities just because you roughed up the wrong guy half a lifetime ago."

"Silke, just because you and I have this twin connection doesn't mean the whole world is abnormal."

"There's nothing abnormal about it. Not our sort of connection, anyway. More people could do it if they tried," she said earnestly. "I've been doing a lot of research on the powers of the developed mind… and that's what scientists think."

"Some scientists." Kooks.

"I've been doing research for you, too," Silke announced. "That's what I brought you in the second bag. Books and videos."

I approached the cloth bags with apprehension and opened the research one with the caution of someone afraid a snake would slither out. And so it did, in the form of a heavy tome called *Reality Bites: Vampyres among Us.*

"Um, and what am I supposed to do with this?"

"Read it, of course."

"I don't have time for fiction," I insisted, dropping the book on the table. I thought of the stack of folders on my desk that awaited me.

"You don't have enough time not to consider every possibility! You don't know when the next person might be turned."

"What do you mean, turned?"

"I was thinking about your being attacked. What if there is a real vampire and the woman who attacked you was recently turned? Then she would need blood."

Remembering feeling a nip at my neck, I shook off the memory. "Silke, there's got to be a more rational explanation for—"

"Open up your mind, Shelley. The world isn't all nice and neat. It's messy and full of nasty surprises."

"I know that! I'm a cop, remember."

"You may be a cop, but you don't know all the possibilities, because you won't even consider anything out of the norm."

"Because I'm a rational human being."

"That's your trouble. I just hope it won't be your undoing."

This wasn't getting us anywhere, and I desperately needed sleep, so I caved. "All right. Just leave the stuff here. I'll try to keep an open mind when I look at it." I didn't promise when that might be.

Pacified, Silke calmed down, gave me an extra-long hug and left.

I started for the bedroom, but slowed as I passed the table and glanced at the paranormal research materials. Skeptic that I was, I knew I wouldn't believe in any of this nonsense, but I guessed it wouldn't hurt to take a look. After all, I had researched vampire cults myself, and I'd just spent the morning wading through the information Commander Aniceto had gathered. If nothing else, this might give me additional insight into Elvin Mowry's mind.

I grabbed a couple of the books and dragged them into the other room with me, where I tossed them on the bed. I was simply going to do my homework.

After stripping into my underwear, I slid onto the

bed with a sigh. Before I could open the first book, a thump on the mattress told me I had company.

"Hey, Sarge, come on here, boy."

But he stayed at the foot of the bed and stared at me out of accusing kitty eyes. I lifted my foot and ran my toes along his side as I opened the cover. He couldn't help himself from purring, but he settled down right where he was. His idea of a compromise.

I started to skim the material.

That vampires—male and female—were generally beautiful didn't surprise me. I'd gotten that out of the books that analyzed vampire cults. Looks were always a major issue. Even with purple hair, Mowry himself was a pretty boy.

According to this book, however, "Becoming a vampire makes one even more attractive and hard to resist."

I raised my eyebrows at that one. Somehow, I was sure seeing someone with jaws dripping fresh blood would pretty much be a turn off to me. I flipped a few pages.

The author wrote, "Vampires can move around with surety in the dark because they operate using a kind of radar."

What, like bats? Ha-ha.

"And all their senses are heightened—sight, smell, hearing, touch."

That must mean they worked on overload most of the time, I thought with a smirk.

"They're faster and stronger than any human, and their healing power is legendary."

So Superman was a vamp?

"Anyone with psychic powers is too tempting to resist."

I guess that made me a prime candidate to a vampire stalker.

"Drinking blood isn't just a way for a vampire to stay undead but to boost sexual energy. Although vampires are unable to conceive a child, they have more than enough sexual energy to spare in any circumstance."

They might shoot blanks but they were expert at sex? Well, that was interesting, anyway.

And in a roundabout way, the sex reference reminded me of Jake.

I slammed the cover down on the book and pushed it away from me just as Cadet jumped onto the middle of the bed with a loud meow. I scooped her to my middle and hugged her there despite her mewling protest. She quickly settled down. Good. Then I slid my toes into Sarge's fur. His side was vibrating with purr.

No more nonsense. Sleep was calling.

And sweet dreams of Jake DeAtley, the man who didn't exist....

She sobs and her eye tears and rolls along her cheekbone. "You're missing it, you're missing it."

Missing what?

"I'm working on your case. I promise I'm going to find the person who did this to you." Even as I say it, I fear I won't really be able to do so.

"Naive," she croaks, for a moment sounding like Silke. "You have to look beyond what you think you know."

I shake my head. "Then who will I be?"
"Yourself."
Maybe that is what scares me most.

Chapter 12

Jake started every time a set of footsteps approached Heart of Darkness, disappointed when it wasn't Shelley.

He couldn't stop thinking about the woman.

He'd awakened to find she'd stolen away while he was sleeping. He'd felt alone, suddenly not a good feeling.

Something about Shelley wouldn't let him be. She was fearless and stronger than most people. That she might be his match in every way was something he hadn't been able to say about any other woman. And she was a straight arrow and true to herself. Sappy stuff, but in the end it all got to him.

Blaise Allcock slid onto a stool at the head of the bar. "The usual."

Jake poured him the house's finest red, which went for more than twenty bucks a glass. Blaise didn't mind the expense.

He set the glass of red on the bar. "Who's watching the store?"

"I haven't opened." Blaise picked up the glass, his hand smooth, fingers manicured, long nails painted a deep blue to match his silky midnight-blue shirt. "No people, no business, no sense in sitting around waiting for my next victim to come in."

Considering what had been going on in the area, Jake didn't think that was particularly funny, but he smiled anyway, just to appease the shop owner, who normally had a thriving business. Most of the bar regulars were victims, but fashion victims rather than the violent kind. Many of them not only wore odd clothing and odder makeup, but they also mutilated their bodies with myriad piercings and multiple tattoos. As far as Jake was concerned, the one ear he'd had pierced was plenty. Blaise was either a damn fine salesman or he had a way of mesmerizing his customers to come back again and again and again.

Mesmerizing…hmm…

Jake stared at Blaise and attempted to read him, but try as he might, he couldn't manage it. He was blocked, stopped cold.

Maybe that should tell him something, but he couldn't be certain. Some people were simply more resistant than others. And Blaise was definitely an odd duck, an effeminate semi-cross-dresser, who—while he didn't pretend to be a woman—certainly played on those pretty looks of his. For some reason, young women were attracted to him. Maybe guys, too.

Not that Blaise did a thing for him.

Which was in itself unusual. Not the sex part. The unreadability factor. He could nearly always get an accurate take on a person's nature. That he couldn't on Blaise made the man suspect.

But before Jake could attempt to sort out his thoughts in the matter, Shelley entered the bar and his attention shifted.

There was something different about her tonight. She was toned down a bit, more natural-looking. More attractive, if that was possible. But she was also more tense than normal. He didn't miss the once-over she gave the place, as if looking for someone. Mowry?

Just seeing her made his blood rush.

Shelley looked every way but at him.

Amused, Jake wondered if she really thought she could resist him. Of course she must. She didn't know who or what he was.

Not yet.

I so didn't want to be disappointed in Jake after last night, but after talking to Mom and reading the report, I was concerned. If he wasn't who he said he was, then who? Why was he tracking down some criminal? Could I believe the story that the person had been responsible for his mother's death? What if he knew more about my investigation than he was saying?

I suspected I might not like whatever was going on with him.

Still, I had to face him sometime.

I chose to do it while he was occupied with Blaise. That way, I wouldn't have to take the heat of his full attention.

I stopped at the head of the bar and opened with "They're not exactly banging down the doors tonight, are they?"

"Blame the perfect weather," Jake said, his eyelids drooping, as if that could hide his thoughts from me. "Every outdoor beer garden in the city probably has a waiting line."

"Of Goths?" I couldn't see it. They seemed to be happiest in a room thick with smoke.

Blaise said, "You're not wearing any jewelry tonight."

Uh-oh. I hadn't properly finished my first do-it-myself makeover. That's what I got for refusing my sister's help. Now Blaise made me wonder what else I might have missed. Had I put on the violet eye shadow or not?

I shrugged nervously. "I was in a hurry to be on time."

Blaise sipped at his wine, his eyes never leaving mine. "Those red crystal chandelier earrings I told you about have your name on them."

Right. The ones that would look like splashes of blood against my throat. "No customers, no tips, no cash."

"I take credit."

But of course my credit card was assigned to me—Shelley—not to Silke Caldwell.

"I've taken a hiatus from using my card. I got a

bit carried away last month." I could feel Jake's eyes on me again, and my pulse rushed to the blood in my throat. "I don't even have it with me."

"You can pay me later," Blaise said. "Or I'll take it out in blood." He laughed at his own joke and added, "I'll even give you a professional discount. Now, that's an offer even you can't refuse."

Take it out in blood? "You're right."

If I continued to refuse, it would simply bring attention to me, which I didn't want. Besides, this was an opportunity to check out Blaise Allcock, one of the key players in this Goth miniempire.

So the next thing I knew, I was following Blaise through the hall door, all the while feeling Jake's gaze boring into the spot between my shoulders.

I glanced back and said, "If Desiree asks, tell her I'll be just a few minutes."

We crossed the hall to the minimall of stores up front along the street. Expecting to see Hung Chung back on duty, I was a little on edge. But the security guard working the building was tall and wiry.

"No Hung Chung tonight?"

"It seems to me you might be relieved that our Asian friend has been removed from the premises."

A reference to the fight, I supposed. No doubt, everyone had heard about it.

"Removed?" I echoed him. "As in fired?"

Blaise shrugged. "You could say that."

"I haven't seen Raven tonight, either," I said, testing the waters by using the dead girl's name. No reaction. "Chung scared her to death."

"Bad technique," Blaise said. "There are better ways to get what you want."

A comment that disturbed me. It was almost as if Blaise thought Chung should have gotten what he wanted....

Inside Taboo Tattoo, I was avoiding looking at the needles laid out in the tattooing and piercing area and was following Blaise forward to the jewelry counter, when I saw a gargoyle among the tattoo designs. Not the same as LaTonya's tattoo, but a gargoyle nonetheless. And on the jewelry counter lay several other gargoyles in the form of pendants.

"Neat gargoyles," I said in Silke's enthusiastic voice. "Everyone seems to be into them."

"Some are. Mowry's group mostly."

Mowry's group. Thora qualified. And I guess LaTonya did, too, from what Raven had told me. But Raven herself? I hadn't yet been able to make that connection. An image came to me—Mowry lifting the glass of wine in a ring-heavy hand. One of those rings had been a pewter gargoyle.

Blaise had gone straight for the dark red crystal earrings, which he snagged from a display. "Here you are."

When he held them out to me, his shirtsleeve opened slightly and I caught a glimpse of the tattoo beneath. Every inch of his skin was covered with beautiful inks. I thought I caught a glimpse of a wing, but the gap in the material closed before I could get a better look.

I focused on the earrings. "They are beautiful." They really were. I took them from him and, looking in the mirror set on the counter, held them up next to my ear. The crystals spilled from tiny carved faces, full and practically long enough to brush my shoulders. Not my taste, not normally—too wild—but an impulse I couldn't quite name made me say "Okay, you convinced me. So you said something about a discount?"

"Keep them as a gift from me."

"I couldn't."

"Of course you can. But here, let me put them on you."

I was about to tell Blaise that wasn't necessary, but the words froze in my throat when I met his gaze. Nodding, I gave the earrings back to him, and the next thing I knew, I was enjoying the feel of his hands brushing against the side of my neck and my earlobes as he fastened the crystals in place.

Enjoying…actually, I was loving it.

I recognized how odd that was even as I looked deep into Blaise's eyes. I couldn't turn away from him, couldn't move. For the moment, I was mesmerized. He broke the connection and set a mirror in front of me. I checked out my reflection as he watched me. I got a good look at those carved faces at my ears, which were tiny gargoyles.

And then, so lightly that I might have imagined it, Blaise stroked the length of my throat. Sensations rippled down where his fingers touched my flesh and kept going to my breasts. My nipples hardened, and sensations lit me from the inside out.

"You really are a beautiful woman, Silke."

I fought the flush of warmth threatening to overtake me. "And you really are some salesman." Disturbed by my reaction to him, I blinked and took a step back.

"Yes, look at all the profit I'm making with my many customers." He didn't bother to keep the irony from his tone as he took hold of me again with his eyes. "I might as well lock up and leave for the night. I could do that. You could accompany me. I can promise you a whole menu of earthly delights."

"Menu?" I asked breathlessly, my imagination already at work. "That's a big promise."

"And a sincere one."

He hadn't broken his gaze. And though I desperately tried, I couldn't look away. The thought that I might want to accompany him, might want to see what his earthly delights might entail, seemed for a moment irresistible. Then I somehow managed to tear my gaze from his and reality came flooding back to me.

What the heck was happening to me? First Jake, now Blaise…

"Hey, listen, I need to get back to work before Desiree notices I'm gone," I said, turning to leave.

"Leave Desiree to me. If she becomes agitated over your absence, I'll calm her."

"Oh. Thanks, but I really must go." I wondered how he might manage that. Did Blaise have some kind of relationship with the bar owner? "I'll pay you for the earrings at the end of the night."

"If you insist."

I was looking down at my hands as I headed for the door—anything to keep from looking at Blaise—and almost ran into a customer entering the shop. I blinked and went on as if I'd never met the blond cop who ignored me, too.

"Can I help you?" I heard Blaise ask, his tone sounding more interested in her than in making a sale.

I raised my eyebrows and fled back to the bar. Jake spotted me the moment I walked in the door. Or maybe it was that I spotted him.

Unsettled by my strange encounter with the tattoo artist, I was glad to see the place was filling up. Our Goth customers weren't lining up for those beer gardens, after all, though maybe the neighborhood regulars and the tourists were seeking summer digs since they were in short supply.

I got busy taking orders, all the while my brain going over what had just happened with Blaise. And with his declaration that he could take care of Desiree if she presented a problem—which she didn't, because she was nowhere to be seen.

But the new undercover cop was. Officer Fred Duran's own mother wouldn't recognize him in black leather pants and jacket and a long black wig. He sat at the bar, about halfway down. I knew he was the plant by the way he too casually swept his gaze over the room, letting it come to rest on me for a significant moment before looking away. He was too close to where I placed my orders for my comfort. I didn't want him overhearing anything personal between Jake and me. Assuming anything personal went down.

Thinking I would simply have to make sure it didn't, I avoided lingering at the bar. As I approached a table of straight customers, I was reminded of Annie. I looked around but didn't see her tonight. Smart girl.

"What can I get for you?" I asked.

No sooner did I place an order than I approached another table, then returned to the bar and traded a new order for the filled one.

An hour of this and Jake said, "Are you trying to make most-efficient-waitress-of-the-year or what?"

"Wow, I didn't know efficiency was frowned on around here."

"Avoiding me is."

I glanced sideways to the cop, hoping he was far enough away that he hadn't heard Jake's throaty reply.

"Not here," I said, my jaw clenched.

"Sounds promising. Where, then?"

I felt as if Officer Undercover were staring a hole through me. And beyond him, Desiree had appeared from somewhere, and she was staring at us, too.

In a slightly raised voice, I said, "Make that Bloody Cosmopolitan a double." Then I took my tray and moved off to deliver the drinks.

With a reduced crowd, I couldn't keep up the busy-waitress routine, so I decided a break was in order. No one was in the ladies' room, so I took refuge in there.

The ladies' room was downstairs in the basement. There was a lounge area sharing space with the furnace, which at this time of year was off. I had to go through there to get to the stalls.

I did my business and was about to come out

when I heard, "Elvie told me the lair is something else," and I froze.

I recognized the voice as belonging to the fuchsia-haired Goth named Sheena.

"Where is this place?" a second voice—one I didn't recognize—asked.

"He said the entrance is on Lake Street. You know, the boarded-up meat market," Sheena said. "I think we ought to check it out."

"Without the guys?"

"Why not? Where's your sense of adventure?"

"I don't know...."

"I don't want to go alone," Sheena complained.

"If I were you, I wouldn't go at all."

The voices faded off and I came out of the stall.

Lair. What kind of lair? One that interested Elvin Mowry. And with a nearby Lake Street address.

Maybe tonight I would find out what happened to Thora Nelson and LaTonya Sanford.

Chapter 13

After I left the ladies' room, I went to find Desiree. I found her in her office. She lay back against her chair, looking weak and wan. At my knock, she lifted her head as if with great effort.

"Silke, what is it?"

Wondering if she was ill—or perhaps simply weak from starving herself to stay so thin—I said, "I need to leave a little early tonight."

I thought to slide out the back way. I didn't want one of the other cops following me and screwing up my plan. I meant to check out the place Sheena had been telling her friend about, and if my guess was right about its use, I would call for backup and do everything by the book. But I didn't want to jump the gun and have my colleagues getting their chuckles at my expense once again.

"You may leave as you wish if you will work late for me tomorrow night. A private party at my place." She stood and walked over to me. "You will be well compensated."

I didn't see how I was going to get out of agreeing to do the private party, so I said, "Sure. No problem." Unless I solved the case tonight, of course.

If we were on her private turf, I might get some useful information out of the bar owner. I wondered, though, if she really was going to be able to hostess that party. I noted how sunken her cheeks were, how pale her skin, how dull her eyes.

We left her office together to the sounds of a commotion—raised voices, knocked-over chairs. Jake was standing in the middle of two half-drunk half-wits—a Goth and a neighborhood regular who were going at each other. The Goth was bleeding profusely from his nose. He ignored any pain he was in as he tried to get past Jake to jump the other patron. Jake put out a hand and stopped him cold.

So fast that I didn't see it coming, he grabbed them both by the backs of their shirts and yelled, "Enough!"

The contentious men started to swing at him, but Jake somehow managed to hold them far enough away from himself and each other so they couldn't do more damage.

I glanced at the cop halfway down the bar. He was watching the altercation closely, but he couldn't break his cover. From somewhere, a tall bouncer I hadn't seen before appeared. Jake handed over the two men to him.

I relaxed. At least I did until I got a good look at Desiree. Still next to me, she'd frozen, her gaze fixed on one of the men—I was pretty sure it was the one whose nose was undoubtedly broken. The blood was pouring from it. Desiree's mouth was open and she darted out her tongue to her top lip as if she wanted to taste it; she was practically drooling. Then she covered her mouth and rushed back inside her office.

It was almost as if she were turned on by the sight of blood. Could she be a member of a vampire cult, too? That would explain why she ran a place like this.

All that vampire nonsense was getting to me. I desperately needed to figure out if Mowry and company were responsible.

Taking Desiree at her word that I could leave, I decided to head out now. I could probably check out the lair and make it back to the bar well before closing. Then Jake and the undercover cop could think whatever they wanted about my absence.

When Jake's back was turned, I grabbed a small flashlight from the bar and dropped the slender metal stick into my skirt pocket. I delivered the last order I'd had filled, then slipped out into the hall, checking to make certain no one—including the cops watching the place—noticed my departure. I quickly crossed to the rear exit that took me to an alley.

The day's heat had remained trapped between buildings, and coming out into it was like opening a furnace door. Either that or my rising adrenaline level was roasting me from the inside out. Fear slid down my spine as I set off, my gaze continually roaming as I searched in vain for other signs of life.

A moment later I was on Lake Street, where I crossed under the elevated tracks and approached the boarded-up meat market in question. The place looked deserted. I took a deep breath to center myself and checked around me to make certain I hadn't missed anything. I was alone. I circled the building and checked for an alarm system—there was none—and for any easy entry.

The windows were nailed down tight and the doors were bolted, including the one on the shipping dock. In frustration, I struck out at it and the bolt swung out slightly, making me realize it was hanging from its latch without actually being engaged.

The door opened easily. I clicked on the flashlight and entered quietly. The space was open and empty and smelled slightly of old, dried blood.

Of course…a meat market.

My stomach lurched anyway, and I swallowed hard to settle it.

I half held my breath and walked around the large open area, finding nothing of interest. Then I swept my intense beam across the floor that was thick with dust…all except for what looked like a pathway to a far door.

My pulse raced along my veins as I made my way across the room, all the time concentrating on picking up the slightest sound.

No way was I going to be ambushed again.

I slowly opened the inner door and saw a set of steps. I followed them down to a basement that looked as if it had been used for storage. At the far end of the room was an old wood elevator cordoned off with a heavy chain-link barrier.

Apparently, someone hadn't wanted anyone using the elevator. Perhaps the structure had grown dangerous with age.

I flashed the light along the elevator. Swinging the flashlight's beam to the floor, I found the lock had been smashed, and further inspection of the area in front of the doors revealed more dust had been disturbed.

Someone had been using the elevator.

My pulse picked up. Had I found it, then? Would this lead me to the lair that Sheena had been so anxious to see?

I thought to stop right then. To return to the bar and get backup. But a noise from below made me hesitate. I listened hard and swore I heard what I thought was a cry cut short.

I should call for backup. I flipped open my phone and saw I had no signal. Damn!

What if someone was in danger? I listened hard but heard no further sound. Maybe what I'd heard was an animal. Rats?

Even so, I slipped through the chain-link barrier. I had to check it out, just in case....

My hand shook slightly as I slid open the doors and quickly swept the inside of the car with the beam. Empty. I walked in and closed the door behind me, then cocked a rotating handle to power the elevator down. The rest of me shook inside when the groan of the old machinery bellowed around me. Not that it was really that loud. Every sound seemed magnified, starting with the blood that rushed through my head.

I had my gun on me, which calmed me a bit.

When the car stopped and the doors opened, I shone my light into the dark hole before me and listened hard. But if there was a woman in pain down here, she was quiet now. This wasn't a subbasement as I had expected, but an oval-shaped tunnel about six feet wide and eight feet high. Steel tracks swept down the tunnel floor.

What in the world…?

Then it hit me. The tunnel was part of the crazy quilt of intersecting freight and mail tunnels built forty feet below street level in the late nineteenth century.

I knew the network ran under the entire Loop area. Everyone in Chicago probably knew about them after the flood. A decade ago, there'd been a leak in a wall banking the Chicago River. The wall had given, and not only had the entire Loop network flooded, but subbasements of buildings, as well. Interest in the abandoned tunnels had been high, and the story had been heavily covered by the media.

I remembered reading that spur lines extended west under and then beyond the river for another half mile or so because of the fish and meat markets that used to occupy this area. The tunnels had been sealed off for more than half a century, but apparently someone had found use for them once more.

The tunnel floor was mostly smooth, but in places it was strewn with debris, chunks of decomposing wall and ceiling. I was careful to keep to the middle area between the tracks, and to avoid stepping on anything that might twist an ankle.

Ahead the tunnel split in two. I took the right branch. And when it split again, again I went right. I kept careful track of every twist and turn. The last thing I needed was to get lost in this maze.

This dark, dank and ultimately deserted maze. My gut was telling me to head back and call for backup. I was risking my life because I couldn't sleep at night without a visit from LaTonya. But ending up dead wouldn't do anyone any good.

Suddenly feeling not so brave, I began tracing my way back the way I'd come.

But before I could get there, I heard something that sounded like loose material skittering along the ground—some of the detritus from a crumbling wall that I'd come across before. Was that a natural sound? The decomposition of the tunnel? Or something human?

Then I swore I heard the whisper of footsteps along the tracks somewhere ahead.

The idea of unexpected company made my mouth go dry. I stopped and clicked off my flashlight and tried not to breathe. Did my best to listen, to pin where that sound had come from. My best effort was met with silence.

No aura of light came from anywhere down the shaft.

How could anyone get around in such absolute darkness?

I removed my weapon from its holster and held it firmly in front of me, aimed into the dark.

Still nothing.

I waited yet another interminable moment before going on, my flashlight low and close to me—a roaming beam would be a warning signal should someone else be in the tunnels. I would have clicked it out, but then what? I needed to see where I was going. All the while I crept back the way I came, I kept my inner radar at alert. I didn't hear another sound, but for reasons I couldn't explain, I felt another presence.

Call it instinct, call it experience, call it anything that fit, but I knew that whatever it was that I'd come looking for tonight was within my reach.

I made another turn, got that much closer to where I'd entered the maze, when my foot landed on loose matter and I would have done the splits if my boot hadn't smacked up tight against an old train rail. I threw out my arms to catch myself and loosened my grip on the flashlight. It went flying, hit the tunnel wall and with a smack, went out.

Damn!

I didn't dare curse aloud…didn't dare breathe… didn't dare take another step until I reconnoitered.

I strained for an entire minute at least, listening for some reaction. But the tunnel remained eerily silent.

Pent-up air flowed from my chest, and I blindly sought the flashlight, crouching and running my hand along the ground. Finally my hand nicked loose metal, spinning the flashlight out of reach.

I reached farther, finally closing my fingers around the comforting tool.

As I snatched it up, a feeling of triumph filled me.

But my relief was short-lived because the light wouldn't turn on. I tried snapping it. Shaking it. Begging silently with it. Nothing worked. It remained adamantly dark.

Great, because that's just how I was going to have to get out of there—in the frickin' dark!

Bemoaning my fate, I was about to stand to feel my way to the next tunnel split, when I heard a scuffle behind me. I started to whirl but something hard hit me in the side of the head and I staggered to my knees. I must have accidentally squeezed the trigger, because my gun went off with a resounding boom and sharp flash of blue light that illuminated a dark silhouette. But one whose identity I couldn't penetrate.

I couldn't focus my eyes.

Couldn't focus my mind.

Couldn't make my body cooperate.

A kick to the head did it every time. But this was the first time I was experiencing it myself.

Before I could recover, my head exploded with more pain—another kick—and my body went numb. Both the gun and the flashlight dropped from my fingers, which went slack.

And then my internal lights went out....

Sometime later I came up from a deep, dark void, someplace far, far away.

My head was still fuzzy and I was floating.

My head hung back as if over the edge of a bed. My legs dangled in space. And one arm hung loose and bobbed a steady rhythm as I moved. But I couldn't move the other arm; it was up against something solid and covered with cloth.

Someone was carrying me! To where? To what? Thoughts raced through my still fuzzy mind as I stirred and tried to fight whoever it was.

His hold tightened. "Shelley, ease up."

"Jake?"

"Yeah, so relax until we get out of here."

How was I supposed to relax when I'd been knocked unconscious only to wake up in his arms? How did I know he hadn't been the one to do the head knocking?

I shoved at his chest. "Let me down!"

He did.

I concentrated on coming up through the cotton-minded world that still cocooned me. Wondering if Jake had followed me or if he'd had his own reasons for entering the underground labyrinth, I said, "I left the bar without you knowing."

"Making assumptions was your first mistake."

I clenched my jaw so I didn't say something I would regret. How many mistakes did he think I had made?

"Did you see who kicked me in the head?" I asked, vaguely uncomfortable because for all I knew, it really could have been him.

"Whoever it was had gone by the time I got to you. Must have heard me coming."

"Damn! My gun—"

"I have it on me. The flashlight, too."

Apparently, the cotton was dissolving, for it suddenly hit me that we were still in complete and utter dark. "How did you know where I was without a light?"

"I saw your beam ahead until it went out."

"Well, there is no light now."

I was dizzy and my head hurt—it felt as if some-one were drilling through my skull—and I still couldn't see. But I could feel my way along the wall, so that's what I did.

Directly behind me, Jake asked, "Whatever pos-sessed you to do something so reckless?"

"I don't have to justify myself to you."

"Surely you answer to someone. Or do you? Could it be you just go off on your own because you think you're the only one who can do whatever it is that needs to be done?"

Words similar to those that I had been hearing from Mom and Silke and Al. What was this? Beat-up-on-Shelley week? Heat shot through me and I walked faster.

"Careful, you don't want to crash into the eleva-tor. It's just ahead."

"How could you possibly know that?"

"I can see in the dark."

"All those carrots your mother force-fed you as a kid?"

"Not exactly."

He had to be joking, of course. Only I didn't think it was funny. Just irritating.

And the feat seemed mind bending until he admit-ted, "I counted turns in the tunnel. We passed the last one just before I let you down. Be careful or you re-ally will run into the doors."

I took his warning seriously and, while keeping one hand sliding along the wall, I reached forward with the other just in time to touch the wall of the elevator.

"We're here."

I was shaking by the time I got into the elevator car. Jake tried to hold me upright, but I eluded his grasp and found the control, then put my back up against the wall as the car vibrated up the shaft.

My head was starting to feel bigger than my body. And more painful. I wondered how many ibuprofens it would take to calm this headache down. I couldn't wait to get back up to street level and fresh air.

As I stopped the elevator car at the basement level, I heard a series of clicks coming from Jake's way. Before I could ask what he was doing, an explosion of light blinded me.

"Here," he said, shining the flashlight at me. It didn't seem to be broken, after all. "You could have a concussion. Let me take a look at your eyes."

He didn't give me a choice, merely cornered me. My pulse triggered but I was too weak to fight him. Thankfully he didn't try shining the light directly into my eyes. He aimed it somewhere over my shoulder, making me wonder how he could then see my pupils well enough to tell anything.

Or maybe that wasn't the point, I thought, my suspicions rising. Maybe he was simply trying to distract me.

"Pupils look even," Jake said, his voice rumbling through his chest and making my stomach do a flip. He moved the light toward my left eye. "It's reacting to the light normally." Then he switched hands and did the same with my right eye. "Looks okay."

Even with the diagnosis complete, he didn't move away. My heart thudded. If he tried something, I wasn't sure I was up to fighting him off.

And then he stepped back and handed over the flashlight.

I snatched it out of his hand, tersely saying, "The gun."

He handed me that, too. "What is it you expected to find down here?"

"I don't know." Had I imagined a cry or really heard it? Or had I been set up? "I was following my instincts."

True, if not totally honest.

Something kept me from telling him about my overhearing Sheena talking about this place in the ladies' room. That something being the fact that I had no idea of who Jake really was.

Or if he'd been the one to stop me from finding what I'd come for. I didn't think so, but trusting my instincts right now probably wasn't in my best interests.

He said, "You'd better come home with me. Concussions can be tricky things, and you should be watched closely for the next twenty-four hours."

"I would rather go to my own apartment," I said back to him.

"Then I'll take you there."

"You need to get back to the bar," I reminded him.

"It's closing time. Besides, I would rather check you out personally, make sure you're all right."

Remembering what had happened the night before after he'd taken care of my wounds, I said, "I'm not in the mood."

Truth be told, I needed to be on guard against making another mistake, especially with a man who was harboring potentially dangerous secrets—his real identity and his true interest in the case, whatever that might be.

The creature stepped out of the shadows the moment the elevator doors whisked closed. Lights weren't really necessary, though they presented a certain charm. Humans, for example, had quite a bit more to them than simple infrared pulses common to all living things.

The woman was exquisite under lamp light.

Silke Caldwell…what had gotten into her?

How had she found the entrance to these well-hidden chambers?

She was lucky to be alive. The bartender had followed her, and he had been her savior.

This time.

Jake DeAtley…what in Hades was he?

His scent had been different this night, and had raised an alarm that had saved the woman from death. Or from a more complicated fate.

DeAtley would need further looking into.

But enough about the man.

Not only was the woman attractive, but she was also strong and sure of herself…and far more intelligent and interesting than the other new ones. It was so difficult starting over, so hard to pick the right companions.

But there was no doubt that she would make a fine addition to the stable.

Maybe that's what she had come for.

Maybe that's what she would get.

Chapter 14

"So where the hell did you disappear to last night?" Norelli demanded of me the next morning, the moment I set foot in the Area 4 office.

As if I was really going to make him my best friend and confide everything in him.

My head twinging a bit—I'd iced it several times and had taken a ton of ibuprofen—I set my briefcase on my desk and put on a puzzled expression. "What do you mean?"

"Doran said he never saw you the last hour before the bar closed."

Officer Fred Doran was the plant inside the bar.

"Maybe Doran had one too many to keep proper track of anyone."

"Doran's no drunk," Walker said.

"Was he drinking his soda straight last night?"

"Well, no, that would have made him look suspicious, coming to a bar to not drink."

I spread my hands in an I-told-you-so manner. "Nothing against him. I mean, if he doesn't usually drink, the booze probably gave him a kick in the head." One a whole lot more gentle than the one I'd received. To keep the headache at bay, I still was eating ibuprofen as if they were candy. "He was simply mistaken."

I could tell Norelli thought I was lying and that he was having trouble keeping himself muzzled.

He locked gazes with me and said, "You need to be wired from now on."

"You're not putting a leash on me, Norelli," I informed him as calmly as I could, "so don't even try it."

He straightened to his full height. "This is *my* case, Caldwell."

"But it's *my* undercover operation, so we're partners. You're not running me. Get used to it."

Norelli grabbed his coffee cup and stormed off. I felt Walker's gaze on me.

"What?" I asked him. "You want a piece of me, too?"

"I would rather have your cooperation. You and me—we're not important. The victims are the only ones we should be thinking about. Are you ever gonna stop being pissed off and try to work with us?"

"I don't know."

The victim comment got to me, though. Wasn't

that why I'd gotten into this situation in the first place—because I couldn't forget about LaTonya Sanford?

I asked, "Why should I give you another chance?"

He gave me a disgusted expression and shook his head. "You can't always be right, Caldwell. No one can. Everyone makes mistakes."

"That's the thing. I didn't make a mistake."

Walker came back with "But we thought you did."

"You *wanted* me to be mistaken because I solved a case you and Norelli dropped."

Walker threw up his hands. "You're not an easy person to negotiate with."

"And Norelli is?"

"Norelli is a good cop. He's solved more cases than anyone in the division. The job is his life, the only one he's got. But he's from another era, when women didn't make detective, so maybe you can understand that and cut him some slack. What's your excuse?"

My excuse? I was about to say I didn't need one when I stopped myself. Walker seemed as if he genuinely wanted to work with me, but I was fighting it all the way. I always seemed to be fighting something or someone.

Especially myself.

Wasn't that what I'd been hearing from every direction lately?

When had this happened to me? When had I become the one who always had to be right? Who always had to win, as Silke insisted I did?

And it could get me killed. I never would have

been foolish enough to rush in without backup before the Sanford case. So maybe they had a point.

"All right, Walker. I'll lay off Norelli if it kills me."

"Good. That's a start."

Only he wouldn't think it was such a good start if he knew how much I was holding out on them. Feeling guilty about what I couldn't—or at least was not willing to say yet—I threw him a bone.

"Tonight, after the bar, Desiree Leath wants me to work a party at her place."

"What kinda party?" Norelli asked as he passed me and set his cup of coffee on his desk.

I shrugged. "All I know is it's private and she asked me if I could work it."

"Private, huh? That means you'll be working it alone?"

"I guess. Unless we can figure out how to get someone else on the inside."

"Or unless you agree to wear a wire. Your decision, of course."

Silence ticked between us while I held my tongue. Then I mumbled, "I'll think about it."

"You do that."

Though I wanted to, I couldn't really find a reason to object.

"I need an outfit that'll conceal a wire," I told Silke. "A tiny microphone with—"

"I know what a wire is. You have to wear one?"

"I'm acting in the spirit of cooperation."

I'd gone to her place straight from work after giving in to a happy Norelli. I'd left as early as possible to leave myself plenty of time just in case I had to go elsewhere to find something appropriate to wear.

"Nice that you've decided to cooperate with someone," Silke said. "And the requirements of the garment would be…?"

"Something not as revealing as a bustier." I tried not to be aggravated by her comment, but I felt my stomach knot at her words. "The mike is tiny and black." I held out my forefinger and thumb to indicate how small. "I need a way to camouflage it."

"I may have just the thing."

Silke brought out a top that was layered and draped and had lots of black beading, some of which was pulled into a fancy flower just below the shoulder. That would provide sufficient cover for the mike.

"Perfect."

"Good." Silke reached into the closet and pulled out a plastic cleaner's bag to cover the top. "So what else is on your mind?"

I threw myself on the sofa bed—open, sheets torn apart, even though it was the middle of the day. I saw that she'd been reading. Books on magic and spells. One called *Wicca: a State of Mind.* More of Silke's woo-woo stuff. I rolled my eyes and flipped onto my back.

"Where should I start?" I mused. "I have so many things to worry about."

Like what would whoever was tuned into me hear. To my chagrin, Jake was working the party, as well. Unless I told him I was wired—and I didn't intend to—he was likely to say anything. Which meant I simply had to keep my distance from him as much as possible.

"I don't mean about the case." Silke sat near me. "I sense something, well, personal is going on with you."

Leave it to Silke to read me. I sighed. "I've been thinking about how I operate with other people. I'm afraid I'm not a very nice person."

"Oh, come on."

"People have been making comments to me lately about my personality. That I'm reckless and that I *don't cooperate.*" I emphasized the last. "I guess I could be easier to get along with."

Silke didn't say anything, and I accepted her silence as agreement with that assessment.

"So how big a bitch am I?"

"You have your moments," she admitted with a smile. "But you're a really good person, Shell. You just need to believe in yourself more."

"What?" Where had that come from? "I know I'm good at what I do."

"Not just at what you *do.* The decisions you make. When people have self-confidence issues, they tend to strike out at others to cover."

My jaw dropped at Silke, the psychoanalyst. I'd never seen this side of my sister's personality before. "Wow, you still remember your Psych 101."

"Not exactly. Something more recent."

"You're taking a class?"

"I've been stretching myself for a while now. And lately, I've been getting, well, counseling."

The way she said it made me wonder the nature of the counseling. "Why?"

"I know you think I'm always happy, but it's not true. I have issues. And working with a counselor has helped me work through some of them. Laura thinks you could use some counseling yourself."

"You talk about me?"

"Well, duh! I'm worried about you, too."

I didn't know how comfortable being psychoanalyzed without my permission made me. But if it helped Silke get herself together, then that was a good thing.

"I don't need therapy to help me find my way," I said confidently. "I know where I'm going and what I want to do with my life."

"Uh-huh."

Okay, that was Silke humoring me. "Explain that 'uh-huh,' please."

She shook her head. "You're not ready to hear it."

My irritation with her growing, I said, "Talk, or you'll be sorry."

"What are you going to do—pin me? You might not like my response."

Now I was getting edgy. This was unfamiliar territory. In the past, I merely had to make an idle threat and Silke would be spilling her guts. She was threatening me back! As if she could hold her own against me.

I glanced at her reading material. Magic spells? Was that what she meant—she would use magic against me? And the "counseling." Suddenly I wondered why she hadn't used the word "therapy."

Uncomfortable with my train of thought, which was speeding faster than a locomotive into uncharted territory, I popped up off the sofa bed, saying, "I should probably leave."

"I thought you wanted an answer."

I bit the inside of my cheek so I didn't say something smart-ass that would stop her from telling me what was on her mind. No matter that we operated in direct opposition to one another, we had the same basic values.

"Okay, give it to me straight."

"It's just that you don't seem to be getting along with people much these days, and I think it's because you're not very happy."

"And you think seeing a shrink again will make me happy?"

"No, a trained professional is simply a sounding board and listens to what's on your mind. Someone who doesn't tell you you're wrong every time you turn around."

I swallowed a gasp. She was talking about me telling her she was wrong. Years ago, I'd supported Silke's right to be who or whatever she wanted. Lately I'd become judgmental, had somehow turned into our mother.

Maybe I did need a shrink.

Uncomfortable now, I mumbled, "I really do have to get going," and gave my twin a quick hug before heading for the door.

"Hey, Shell…about tonight…it's going to get dangerous."

"It'll be okay," I assured Silke, knowing she

would tune in for a blow-by-blow whether or not I wanted her in my head.

"And the danger isn't the kind you know."

"That's clear as mud."

"Those books and videos I gave you—"

"I looked some of them over," I said, trying not to sound annoyed.

"Then you know you can't just cuff a vampire and bring it in for trial. You have to kill it."

I sighed and shook my head. Silke really was starting to believe her own fantasies.

Suddenly, I felt her reach across the room to hold me. I swore I felt enveloped by her warmth and love, making me feel she was right there, touching me, when she hadn't even moved.

I blinked at her and took a step back. "That was a new one."

"I told you I've been stretching."

Magic and spells, Wicca, counseling…for what? To become a witch?

I didn't ask.

I simply left.

Silke waited until after dark to tune into her twin—she'd thought she'd give Shelley some private time before intruding—but station SHELL was closed for the evening.

"Shell, you're going to make me sick not knowing."

Silke concentrated and used all her energy to send that message over and over, but she knew it wasn't being received. Shelley was an expert at tuning her out.

Several times over the next hour, she tried tuning in to find out what was happening at the bar, but her hardheaded sister wouldn't let her in.

"I got you into this, and all I can do is sit here and worry."

Wait, perhaps, for Mom to call to say Shelley had been hurt on the job this time. Or worse.

Her imagination blossoming, Silke paced her studio. Envisioning her twin drained of blood, she couldn't settle down. Not when Shelley didn't know what she was dealing with.

"I should have made her understand. I should have made her believe me."

Shelley obviously hadn't given the books and videos any credence. With nothing else to do over the past few days, Silke had been continuing her research…and looking for optimal means of protection.

If one could really protect oneself from evil.

When she couldn't stand it any longer, Silke raided her wardrobe for something she hadn't worn to the bar. She was going to find Shelley at Heart of Darkness and try to stop her from working that after-hours party at Desiree's. And if she couldn't stop her, then she was joining her. She found the perfect garment in the back of her closet—a backless floor-length purple velvet dress with a deep hood. Wearing this dress, added to a change in her makeup and hair color—she had some violet spray that should cover the red—no one would ever recognize her.

Her heart thundered in her chest and her stomach felt twisted into knots. Shelley was the brave one, but she was nearly as closed minded as the cops who'd laughed at her.

Someone who knew what was what had to watch her twin's back, and Silke only hoped she was up for the job.

The creature was bored waiting for the bar to close and for party time to start. The only entertainment was the mysterious woman in purple velvet who'd walked into Heart of Darkness a short time ago. Lovely in candlelight, she stirred the senses…including a vague sense of recognition.

Come closer…

She'd been lurking in the shadows, and her gaze kept stretching across the room to the waitress. They had that in common—Silke Caldwell as the object of their attention.

But what was *her* interest?

Moving closer, the creature was startled by the woman's scent. It couldn't be, but there it was. The woman in purple and the waitress…the two women were the same. The one in purple must have felt the piqued interest, for she turned, eyes wide, to meet it.

The creature read in the open gaze that this one was aware.

As if she sensed that acknowledgment, she turned to push through the crowd. She had a beautiful back, a long, elegant spine punctuated with a gargoyle tattoo.

Thump-thump…thump-thump…thump-thump…

Her heart raced as she pushed through the crowd to get away.

Smiling, the creature followed.

Chapter 15

I wasn't in top form after working double duty for a couple of days and nights, so the wire gave me some comfort. If I got into trouble, at least someone would know about it. I wondered if this party was going to be a waste of my time or if I would actually learn something of value. I planned on scoping things out and seeing what I could find out about the owner of Heart of Darkness.

Seeing Desiree drooling over the sight of blood still had me creeped out. When I'd gone home earlier, rather than taking a nap as I'd needed to, I'd done a refresher reading about vampire cults instead. To my horror—although why I even had a sense of horror left considering the kinds of things I'd run into on the job—I had found an account of one young woman so addicted to blood, so convinced that she was the real thing, that she'd refused to eat food. Her parents had thought she was simply anorexic. Health-care providers hadn't been able to help her. Her body had slowly but surely shut down. In the end, the young woman's obsession with the idea of being a vampire had killed her.

The story had reminded me of Desiree. She was so thin and pale and lately so wan that I swore she was starving herself to death.

But she sure had been interested in that blood, I remembered, pulling up in front of her place, which was located a half mile west of the bar. It was a weird, sparsely populated area between a historic district and pockets of new condominiums and converted warehouses.

Desiree's home was actually an old lone graystone mansion, which was visibly crumbling from the outside. There was a deserted-looking firehouse on its south, a park on its north, so she had virtually no neighbors. The rowhouses across the street hadn't yet been gentrified. Some didn't even look occupied. Parking wasn't a problem, which was good, because everyone seemed to be arriving at once. Patrons of the bar were mixed with a few others not in Goth disguise, including people I'd never before seen.

The undercover team had arrived, as well, to stake out the mansion from the outside. As I got out of my car, I saw theirs pull up almost directly across the street. Tonight Norelli and Walker were taking a big chance doing the stakeout themselves. Hopefully Desiree wouldn't spot them. Or Jake.

Avoiding looking directly at the detectives, I headed up the concrete steps. Before I could get inside, Jake appeared from somewhere to hold the door open for me.

"Thanks," I said, squeezing by him.

Despite the fact that I'd mentally put him on hold, my body didn't seem to know that. When flesh touched flesh just for an instant, my reaction was like a kick in the gut.

Right behind me, he asked in a low voice, "So are we friends or…"

His breath caught me square in the back of the neck and I froze in place.

"…acquaintances…"

I swallowed hard.

"…or strangers?…"

Thankful I hadn't yet turned on the wire, I said, "I'll get back to you on that one."

I took a steadying breath and headed straight for Desiree.

Wearing a low-cut diaphanous black gown that left nothing to the imagination even in the dim, atmospheric lighting, Desiree stood in the middle of the foyer.

"Ah, Silke, there you are. Since you haven't been here before, familiarize yourself with this floor. Jake will be setting up the bar in the south parlor. And I have a caterer preparing appetizers in the kitchen. You can help set them up in the dining room."

"Sure."

Taking a look around was a priority, but I wasn't

going to limit myself to the first floor. I would find an opportunity to get upstairs, as well.

The mansion was dark and musty, as if it hadn't had a good spring cleaning in years. Huge twin front parlors sat across from each other on either side of the parquet-floored foyer, where a wide staircase led the way to the second floor. One parlor was adjacent to the dining room, the other to the kitchen and back stairs to the upper floors. The antique furniture reminded me of a mausoleum and contrasted with the sudden blast of modern techno music.

I squeezed my ears shut against the raucous sound, thinking it would be a miracle if the cops outside could hear anything over that. Which reminded me I needed to turn on the equipment and insert the wireless earpiece so I could hear Norelli. A trip to the powder room tucked under the stairs helped me accomplish that in private. I fluffed my hair around my face to camouflage the tiny receiver.

Someone banged at the door, making me jump. "I'll be right out!" I yelled a little too harshly. I flushed the toilet and ran the faucet to make it clear I was using the facilities.

"Hey! Watch that!" Norelli groused through my earpiece.

"Sorry."

Grinning, I left the powder room to a desperate-looking young woman and headed for the kitchen.

For the next twenty minutes I was too busy setting out appetizers and helping to pass out drinks to do any investigating, despite the fact that Norelli prompted me a couple of times. I took pleasure in ignoring him. There wasn't a whole lot I could do on this floor, not with so many people around.

I, who hated my twin tuning in on my life, was cooperating to let strangers listen in. Thinking about Silke, I concentrated for a moment to assure her I was okay, but I didn't feel her presence.

Now, that was odd....

"So what's going on?" Norelli asked me, jolting me back into the moment.

"Not a good time," I murmured in return. Did he actually expect me to describe the scene and take a chance that someone might overhear me and know what I was doing?

I waited until the mansion's lower rooms were filled with people talking or dancing. As I scanned the room, I felt someone watching *me*.

I turned to see Blaise leaning against the doorway, his blond hair waving along the shoulders of his white poet's shirt with split sleeves revealing glimpses of his tattoos. His gaze was glued to me, and as I had the other night when he'd fastened the red crystals to my ears, I felt an odd stirring, a rushing in my head. And this time he wasn't even touching me.

Blaise curled his fingers toward me, inclined his head toward the dance floor. I looked that way, saw the couples in what appeared to be mating rituals. They were all over each other, hands groping, pelvises grinding, mouths locking. The music was pulsing sex and so were they.

A yearning whispered through me....

Frowning, I fought it. I wasn't interested in Blaise Allcock. I wanted Jake. The very thought startled me, but there it was—the answer to his earlier question.

So I smiled at Blaise and shook my head regretfully and mouthed, "Sorry, I'm working." He could make of that what he would, but it was the best I had to offer him.

I passed out drinks and worked my way toward the dining room, thinking that I was more earthy than I'd realized.

Glancing back at the dance floor, I saw Desiree slithering up against her partner, whose back was to me. It was dark, but the blond hair and shirt were hard to miss. Blaise had already moved on.

I picked up some empty platters that I took to the kitchen and set down on a counter near the back stairs. "Any more food to bring out?" I asked the caterer.

"It'll be a while," she said without so much as looking up from her work. "Come back in about fifteen minutes."

"Will do."

Fifteen minutes upstairs wasn't a great deal of time, but it would be a start. And if I was missing any longer than that, someone was bound to notice. Making certain her attention was otherwise engaged, I slipped up the stairs, careful not to make any noise. A whiff of fresh air brought my attention to a window halfway up—it was open several inches.

The second-floor hallway was dark and oddly cool, probably in contrast to the body-heated downstairs.

To shake off the uncomfortable feeling I got entering Desiree's private quarters, I decided to talk to the cops-at-the-curb unit.

"Hey, Norelli, in case you're wondering why it got so quiet," I said softly, "I didn't leave, okay? I'm upstairs on the second floor."

I couldn't stop myself from pushing some buttons after Norelli had complained about my absence from the bar last night. If I was too nice, he would be suspicious.

An observation that reminded me of my conversation with Silke. Frowning, I wondered why I hadn't been able to feel her knocking at my head in a while. I knew how worried she'd been. I couldn't believe she would really stay off the twin-mind-meld airwaves tonight. After all, she had been the one to warn me of danger.

Creeping down the hall gave me the oddest feeling, as if I were entering another world. A dark, airless world. This floor felt sealed off. The windows were covered with heavy velvet draperies that let in not a peep of light from the street.

"What's going on?" Norelli demanded.

"I'm looking for her bedroom."

I peered in one room after the other, using my own personal flashlight rather than the one from the bar that I'd returned. One room was empty, another was stacked with boxes, but all were musty and airless.

And then I found the master suite, the entry of which was a combination sitting and dressing room. I found a switch and turned on the room light.

"The walls in here are purple," I murmured for

Norelli and Walker. "The carpeting and chaise are bloodred." As were dozens of candles of every shape and size resting on surfaces and metal stands. I turned and nearly ran into a winged gargoyle perched on a black marble pedestal. "Shit!"

"What happened?"

"A gargoyle!"

"Ooh, don't let it getcha."

"Kiss my…" I coughed. If I said butt, no doubt Norelli would make something of it that would piss me off worse.

Continuing my search, I couldn't help but wonder at the significance of the gargoyle and the unsolved murders. The closet revealed only clothes like those Desiree wore to the bar. The materials were either black or jewel tones of red, purple or deep blue.

Desiree certainly had her style down, I thought, moving to the doorway of the inner room, where I switched off the dressing-room light and switched on the one in the bedroom. I don't know why I was surprised that the red carpeting, red satin sheets and red candles provided the only pinpoints of color.

I continued my narrative. "The bed is curtained in heavy black velvet like the spread."

My gaze lit on a trunk next to the bed. It was beautifully carved of rosewood. Something drew me to it. I lifted the lid and revealed dozens of leather-covered books. But when I opened one, I saw handwriting rather than print.

"Journals."

"What?"

"You know, like diaries. A bunch of them in a

trunk next to the bed. The handwriting is hard to read, though. Kind of old-fashioned." Then I found a date. "According to this, it was written at the turn of the century. The end of the nineteenth century."

"Then why are you wasting your time on it?"

I paged back to the inside of the front cover. "According to this, the author is Desiree Leath."

"So the broad's sentimental. Musta been her great-grandma's."

"Must have been."

I replaced the journal and closed the trunk and took a look at the rest of the room.

"There's a single plush black chair in front of a small table covered with a dark-red-and-purple fringed scarf." Drawing closer to it, I said, "Now, there's something odd—the table is loaded with makeup, but there's no mirror."

"Maybe it broke when she looked into it," Norelli said with a guffaw.

Grimacing, I thought to say something smart-ass back to him when I heard laughter floating down the hall.

"Damn!"

"What's wrong?"

"Someone's coming." Desiree, no doubt. I looked around wildly for another door, but there wasn't one. "There's only one way out of here. I'm trapped."

"Don't panic. Look for someplace to hide."

I switched off the room light and thought about the closet in the dressing room. But what if Desiree had come for a change of clothing?

The voices drew nearer.

"The bed!"

I ducked under it and prayed whatever she had come for, it wouldn't take her long to get it. My heart pounded so hard, I feared I wouldn't be able to hear them.

No such luck.

The footsteps stopped in the other room and Desiree moaned, "Oh, yes, touch me there."

I peeked out from under the bed skirt to see Desiree silhouetted by a soft table light she'd turned on. The lamp shade was of red glass beads, and a silky red scarf floated around it. The room seemed to be on fire.

As were Desiree and her companion. Lips locked, the two twirled and, as they fell together on her chaise, Desiree on top, waves of blond hair spilled over. Great. Blaise was with her, and even from my cockeyed view I could still see enough of Desiree to know she was opening the front of her gown.

I grimaced. They were going to do it right there!

Disgust quickly replaced fear. The good news was they weren't going to do it on the bed above me.

At least I hoped not.

I pulled back away from the bed skirt so I wouldn't be tempted to watch. But I couldn't help but hear. Desiree was a very lusty, very loud lover, far more so than her sex partner. I tried to shut out her moans and sighs and shouts—yes, shouts. Plural. I don't know how many orgasms she had, but they seemed to go on forever.

Okay, so despite my disgust at being forced to eavesdrop, I was a little impressed. I didn't know a woman could have that many orgasms that close together, and Jake had done a pretty incredible job on me the other night.

Just when I didn't think I could stand to listen to one more scream of passion, I heard Desiree say, "Your throat...it's so very tempting. I can't wait any longer. Arch your neck for me. Yes, that's it...."

I couldn't help myself. I *had* to look.

"What the hell's going on?" Norelli demanded to know.

Not that I could chance telling him. The earful he must have gotten gave him the score.

At least until now.

What I saw made my stomach twist. Desiree's eyes seemed to glow as she opened her mouth wide, and as she dipped her head I caught sight of teeth too long to be real. Had she put in those crazy contact lenses and some kind of bridge with extended canines? That mouth quickly closed over the offered throat.

Part of me thought to stop whatever was going to happen, but before I could move, Norelli was saying, "Don't break cover until you see what's really happening." I knew that if I moved too soon, we wouldn't be able to make a case against her.

The twisting and turning on the chaise grew frenzied, in what sounded like a mutual orgasm that lasted so long and was so loud that I felt shattered when it ended. I peeked out again just in time to see Desiree lift her head. I scowled in disgust when I saw the blood smeared around her mouth. Her long, pointy tongue was trying to lick every drop.

And she seemed to be staring my way…as if she knew I was here!

When she smiled this time, her teeth looked normal, and I wondered what she'd done with the fake ones. "I knew you would be delicious," Desiree murmured as she rose from the chaise. "And an audience makes it so much better."

She did know I—or someone—was here! But how?

Desiree's gown was open in front and I could see her body, which didn't look quite as thin as I thought it would. Without even closing the garment, she wandered to the door, saying, "I must see to my other guests. I'm sure you understand. Rest for as long as you need to recover and then join me downstairs. You need to eat to regain your strength so that I can savor you again very soon."

She threw a kiss my way before undulating out of the room. A moan came from the chaise, and a white-garbed arm spilled over the edge.

"I'm going out," I whispered, getting to my feet and creeping to the dressing room.

"Be careful!" Norelli ordered. "I don't want to do more paperwork than I have to."

"Nice." I hurried to make certain that Blaise wasn't dead.

I stopped in shock when I saw Desiree's very-much-alive sex partner sprawled across the chaise— a blond woman who was still writhing her hips in ecstasy. Her pant zipper was down and I could see dark blond curls peek out from the gap.

"But Desiree left too soon," she said, noticing me.

Her tongue darted quickly over her lips. "I need more. You can help me."

"Jeez, it's a broad," I heard Norelli say to Walker, "and I think she's coming on to Caldwell."

The blonde arched her neck and I saw twin holes from which thin streams of red oozed down to her naked breasts. She trailed long fingers through the blood down to a peaked nipple and arched her neck to me.

"Please," she said, trailing her hand back up through the red smears up to her neck. "Taste me and I'll let you do anything to me you want."

I nearly choked at the offer. "You look like you've lost a lot of blood. You should let a doctor check you."

"You don't understand, do you?" The blonde wiggled around on the chaise as if in dire need. "I must have *more*."

Staring at the oozing blood, I couldn't stop myself from saying, "What you want is sick."

"Come on, Caldwell," Norelli urged. "Loosen up. Give us a little lesbo action up close and personal. It's damn boring out here."

The woman sighed and appeared disappointed. "Oh, you're one of those. Open your mind, honey— it's the only way to fly. You really should try it sometime."

She was sliding her hand down into the front of her pants. That was all I could take. I bolted out of there as fast as I could.

"What's going on?" Norelli demanded to know.

"I'm leaving the scene. That might have been some sick shit, but it was consensual."

"What kind of sick?"

"The kind where the hostess gets off while she sucks her guest's blood."

"Mother F!"

"Right. But both parties are alive and apparently happy."

"I don't know about that. The fangbanger apparently wanted you, Caldwell."

"Go to hell."

"Hey, some girl-on-girl action might loosen you up, and—"

"I can't hear you, Norelli," I singsonged and removed my earpiece and pocketed it.

Silently, I descended into the kitchen, careful not to give the caterer a clue as to where I'd been. "I'm back for those appetizers."

"Right here," she said, indicating a couple of loaded trays.

Smiling tightly, I transferred the snacks from the kitchen to the dining-room table.

I don't know how I worked the rest of the party without giving myself away, but somehow I managed it. And every once in a while, I caught a glance of the bar owner. Desiree glowed from the inside out. No longer wan, she was more beautiful than ever, vivacious, the life of the party. Her guests seemed drawn to her, as if they wanted a piece of whatever it was she had to offer.

Or maybe that was just me imagining things. If nothing else, she had regained her strength.

As if the blood had worked some magic on her.

Eventually the blond sex partner came back

downstairs. She was obviously still turned on and ready for more. She looked right through me, and I was relieved that I saw no hint of recognition. When she tried to get close to the object of her desire, Desiree merely tolerated her fawning. I sensed the bar owner was already looking for another sex partner. Someone else who would indulge her sick fantasies.

Only Jake sensed my disgust. I could tell, even though he didn't say anything to me during the rest of the party. Around 4:00 a.m., most of the guests were gone and I was beyond exhausted. I noticed Desiree had disappeared, undoubtedly with another fangbanger, as Norelli had dubbed them.

We were cleaning up when Jake broke the silence between us and asked, "So what happened to get you so upset?"

"Nothing," I lied. Norelli was still listening in and I wasn't about to give him an earful.

I dropped the last of the wandering beer bottles into a plastic garbage bag and left it against the wall behind the makeshift bar.

"It's something," Jake insisted, setting stemmed glasses of various shapes in a plastic carton that would go to the caterer in the kitchen.

"If you say so."

Not wanting to be pressed further, I walked off and headed for the powder room. I felt Jake's gaze on me all the way. Under different circumstances, I might be turned on, but tonight had been way too weird for me.

Once inside the powder room, I spoke in a low voice. "Norelli, we'll be cleared out of here in a few minutes, so I'm signing off. You and Walker go home. I'll catch up with you tomorrow."

Hopefully, they would actually leave. I should go back to the office, of course, to turn in the equipment and to write up a report. But it was half-past four in the morning, coming up quickly on dawn.

Screw the report. It could wait until tomorrow.

I needed some sleep. More than that, I needed a drink. I thought about having a double of anything before I left, but decided I didn't like the eerie atmosphere of the place. And I didn't want to give a certain bartender the chance to give me the second degree.

Jake was standing at the cleaned bar, looking ready to leave.

"I'm gone," I said.

"Desiree won't like it if you leave before she dismisses you."

I wasn't liking Desiree much at this point, but I kept that thought to myself. "If she shows, tell her I was all played out." And let her do with that information what she chose.

Jake didn't argue and I took off.

First thing I did when I got outside, I checked for Norelli's car. Gone. Good. I didn't need him ragging on me for removing the earpiece. I was too tired to fight with him.

But not too tired to remember what little I'd seen go on in Desiree's quarters as I drove home. The violence of the sex act had sickened me, as had my inability to do anything to stop it. Well, legally, anyway. There were lots of sick bastards in this world.

I knew that. I just didn't want an up-close-and-personal look at their perverted activities.

I was grateful to find a parking spot practically in front of my doorway. I didn't have much left in me as I climbed the stairs to my apartment. To my shock, Jake was waiting for me in front of my door again.

"It's late, Jake."

"We need to talk."

"Tomorrow."

"It is tomorrow."

He was blocking my path. If I didn't give in, I might never get inside my apartment.

"All right. Come in. I'll give you five minutes."

Once inside, I looked for the cats, but they weren't waiting for me at the door as usual. Sarge was sitting in the bedroom doorway, his eyes wide as he stared at Jake. In the middle of the living area, Cadet made a weird growling sound, fluffed out her tail and ran into the bedroom. Sarge whipped around and followed her.

"That's weird. They're usually okay with strangers. Sarge, Cadet, din-din. C'mon, kitties, come out and eat."

But the cats didn't respond. I set out their food in case they changed their minds and then I poured myself a drink. Not the red wine I might normally choose, but a shot of straight *añejo* tequila, aged long enough to be reminiscent of whiskey.

"Want some?" I asked Jake.

"Don't need it."

"Well, I do."

I downed the shot and appreciated the burn as it hit my gut.

"So talk," Jake said.

"I thought you were the one who wanted to do the talking," I said, feeling my body relax from the tequila.

"I will, but you go first. What happened at the party that got you so upset?"

"I was an involuntary Peeping Tom. I got a load of Desiree in action."

"Action?"

"Sex with a twist." Thinking about it, I poured myself a second shot and downed that one, too. "She mainlined her sex partner's blood."

"That would explain it."

I threw myself down on the sofa. "There's some explanation here?"

"When Desiree rejoined the party she was so much more…vital than she has been all week."

I shivered. "What she did was disgusting."

"I agree. But feeding on human blood is what vampires do to stay undead."

Chapter 16

There was that vampire thing again. And Jake was staring at me straight-faced. Surely he meant vampire *cult*.

There was only one other possibility I was willing to consider. "You mean in mythology."

"I mean in real life."

I was afraid of that. I shook my head. "Jake, I'm too blasted tired for this."

He sat in the chair across from me, his elbows on his knees as he leaned toward me. "You have to face it, Shelley. You've seen Desiree—in action, as you called it—for yourself. How can you not believe what I'm saying?"

"You want me to believe that Desiree is a vampire. A real, bloodsucking vampire."

"You witnessed the bloodsucking part for yourself."

"We almost saw Elvin Mowry do the same thing to that girl Annie."

"Not the same," Jake argued. "He's playing at it, imitating the master."

I frowned at his use of the word *master,* but I didn't question it. Was that supposed to be like the *sire* I'd read about?

Still not believing him, I said, "So, you think Desiree is our murderer."

"I didn't say that."

"Then what *are* you trying to say?"

"Just that not every vampire is a murderer, so I'm not ready to jump to conclusions about Desiree. Vampires don't need to kill to stay undead. Instead, they develop a parasitic relationship with a donor. Or with multiple donors. But they don't drink enough blood to kill them. That would be wasteful."

I decided to humor him, to see how far he would take this twisted fairy tale. "Then why are people dying?"

"There are psychopathic vampires just like there a psychopathic humans. But I think the one you call a murderer is a vampire who wants companions, so he or she is turning young women to serve him or her."

"Like a harem? What about the homeless men who've died?" I asked, before realizing I'd told him something that maybe I shouldn't have.

I watched Jake register the new information. He didn't challenge me, but he looked disappointed, as if he'd expected me—a cop—to tell him everything.

He finally said, "The new ones need to feed and they don't have control of their appetites yet. That takes time. And practice. In effect, they're greedy children. And the master hasn't managed to rein them in."

I felt as removed from these crazy suppositions as if I were listening to Jake tell a ghost story. "This is all too unbelievable."

I whipped off the couch and considered getting myself another drink. Then I thought better of it. That might make me too vulnerable to Jake. I'd been suppressing feelings for him since Mom told me that Jake DeAtley didn't exist. But now my mixed emotions were tearing me up inside.

"I know you don't want to believe that vampires really exist," Jake said, getting up and stepping into my path. "But you need to start thinking outside the box for once in your life. I want you to know what you're up against. This vampire is devious and dangerous. This one will do whatever is necessary to stay undetected by humans. That means you're not safe."

"It sounds like you know a lot more than you've been telling me," I said, unconvinced I was in great danger.

"You're right. I am familiar with this particular vampire's style—drinking from the median cubital vein, the one in the elbow where medical types draw blood."

He turned his arm and indicated the very spot I'd seen Thora cut. And it was the place that Mowry had intended to cut Annie, though it wasn't where the homeless men had been drained. The homeless men had gotten it in the neck, the way I'd seen Desiree bleed the blonde.

Not that I actually believed in real vampires.

But Jake went on. "I've been moving from country to country trying to catch up to the killer vamp, but I'm always one step behind. When I got to Chicago, I did some checking on Desiree. I couldn't find anything to indicate that she was in the right place at the right time. It doesn't eliminate her, but it doesn't incriminate her, either."

"Let's just say that I believe you." Which I didn't, of course. "You've known Desiree was a vampire. How?"

"Let's call it…vibrations," he said cryptically.

"How many other vibrations have you recognized?"

"Here? Only one other, but he seems to have vanished. But again, that doesn't prove anything. He could simply have gone underground."

That reminded me of the tunnels under the city and Sheena's reference to them as the lair that Mowry talked about.

"If the master is very, very old and adept at being a chameleon, I probably wouldn't be able to sense enough to make an identification. "

"What are you, some kind of vampire slayer?"

"My mother was a vampire."

It took me a moment to register Jake's meaning. That *he* was a vampire?

"Right. So where are your fangs?"

Jake glared at me and moved closer.

I stepped back, away from him, saying, "Come any closer and I'll flatten you."

Heat seared me and I recognized it as anger. Anger coming from him. The heat dissipated but the fear it wrought in me didn't. Jake was a dangerous man, but of course I'd known that all along.

I was ready for him, though after seeing him at work in the cult's nest taking care of Mowry's minions, I knew how strong he was. Could I take him on some tequila added to a day filled with exhausting stress?

But he wasn't making his move, and I was grateful for that.

"I'm not a vampire in the truest sense. My mother was already pregnant with me when the master got hold of her. My blood was affected, but not to the same extent, because somehow I didn't 'die' as she did while being turned."

His voice was calm but I read pain in his eyes. It gave me the oddest feeling, as if I should comfort him. He moved away from me and stopped in front of the window, where he stared out into the dark.

"Normally, she wouldn't have a choice but to follow and to do as commanded," he went on. "But her hormones were all screwed up due to the pregnancy—at least that's her theory of how she fought it—and the master wasn't able to hold on to her."

"And she never identified the master in any way?"

Jake faced me and shook his head. "She didn't want to put me in any more danger. She knew how angry I was at what she had to do to survive."

"So you're saying your mother used humans for their blood."

The repulsive words stuck in my throat. I could hardly believe I was giving them credibility, but when I looked at Jake, he appeared absolutely serious. And tortured by what he was telling me.

"My mother hated having to feed. She swore to me she never killed anyone. She stayed on this earth for me, Shelley. To give me life. To protect me. She made sure no one ever turned me."

I remembered his reaction to the cut on my arm, when my blood had bubbled with the hydrogen peroxide. "But if she was turned while you were inside her…"

"I told you I wasn't a vampire in the truest sense. I've never tasted human blood myself. It's not that I haven't been tempted, but when I can think clearly, the idea repulses me. And I don't need to drink blood to stay alive."

"You've been tempted?" The thought made my stomach turn over.

He began pacing again, as if trying to flee the truth.

"I imagine it's like a recovering alcoholic wanting liquor or a recovering drug addict needing a fix. Only I'm not recovering in that sense of the word, because I've never gone there. But I am aware that blood could be an addiction for me, just like liquor or drugs would be to an average human."

Average rather than normal. Good choice of words. I listened to him go on with a sense of unreality. As he spoke, I became more distant from the situation. I felt as if I were viewing this scenario from afar. Like watching a movie.

A really bad B movie in which I was the star.

"I can see you still don't actually believe me," Jake said. "Remember your first night at the bar and your encounter with the groper? How do you think I knew about the how-many-bones-in-the-human-hand comment? And I'm the one who heard the voices that led us to the vampire cult's hangout. I didn't need a light to find you in the tunnels. My senses are all heightened. And my speed and strength."

"Just like a vampire?"

"Exactly like a vampire."

"So you can't go out in sunlight?"

"My skin is sensitive to sunlight, my eyes more so, but I'm not a creature of the night. And I don't need blood to survive. I age normally, too, although I assume I'll die like a normal person. I won't test out that theory until I have to."

If he thought I'd be amused by his tall tale, he had another think coming.

I felt...let down.

I'd liked Jake. I'd felt challenged by him. But now I was wondering how I'd gotten so deeply involved with a nutcase. A nutcase who was playing me for some reason.

"I told you I was after the one responsible for my mother's death, the master, the one who turned her. Her conversion wasn't voluntary. And she couldn't stand the life. So once I was grown and able to be on my own, she simply walked into the sun and committed suicide."

He'd told me before that she'd burned to death; now he was talking about vampire suicide.

It was all too much for me to take in.

"You've given me a lot to think about." Not that I actually believed any of it. But perhaps there were truths I could learn from his story if I was less exhausted and more sober. "I want to think about it alone. In case you didn't get it, that was your invitation to leave."

"I'll go. I can understand your need to think about this. Only don't think too long."

Though I wondered if Jake had some time limit for me, I didn't ask. What was the use? This whole thing was insane. *He* was insane.

Or very, very clever.

But try as I might, I couldn't think of Jake as a criminal. I didn't really think he was trying to trick me. Either he was sincere but misguided or he was out of his mind.

The moment the door closed behind them, the cats reappeared.

"So what's going on with the two of you?" I asked, realizing they were staring at the door.

They still seemed stressed.

Just like me.

My psychic cats must have been sensing and absorbing it themselves.

I threw myself in bed fully clothed and slept awhile, but I hadn't adjusted the blinds and the morning sun crept through them to wake me. Sarge had wrapped himself around my head, and when he realized I was awake, he started purring and exercising his claws in my scalp.

"Hey, watch that!" I warned him, taking his front

paws in my hand so he couldn't continue. "No, Sarge." He stopped flexing but kept purring anyway.

As did Cadet, who was tucked into the small of my back.

For a moment, I enjoyed the closeness of my cats and refused to think dark thoughts. But dark thoughts battered my mind until I decided I had to face them.

I looked over at the clock and groaned. I could have slept another hour before reporting in to work. Then my gaze lit on the stack of books that Silke had loaned me.

Silke…where the heck was she?

I concentrated, but I didn't sense her.

And my trying to sense her made me think of what Jake had said about sensing the master vampire.

Pure logic would say that if my sensing Silke was real, then Jake's sensing vampires could be real. If there was such a thing as a real, scary-flick-type vampire.

What if…?

I couldn't help myself. I disturbed the cats while reaching for *Vampyres among Us* and turned on the bedside lamp. I thumbed through the book. When I got to the how-to-destroy-a-vampire section, I couldn't help myself. I stopped and stared at the first lines of the chapter for what seemed like forever.

Vampyres must be destroyed rather than killed, because they are already dead. A stake through the heart is rather like pinning a live butterfly to a board. The stake holds it still, but once removed, the undead walks again.

I almost closed the book then, but I didn't. Something made me continue to read about what the author described as the final death: cutting out or otherwise destroying the heart, dismemberment—severing heads from the body being the only real way to assure destruction here—acid or holy-water baths, fire or exposure to the sun.

"This is some sick stuff," I told the cats.

Closing the book, I patted them both, then got up and hit the shower. I scrubbed every trace of makeup from my skin that I hadn't gotten the night before, every hint of bloodred color from my hair.

What I couldn't wash away were my thoughts. What Jake had told me. He'd first said his mother had burned to death. Last night he'd said she'd given up the life she'd hated by walking out into the sun.

According to Silke's reference manual, a vampire would have had a slow, agonizing death as her skin set on fire and she self-combusted.

"No...no...no...!"

I couldn't go there. I was a rational person.

And yet there was Silke, and my deepest, darkest secret. Mom knew about our connection, sort of, but she didn't know how strong it really was. Hell, *I* didn't want to know, even now.

If I had to face what I was, then I had to face what else might exist out there.

And I just wasn't ready.

How could I believe in any of this vampire stuff? How could I believe in Jake?

But even as I thought it, all that I'd absorbed over the past several days nagged at me, and I wondered if I really could believe in my black-and-white world anymore.

So as I dried my hair and dressed for work in a conservative navy pantsuit, white shirt and leather ankle boots, I tried to get it together. I had to face Norelli and Walker this morning. I would have to listen to their crude comments and cracks about the blonde coming on to me.

Before that happened, I had to decide how I would respond. As Mom would say, if you wanted to get along in life, there was just some crap you had to shovel in order to survive.

I slipped into a shoulder holster and checked my piece before securing it. I stared at the gun—a weapon of death, but not for the undead, not according to *Vampyres among Us.*

Before leaving for work, I tried to contact Silke the boring, normal way, but her machine came on, announcing that she wasn't available. I left a message for her to get in touch with me using any means possible—yeah, even the mind-meld pathway that I normally avoided—as soon as she heard this.

Mom was in the Area 4 office waiting for me when I walked in the door a half hour later.

Norelli and Walker were there, too. As I set the department spy equipment I needed to return on my desk for the moment, I could tell the detective tag team wanted to torture me with the details of last night's operation, but they remained strangely silent.

A reason for me to smile—Mom must intimidate them!

"Commander," I said formally, "what brings you here?"

"I wanted the details of last night's undercover operation in person," she said, giving me a hard stare. "Why don't we get a cup of coffee and you can fill me in."

I led the way to an empty interrogation room we sometimes used for breaks. Somehow I figured she'd already heard what had gone down the night before. What would Mom think if I tried talking out the vampire stuff with her? If I told her about Jake's claims? About my research?

I poured two cups of coffee and handed her one and realized Mom wasn't here about the job when she said, "It's Silke."

The back of my neck prickled. "Do you by any chance know where she is?" I was hoping that she was holed up at Mom's, hence the worry on her part.

"Then you don't, either?"

My heart began to thud for real. "I have her keys. If I don't get her by the time I leave here, I'll swing by and see what's what."

"How soon?"

I wanted to go now, but I couldn't see how I could justify leaving before I tied up last night's loose ends. "As soon as I write up the report, okay?"

"Of course. I'm sure I'm worried for nothing. I just can't get a hold of her on her cell phone or at home, and that's odd for Silke not to return a call as soon as possible."

I tried to soothe Mom by telling her Silke was fine, but I found myself calling Silke's number several times while I wrote the report from last night. Paperwork, paperwork, paperwork. Cops sometimes drowned in it. When Norelli and Walker dug into me about Desiree and the blonde, I didn't even have the heart or the focus to give them a hard time back.

They kept trying, though.

"I can't wait to see what you have in store for us tonight," Norelli said.

"Do you think you can disguise me as one of those Goths who hang out in the bar?" Walker asked. "Then I could be a witness to whatever goes down."

I gave his robin's-egg-blue suit jacket a significant look. "You'd be willing to shed your pretty clothes for basic black-and-blue?"

"They get rough, do they?" Walker asked. "Other than the bleeding thing, right? Sounding interesting."

I didn't think he meant it. Something told me he was trying to lighten the mood. In an odd way, I got the feeling my partners had softened toward me just a little.

At least I wasn't tense about them when I left the office after turning in the equipment and my report. But I was stressed as hell about Silke, wondering why she'd chosen now to do a disappearing act. If she'd chosen to do so at all. I remembered her telling me that "they" could find her if they wanted....

As I drove to her place, I used my cell to check my messages, both phones. Nothing. Maybe she was simply acting out. She'd come to me for help and I had pushed her out of the case. Maybe together, we could make sense of what was going on.

Only Silke was gone.

Her apartment was a mess. Not the kind when there'd been foul play, but the Silke kind. Stuff all over. Including her Goth makeup. And her closet seemed torn apart, as if she'd been looking for something specific.

My gaze lit on the books she'd been reading. One had been left open. I glanced inside and saw something about creating a simple spell to control the elements. Well, if she'd been messing with Mother Nature, I didn't know about it. We had a sunny summer day going for us.

So why was I so nervous about what she was up to?

I feared she'd decided to come to the party to play I Spy for herself.

"Silke, where are you? I would do anything to get one of those messages that make me so cranky."

But of course the internal airwaves were silent. And I was beginning to feel really, really sick inside. If something had happened to her, I knew I had only myself to blame.

When had I disconnected with Silke?

When had I stop listening to that inner voice that told me when she was in trouble?

When had refusing to be open become part of my nature?

I thought about it and realized this went all the way back to my roughing up Silke's wanna-be boyfriend. I'd been wrong and wouldn't admit it then. And now, after all these years, I simply didn't know how to be wrong anymore. That's where the attitude came from—the one Silke and Mom and Al had all noted. Rather than accept failure and learn from it, I'd rejected the possibility of failing. Just as I'd rejected the gift Silke and I shared. In a way, I'd rejected her, the other half of myself.

My eyes filled with tears.

My life was looming before me like one big toilet bowl. I had no idea if I could actually resolve this case and put my ghosts to rest. Mom and I had an uneasy truce, but I didn't know how long that would last. I'd been keeping everyone at bay. And now I feared something horrible had happened to my twin.

Losing Silke wasn't an option.

I climbed onto her open sofa bed and hugged the pillow still sweet with her scent. Closing my eyes, I inhaled slowly.

Silke, where are you?

No response.

I concentrated on seeing her, not Goth Silke, but my twin Silke, my mirror image.

I know something's wrong. Help me to help you.

Nothing.

Years ago, we'd taken yoga together. We'd learned to meditate. Well, I'd learned the theory anyway. The practice kind of drove me nuts. But I remembered the mantra. I lay back on the bed, eyes still closed, and relaxed my body. Then relaxed my mind.

For the first time since we were adolescents, I opened myself to what I feared most.

My breath came slow and deep as I opened the door to my subconscious. Over and over, I called to Silke as I felt myself drifting…searching…aware.

Suddenly I lay in a bed, not here, but someplace tomblike with flickers of light…torches whose flames licked the dark. I couldn't move; my wrists and feet felt secured.

Silke, is that you?

Shell…?

I almost cried when I felt her.

Are you all right?

Afraid…

The word drifted through my mind. I didn't think she actually said it, but I felt it like a cold fist closing around my heart. The darkness crowded in on me, and I could hardly breathe. I almost panicked out of my altered state. Somehow, I calmed myself and stayed there.

My mind was whirling. Hard to focus. Harder to form actual words. Drugged?

Silke, did they drug you?

I felt her assent rather than heard it. And then I felt her, as if she were inside me.

We were confused, disconnected from everyone but us.

We were one.

Then suddenly no Silke. I shot straight up with my heart pounding like mad.

"Silke…where did you go?"

I couldn't complete the unthinkable.

I knew the murderer had her. I also knew she had one chance of getting out alive.

Me!

Chapter 17

Willing to do anything to get Silke back safe, I didn't run off half-cocked.

I tried Norelli. I would take any help I could get, assuming I could get him to believe me. But Norelli's voice mail answered; he must have gone out on another case.

"Norelli, this has to do with the murders. My sister's been snatched and I'm after her. You get this before you hear from me again, call me on my cell."

I left the same message for Walker.

Even though it took more precious time than I wanted to lose, I prepared properly for battle. Under my suit jacket, I carried not only my gun and holster, but also attached to my belt were handcuffs, a sheathed knife, a tactical light and telescoping steel baton, a stun gun and a canister of Mace. I'd also stuffed a half-dozen throwing stars that I'd bought in Chinatown in my breast pocket.

The problem was, what if Jake had been right and a standard weapon wouldn't work on the killer?

I still didn't believe in vampires, but I wasn't going to let anything get by me, so as I set out, I stopped at the nearest Catholic church and then the local hardware store for additional "weapons" just in case. No point in taking any chances.

Nothing—and I mean nothing—was going to let me lose Silke.

Armed and dangerous, I was driving straight for Desiree's mansion before deciding that perhaps I should have alerted Jake. I'd discredited his vampire spiel, but now I wasn't so certain about anything. I had to admit that no matter how it played out, I would feel better with backup, and I'd never had better than Jake. Besides which, I couldn't do what I might have to do if I made this official.

Calling Mom was out of the question, too. I didn't want to freak her out, at least not until I figured out what was what.

I took out my cell phone and keyed in Jake's number. No Jake, though. Just voice mail.

"It's me. Silke's gone. I think she's in danger. I'm going to get her back. I'm starting at Desiree's." About to hang up, I quickly added, "I would feel better with you watching my back."

But unfortunately, it looked as if I was on my own.

I was acting all brave and macho here, but part of

me knew I could be killed. And to my surprise, I couldn't stand the thought of dying without ever seeing Jake again.

By the time I turned down Desiree's street, the afternoon shadows had grown long, but it was still full daylight. Jake had said he was sun sensitive, but I'd never seen him after dawn.

And maybe now I never would.

I left the duffel bag with its oversized weapon in the trunk of the car and stared up at the gray-stone building that looked shuttered and deserted.

Desiree was in there, I was certain…but what about Silke?

Now that I'd opened the floodgates, radio SILKE was sending out signals again, though they were sporadic and frightening. I got the definite idea that she believed she was in the hands of a real vampire.

All kinds of scenarios played through my head. Like Silke looking for me at the mansion. What if Desiree had been in the throes of her blood lust when Silke had met up with her?

What if the bar owner had figured out there were two of us and had decided that was one too many to make her feel safe? A cold hand wrapped around my heart as I took the front steps two at a time.

Forcing a woman to do something she didn't want to do was Hung Chung territory. Or Elvin Mowry. But I couldn't discount Desiree, not until I checked her place for myself to see how deep she was into the cult.

I'd had no reason to notice the night before, but Desiree didn't have a doorbell. Instead, I was met by a big brass knocker—a winged gargoyle that seemed to stare at me hungrily as I waited for someone to answer.

No one did.

I tried the handle. Locked. Too bad. I was going in and without a frickin' search warrant. Nothing would stop me, not even if I had to kick down the door. Before putting my foot in jeopardy, however, I circled the building and looked up to see if that window along the back stairs was still cracked. It was. No ladders lying conveniently around. But there was a downspout that ran along the back of the building from the gutter on the roof straight into the ground.

Hoping that it would hold my weight, I tested it. Though old and loaded with peeling paint, the galvanized metal seemed sturdy enough. I reached high and hooked a hand in one of the metal hangers that attached the downspout to the building. I tugged. It didn't budge, so I hung on to it with both hands and slapped both feet against the wall tight to either side of the drain. My climb from hanger to hanger a half floor up wasn't pretty or smooth, but I managed it.

I paused to get my bearings, then reached out and grasped the sill of the open window. I slid my hand inside to find a better grip. Transferring the other hand over was a scary prospect, I was off balance, leaning way over sideways. And when I unhooked my right foot from behind the pipe, my body swung fast and slapped against the wall with a thud.

What was another bruise or three?

I grabbed on to the sill hard and pulled myself up, listened a moment to make certain the coast was clear, then stuck my head through the opening and used my shoulders to inch the window up higher so I could drag my body through.

I landed on the stairs as gently as possible. I paused to catch my breath and concentrated hard to sense Silke's presence. Nothing. Either she wasn't close by or she was passed out again.

The house was silent, the upstairs as dark as it had been the night before. I crept up the half flight and down the hall, leaving the fleeting light from the window behind me. Shadows layered over shadows. I imagined I heard them breathing. The very house seemed to be gasping for breath.

But no, just me.

Sounds I was making magnified themselves through my head. My heartbeat grew more rapid as I approached Desiree's chambers. The door creaked open to reveal the dressing room empty but alight with candles. The room beyond was as dark as a tomb.

Before I could get to the bedroom to see if Silke lay between the bloodred sheets, an angry voice whispered in my ear, "How dare you violate my property?"

I jumped and whirled and came face-to-face with Desiree herself, her beautiful face twisted into a grotesque mask of anger. Surreptitiously, or so I thought, I reached for a weapon. Lightning fast, Desiree had hold of my wrist, her grip so tight I thought she would snap it.

How could a woman so slight be so strong?

Even so, she didn't give my wrist that sharp twist

that would break the bones, so I tried to relax, to sound normal. "The question is, who are *you?* Are you simply a bar owner into perverted sex acts or is there more?"

"Silke?"

She released my wrist. The anger in her face faded to puzzlement. And worry, though undoubtedly that was for herself. Okay, so she didn't have my twin tied to her bed and probably didn't know where Silke was. Which didn't exactly clear her of all wrongdoing.

"Silke disappeared last night," I said. "I'm her sister, Detective Shelley Caldwell. I've been the one working the bar the last several days."

Desiree's eyes closed and her head hung forward as if she were defeated. "The murders…the innocent girls…"

"And more," I said without giving her the specifics of the homeless victims. "What do you know, Desiree? You need to cooperate."

She said something low and passionate in French, then told me, "This never changes, no matter where I seek shelter."

"Are you saying you're the murderer?"

"No! I do not kill!"

Odd the way she stated her denial. A worm of discomfort crawled up my spine. "I saw you and the blonde last night, Desiree. I know what you did to her."

"Ah, so you were under the bed. Did you enjoy watching?"

"I was disgusted."

She dropped her gaze. "I try not to feed—sometimes I think to simply fade away—but survival instincts are strong." She said again, "But I do not kill."

Which reminded me of Jake's assurance about vampires, how they normally didn't kill their sources of food, but instead used them as blood donors. I tried to swallow the explanation, but it stuck in my throat.

"Start from the beginning," I suggested.

"Not relevant. You were not even alive when I was made."

Jaw clenching at the last, I said, "Try me."

"You know what I am. I've been this way for so long that I do not remember the other. When I was like you."

The bar owner was intimating that she was a vampire. So was everyone crazy but me?

"What are you now?" I asked.

"A woman who has nothing to live for. I did once, long ago. His name was Charles, and he didn't care what I was."

Desiree moved around the room, and as she spoke of her former lover, she glowed with beauty. Her eyes glowed also, for just a moment.

And then the light went out.

"Charles would have let me bleed him to survive, but I wouldn't use him that way. It would have changed him. And I loved him too much to let him see me like that."

Caught by the passion in her tone, I was moved. And I thought about Jake. Could I ever feel that way about him? Would I get the chance to find out?

"My master couldn't tolerate my obsession for a human. Francois drained Charles's blood and killed him. First I wept until there was nothing left in me but the thirst for revenge. And then I returned the favor."

"You drained Francois's blood?"

Laughing, Desiree stopped in front of me. "That wouldn't have destroyed him. I cut out his heart."

"You realize you just admitted to a crime."

"I killed no one. Francois was undead. I merely destroyed his remains. Do you think to see that I am punished, sister-to-Silke? Nothing is worse than existing as I have all these years. When Charles died, I had made a vow never to drink human blood again, but I am too weak...."

"You expect me to believe you're a real vampire."

"I expect nothing of anyone but the worst, including myself. When the urge gets overwhelming, I do what I need to." Again, she said, "I do not kill," as if that would somehow excuse her from the things she did do that she hated so much.

Like Jake's mother...

Not wanting to see her as some victim, I shook away the pity that threatened me. "Who does kill, Desiree?" I was certain she knew. "Elvin Mowry? Hung Chung?"

"I can't tell you anything more."

Desiree turned away from me, and this time I grabbed her wrist so she couldn't leave. She snarled and struck out with such surprising quickness and strength that I went flying. My shoulder hit the gargoyle and when I landed on the floor, it was teetering on its pedestal and grinning down at me.

I scrambled to my feet away from it.

"The one I'm looking for does kill, Desiree. You know that. LaTonya, Thora, Raven...maybe others. He needs to be stopped."

"I cannot help."

"Can't? Or won't?"

"He's far older than I...far more powerful."

He. Despite the fact that I'd had to consider Desiree a suspect, I'd been pretty sure the murderer was a man.

"I cannot help you. He will sense me coming and will vanish. You'll have to locate his lair yourself."

"His lair?"

But before the words were out of my mouth, Desiree had vanished into thin air. "Desiree?"

There was no answer. I rubbed my tired eyes, but there was no denying the fact that Desiree had vanished before me, just as *Vampyres among Us* said vampires could. If I believed in vampires.

I was beginning to wonder how I could not.

I searched the rest of the house for Desiree or signs of my sister and found neither of them. Desiree was just gone. But she had mentioned a lair before doing her bizarre disappearing act. The same lair Sheena had heard about from Mowry?

Those tunnels were extensive and my first venture into them had been a bust. I needed help...lots of it. Especially since I was starting to feel a little crazy myself.

As I drove off toward Lake Street, I tried Jake's number and got his voice mail again. I didn't bother to leave a message this time.

After parking directly in front of the boarded-up meat market, I got the duffel bag out of the trunk. Fear held me in its clammy palm at the thought of going back in the labyrinth alone.

This was Silke's life and maybe my life, and whatever I found or didn't find, I had to chance being wrong. But first I would try to get help. I called Area 4 and got Norelli.

"Norelli. I need backup and now. I got a lead… and the murderer has my sister."

"You know that how?"

"I just know it. Trust me."

I gave him the address. He said he and Walker would be there, but he didn't sound as if he had a fire under him, and I didn't trust him. So I did the only other thing I could. I called my mother. Unfortunately her voice mail picked up. Without giving her any but the barest details so she wouldn't panic over Silke, I left a message asking her to send in the troops as soon as she heard this. If I was wrong about my instincts, I didn't care anymore. Silke was in danger and I couldn't let my ego get in the way of saving her.

Jake had slept like the undead. Something had awakened him, but he wasn't quite sure what.

It felt as if he'd been on the move forever looking for his mother's maker, when it had been in truth less than a decade. A decade since his mother had decided she'd had enough, that as much as she loved him, she couldn't continue living like a ravaging animal.

And, Jake suspected, she hadn't wanted him tied to her any longer.

He had, of course, refused to leave her, to start a life of his own. Not when she'd needed his protection. He'd covered for her and had protected her when she'd slept from the time he could put two and two together. She'd always wanted what was best for him, and in the end, he feared she'd thought it best if she was out of his life for good.

But she'd been all he'd ever known. He hadn't had anything to live for but to seek justice by destroying the undead creature who had turned her.

He'd traveled from country to country, city to city, alone. Always alone. And just when he thought he would be alone forever, that there was no one on this earth who could challenge him, who could surprise him, who could, most of all, accept him as he was, along came Shelley Caldwell.

Detective Shelley Caldwell…just his luck to fall for a cop.

Cops had rules, and in his world, the rules were all twisted. Shelley didn't understand. She didn't want to. He couldn't blame her. But he couldn't help but yearn for what he'd never had—a true relationship with a woman. With *this* woman.

He was used to taking what was offered and then going on, not involving his sex partners in his mess of a life, fearing one of them might get caught up somehow and be turned into another creature of the night.

But he wanted Shelley for more than sex.

Laughing at himself—knowing that Shelley

thought he was a freak—he picked up his cell to check for messages. His gut tightened the moment he heard her voice.

And when she got to "I'm starting at Desiree's," he swore loud enough to shake the foundation of the building.

Waiting only to make sure there wasn't more he needed to know, Jake grabbed his clothes and shoes and dressed his naked body as he flew down the stairs.

Fear drove him.

Shelley wouldn't stop until she got to the master, and then she would descend to her own personal hell.

Shoving on sunglasses to protect his light-sensitive eyes, he drove like a madman, which he was. He couldn't let it happen to her. He could give her up if that's what she wanted, but he couldn't lose her this way.

So when he got to Desiree's and the door was locked, he didn't let it stop him. With one powerful kick, he slammed the panel practically from its hinges.

Knowing Desiree would be compelled to answer, he used the high-pitched tones that no normal human could hear. No one but Shelley, it seemed.

A moment later Desiree joined him in the parlor, careful, of course, to stay away from the windows, where the last blush of light innocently threatened the room. And her.

"She's not here, *chéri*."

His eyebrows shot up. "'She'?"

"Whichever sister you're looking for."

Then Shelley had been here. "What did you do with her?"

"No harm came to her. I sent her on her way." Desiree stared at him and stepped close, sniffing the air around him. "What are you?"

One vampire always recognized another, but Jake wasn't a vampire. His heart still beat blood through his body. He was alive.

"I'm someone trapped between two worlds."

Desiree blinked and though she couldn't possibly understand, in a way she must, for she said, "I sensed you to be different from the first...."

"I need to know where Shelley went."

"She seeks her sister."

He knew what that meant. "Where is the lair?"

"If I tell you, he will have me destroyed."

"If you don't, I'll destroy you myself," Jake threatened, stepping closer. "And trust me, Desiree, as fast as you move, I can follow. As strong as you are, I'm stronger."

He expected to smell Desiree's fear, but he didn't. He sensed something different from her. Approval?

"You will see that he is stopped?" she asked.

"Or die trying."

She told him, and Jake was gone before she'd finished her sentence.

Wild images whirled around me: fire and swirling smoke...distorted figures...thump-thump, thump-thump...Silke struggled frantically, bindings tearing into the soft flesh of her wrists—

* * *

I gasped and blinked out of the momentary trance, Silke's terror filling me. "Silke!"

Hauling the duffel bag with me, I pushed away from the car toward the building. My twin was here. I could feel her. Panic welled in her, and I was having trouble breathing. As much as I wanted that backup, I couldn't wait for it to arrive. I pulled out my cell and called Norelli again.

When he answered, I asked, "Where the hell are you?"

"On the way. We got caught in traffic. We'll be there in ten minutes."

"I can't wait that long!"

I told him how to get inside and down into the tunnels. Not knowing where I would go from there, I prayed that was enough for them to find me.

Once inside and down to the basement, I headed to the elevator but followed tracks leading to the other side of the room and around a corner I hadn't noticed before. I saw a door barely visible in the darkness. It opened easily and I could see stairs going down. I decided to take them, thereby avoiding the mechanical noise that would alert the killer. The stairwell was long and steep and choked with dust. I waited until I got out the lower door to stop, to breathe deeply and to concentrate.

Silke, I'm here. Help me find you.

Her thoughts were muddled, but somehow I managed to follow them, this time taking the left branch of the tunnel.

I had a lump in my stomach and another in my

throat. This was it. I knew it. I was not only going to find Silke, but at last I would also come face-to-face with the murderer.

A second turn and I heard a splatter along the tunnel floor, as if someone kicked broken concrete. I psyched myself for trouble, if that was possible. My holster and the duffel bag were open, the disparate weapons ready. I held the tac-light—now attached to a baton—in one hand, a can of Mace in the other.

I stepped cautiously forward, my heart thudding against my ribs. This time I had followed procedure and still I was going it alone.

Where the hell was backup when I needed it?

Suddenly, my light picked up a familiar form as he walked toward me.

"Well, if it isn't Hung Chung," I said sarcastically. "You left the bar without saying goodbye."

"I'll say good-night instead. Permanently."

"Deal."

I whipped the baton around and whacked him in the face. He seemed startled. And then majorly pissed off.

With a loud yell, he came for me, swinging and kicking in best martial-arts style. I danced backward and slashed at him with the baton—leg, body, arm— but then he got a lock on the weapon and yanked it hard. Not wanting to let go of my only light source— not to mention a weapon that could be turned against me—I went spinning and crashed into the tunnel wall, falling on my butt.

At least I was still hanging on to the damn baton.

Chung came directly for me. I was still recovering,

so I did the only thing I could under the circumstances.

I held out my other arm and, aiming for his face, squeezed my trigger finger. He yowled as he sucked in the stream of Mace. I closed my eyes and even held my breath for as long as I could so I wouldn't be affected. I didn't want to open my eyes until the pepper spray had settled, so I blindly released the handcuffs from my belt, rose and plunged forward. My shoulder hit him hard in the chest. He toppled over, taking me down with him. Just in case he had more left in him than I imagined, I cracked open my eyes and punched him in the neck with my knuckles, not hard enough to smash his trachea, but hard enough to stun him into thinking he couldn't breathe.

Gasping for air now, he threw his hands up to his throat as if they could relieve his distress.

"Thanks." I clipped one wrist with a cuff, and made sure he was still breathing. He deserved not to breathe, not after what he'd done to Raven and Thora and LaTonya. I didn't want to think about what he might have done to Silke or I would be tempted to kill him with my bare hands.

Instead, I rolled him onto his face and yanked that arm behind his back. "Give me the other hand or I'll break this one."

He swore at me and clawed at the tunnel floor, as if trying to escape, but he would be fighting the effects of the Mace for a while. I planted my knees solidly in the middle of his back, grabbed the flailing arm and mastered it.

Click.

He was mine.

I flipped him onto his back. Grabbing the tac-light, I shone it in his face. His eyes were squinched and tearing, and mucus ran from his nose and spit-tle from his mouth. The fluids dripped down onto his shirt and the gargoyle pendant he wore.

"My sister—where is she?"

He began to cry and slobber and mutter to him-self.

"C'mon, Chung, I know you have her. You didn't kill her like the others, did you?"

"No," he wailed. "No, I won't."

At first I thought he was answering me, but then I realized he wasn't even here anymore. He was in some other world. A real loony-tune. Then again, what murderer wasn't? And at least I had him. But he wasn't going to talk, not for me.

I slid off him, pulled a long plastic cable tie from the duffel bag and used it to bind his feet together. Primitive but effective. The only way he could get that thing off was to cut it, an impossibility as far as I was concerned.

I stood and concentrated on finding Silke. When I sensed her presence somewhere nearby, I sighed with relief that she was still alive.

"I'll be back for you, Chung," I said. "Or maybe someone else will find you first." If backup ever ar-rived and managed to find this tunnel.

I shouldered the duffel bag—not that Chung could do anything to it with his hands behind his back, but I wasn't about to get sloppy now. Picking up the baton, I felt something sticky on my hand. I flicked the beam over it and realized my hand was smeared with blood.

From what? I hadn't wounded Chung.

I flashed the light over him one last time and caught sight of twin holes on his neck. Several sets, actually. No blood there, though.

The maze of tunnels in this direction proved to be as intricate as the first route I'd taken. The difference this time being Silke. I was honing in on her like a bloodhound with a scent. I didn't let my guard down, though, not for a minute. For all I knew, Elvin Mowry and his followers could be around.

Those holes in Chung's neck bothered me, though. Holes like those found on the two dead homeless men. I hadn't seen anything like that when I'd fought him before. And Chung wasn't exactly Mr. Attractive. The other cult members all were.

So was Hung Chung the exception? Or a conclusion that I'd jumped to?

I thought about it as I picked my way forward. He had a couple of tattoos, but no gargoyles. Only the pendant. I couldn't remember seeing the pendant before, either, and I'd been up close and personal with him.

It occurred to me that the gargoyle could be a symbol of control, of belonging to another being. Desiree had said Chung wouldn't bother anyone anymore. Perhaps when Chung had been with her all night, it hadn't been the romp I'd imagined. But Desiree had denied being the murderer—I'd believed her—and she'd sent me here.

As to the bites on his neck...

I remembered Jake telling me that the new ones needed to feed and didn't have control of themselves, the reason they'd killed the homeless men. To believe that, I would have to believe in vampires, I thought uneasily. For the sake of argument, I gave the possibility credence. What if the new ones had been feeding off Chung? Was this his punishment? Had Desiree given him over to the master?

If Chung was being controlled, which seemed possible, then who was the murderer?

Over the past days, I'd felt my will affected several times by various people at the bar. And since I didn't believe Desiree was guilty...

As I moved on, an image came to me and the pieces began fitting together. Suddenly, I knew and I couldn't imagine why I hadn't figured out the murderer's identity sooner.

A mechanical screech echoed down the tunnel behind me. The elevator. Backup, at last. Or so I hoped. It could be anyone coming down here. Another cult member. And I was too close to reaching my sister to go back to find out.

Channeling Silke the best I could while on the move, I sensed she wasn't alone, but I got no specifics. Mace wasn't going to work this time, not when I was trying to round up my sister while fighting off anyone who tried to stop me.

Going in alone made me jittery, and I wished yet again that Jake was here to get my back.

I pulled out my gun and prepared myself for the fight of my life.

Chapter 18

The one he wanted more than anything was making her way through the labyrinth to him now. He was ready for her. The new ones were also. They guarded the entrance. She would have to get through them to get to him. He was looking forward to being entertained. Chung had telegraphed her presence, but now he could sense her himself.

His plan had worked.

"You are a pretty thing," he said to Silke, who was fully awakening from her drugged state for the first time since he'd abducted her. "Exquisite, really."

He'd been taught to appreciate beauty in all its forms from the time he was a child. His mother had seen to that. She'd also seen to his sensual upbringing, again from his childhood. She'd been turned while in full bloom, but she'd resisted allowing him to join her in blood until well after he'd reached manhood. He hadn't understood why she'd held back until after she'd turned him in a fit of uncontrollable passion. Then he'd understood. After that, she'd no longer been enough for him. She'd been greedy, though, and had wanted him all for herself. He'd never found another companion her equal.

Not until now.

"It's your twin who excites me," he told Silke. "She's clever and strong and single-minded. I knew she would come for you."

"You used me to trap her."

"Clever girl."

Silke gasped. "My fault."

"Indeed."

"I won't let you—"

He interrupted with a laugh sharp enough to cut. "Do you really think you have anything to say about what I do?"

Silke stared at him as if he was evil incarnate—and perhaps he was—but no more foolish threats escaped her full lips.

Good. It wouldn't be long before both sisters were under his power. A unique experience, tasting two sides of the coin at once. His groin ached from fantasizing about the experience of immersing himself in sweet blood and mind-blowing sex with them both, the reason he'd left Silke untouched to this point.

"You'll never have either one of us," Silke suddenly said.

Either she was more clever than he'd given her credit for, or she'd just read his mind. "I take what I want," he declared.

"You don't know Shelley."

"I'm looking forward to the experience."

"And if she can't stop you, *I* will."

He looked at her hands and feet bound to the bed and sighed. "An idle threat."

"Don't ever underestimate a Caldwell woman."

But he was no longer listening. He could hear the other one, her footsteps light along the tunnel. Her breath coming in shallow bursts.

And, oh, her heart.

Thump-thump...thump-thump...thump-thump...

Practically salivating in anticipation, he signaled to the new ones—whose names he'd already forgotten—to be ready. They would test her mettle. He expected her to triumph. They were expendable.

Before dawn, he would have the only woman he'd craved to distraction since destroying his own mother.

Flickers of light like those I'd seen when connected with Silke drew me down the tunnel.

I was close to finding her. It was getting hard to breathe, though not due to lack of air.

Fear stole away my breath.

Fear that I wouldn't be on time, that I would fail to rescue Silke, that she would be lost to me before I had the chance to tell her what an idiot I'd been.

I took as deep a breath as I could, and tightening my grip on my gun, I turned into an intersecting tunnel.

And came to a dead halt when I set eyes on the lair ahead—a hedonistic boudoir of dark velvets, bloodred satins and pale, sheer hanging fabrics. I raised my eyebrows. The decorator must have spent a fortune at Whorehouses-R-Us. When I took a better look at the canopied bed, my momentary humor dissipated.

Silke was gagged and tied to the bed like a satanic sacrifice. From each of the four posts, a winged gargoyle grinned down at her. She was giving off vibes like crazy, trying to make me turn back.

"Don't worry, Silke," I said in a low voice. "I'm prepared for any kind of trouble." I stepped forward, adding, "Bring it on."

Okay, so maybe I shouldn't have said that. Maybe if I hadn't challenged the fates, I wouldn't suddenly be facing two guardians of the keep who seemed to have appeared out of nowhere.

One young woman was of average height and dressed in a tattered Goth dress. Her skin was pale, contrasting with her smeared, dark-rimmed eyes. The other young woman was tall with caramel skin. She was dressed in basic black—athletic pants and a T. They both looked eerily familiar.

"Thora? LaTonya?" I asked disbelievingly.

I stared at them. What were they doing on their feet, walking around as if they were alive? Impossible.

"How do you know LaTonya?" the black woman demanded.

I blinked and caught my breath. She'd answered to the name of the dead girl.

"I know your mother," I said, my mind whirling, allowing for crazy possibilities. "She grieves for your loss. When you disappeared, I looked for your murderer."

"Now you don't have to. You got me," she said, giving me a wide smile. Her teeth looked sharp, especially the incisors. And her eyes seemed to glow in the dim light.

I didn't know how this could be possible, but if by some miracle she'd been brought back to life…

Even as I thought it, I knew it couldn't be true, and yet I said, "Help me get my sister out of here, La-Tonya, and I'll take you back to your mother." I wanted to believe that it was possible. "And you, Thora, I'll take you anywhere you want."

"I know you will."

I started when Thora's eyes began to glow and her incisors elongated. I tried to tell myself I was seeing things, but I knew I wasn't.

From the bed, Silke was messaging me: *Vampire, run!*

I didn't want to believe it, but what other explanation was there? Even so, when a high-pitched whine seared my ears and the two stepped toward me menacingly, I held out my very normal, sure-to-stop-a-human gun.

"Halt right there."

Thora and LaTonya looked at each other and laughed sardonically. As if giving her partner permission, LaTonya leaned back against a pillar and tilted her head at Thora, who licked her lips and smiled wider.

When Thora attacked, I whipped her with the baton, but she easily pulled it out of my hand and tossed it behind me. I tried kicking her away, but she bounced back, and an eye blink later, she was on me. Literally. Her clawed nails dug into my neck, and I couldn't budge her. When she opened her mouth and gave me a gander at those incisors, I knew where she was aiming them. I tried to keep her from sinking them into me, but I wasn't strong enough. Sharp little knives cut into my throat, and I could hear Silke screaming in my head to stop her before she killed me.

Without acknowledging what I had to do, I squeezed the trigger. Thora let go and jerked back, looked down at her bleeding thigh and touched the wound.

I expected her to fall.

Run! Silke screamed in my head. Though a little woozy, I wasn't going anywhere without her.

Her expression furious, Thora said, "That hurts!" and came at me again.

I backhanded her with the gun, but steel on jaw didn't faze her. She grabbed me by the throat again, and this time picked me up off the ground and shook me like a rag doll. I got off another couple of rounds. Didn't miss her once. Holes and red blotches bloomed in her clothing, but she didn't go down. Shit! Vampires bleed. The next thing I knew, she threw me to the ground and was on me, mouth smacking open, her fetid breath on my face, leaving me no choice but to trust what everyone had been telling me.

That Thora was one of the undead.

She clamped her mouth over my neck and began to suck. I felt the blood rush through me and into her. For a second, my eyes closed and I swayed into the sensation. Silke jerked me out of it telepathically, and I knew if I didn't do something *now,* I would die.

I dropped the gun and reached into my pocket to withdraw what had been, in my opinion, a questionable weapon. But the moment I touched the crucifix to the side of her face, Thora screeched and drew back, her cheek smoking and smelling of burned flesh.

I fisted the crucifix and, as hard as I could, swung again. The wood plunged straight into her chest, and *I* prayed that whatever God she believed in could forgive her for what she'd become.

Screaming, Thora rolled away from me, crawled a few paces and got to her feet. Arms flapping, chest smoking, she stumbled back into the boudoir until, with a choked cry, she fell face forward to the carpeted floor. She jerked once as the crucifix hopefully destroyed her heart, and then went still, smoke billowing out from under her.

I was having trouble breathing now, both from the exertion and from the realization of what had just happened. Of what was certainly going to happen again with LaTonya, who lowered her head menacingly at me. I remembered the photograph of her I'd used when trying to find out what had happened after her body had disappeared. She'd looked so young and innocent. I mourned inside for that girl she had been.

But she wasn't that innocent girl anymore, and I had a sister to save.

"Now you just made me mad!" LaTonya said in the whiny voice of the teenager she no longer was. "I'm not even hungry."

This wasn't LaTonya, I told myself again. This was some kind of monster.

"Thank you," I said.

"For what?"

"For making this easier."

I hadn't wanted to believe, but how could I not?

I reached into my other jacket pocket and wrapped my hand around the second object I'd picked up at the church. The vial of holy water popped out as she rushed me.

Seeing it, LaTonya screeched, "Oh, no!" and grabbed my wrist.

She squeezed until it went numb, but I held my arm stiff and kept my fingers locked by sheer will. I let her push at me and push at me until we were right up against the wall. Then I freed my arm muscles so my hand—and the glass vial—smacked into the concrete.

The glass smashed into shards and the holy water doused her legs. Her scream echoed through the tunnels as her flesh began to smoke and dissolve before my eyes.

Her face literally disappeared.

"Shit! Shit! Shit!"

I pulled my stun gun and shocked the body into dropping. LaTonya wasn't there anymore—I knew that—but I still didn't want to see whatever was left of her suffering as the flesh fell from her bones.

Noise from the tunnel I left behind caught up to me. Other cops? How was I going to explain what had happened here? I wondered, driven to get Silke out and fast.

"I'll have you free in no time," I promised her, pulling the knife as I rushed over to the bed and set down the duffel bag.

Her eyes were wild and she was shaking her head at me.

"I know it's horrible, but it'll be all right."

Vampire, she telegraphed.

"I know. I think I finally believe you."

I used the knife to free one of her arms, and it fell limply to the bed. Silke was still rolling her eyes and making urgent sounds through the gag.

"Oh, sorry."

I set the knife down on her chest long enough to pull the material from her mouth.

"Behind you!" Silke croaked the warning.

I whirled and gasped as a blur became a shape and I realized I was looking at the real master vampire, the only person other than Jake or Desiree whose power I had felt.

"Very well done, my lovely. You don't disappoint."

"You do, Blaise."

I guess it had been difficult for me to see the effeminate purveyor of personal decorative arts as a powerful killer. Then again, the decorative arts involved mutilation, if of a civilized kind. He wore his own work on his arms, now revealed fully to me for the first time, and I noted he'd used pigments that glowed in the dark that revealed images to match the ones he'd given to his victims.

There was LaTonya's winged gargoyle, Raven's blackbird, Thora's pin.

"You took the lives of those young girls."

"No, Shelley, you did that."

I was aware of Silke's having picked up my knife. I moved deeper into the chamber, drawing attention away from my twin so she could cut herself free. Movement from the section of tunnel where I'd left LaTonya's body caught my eye, but I didn't dare turn away from Blaise Allcock to check as to the source.

I said, "I destroyed what you made of them— bottom feeders like yourself."

"I certainly hope you can curb your tongue once I turn you. I would be very disappointed if I heard such drivel from one with such potential."

"Turn me? Not in this lifetime."

"Well, that is the point, is it not?" Blaise stepped closer and caught my gaze. "To make you and your sister my companions for many lifetimes."

"How many women have you done that with— and where are they?"

"A vampire needs variety in his life. And you destroyed my latest works of art."

"Art? You took a bright young woman with a future and destroyed her. I remember how horrified I was when I found her body—"

"You found her?"

"Surprise. I'm a cop. My informant, Junior Diaz, called me after you drained her blood. You killed him, didn't you? But you used your strength to break his bones rather than suck his blood. Why?"

"Naturally I didn't want his death raising questions in the right direction." Suddenly, he frowned at me. "Where are the earrings?"

The ones with the little gargoyle faces, symbol of his projected control over me? "I decided I didn't care for them, after all."

"They were my gift to you!"

His gaze caught me and held me, and I felt some of the tension drain from me. He was trying to mesmerize me as he had while putting the earrings on me.

"Stop that!"

"I haven't even started," Blaise told me.

I knew he thought he had me. He seemed to light from the inside out. And his eyes…they burned for me, literally.

I was trying to fight him, but it became more difficult as he moved closer. One more step and I would have to draw a weapon…only which one? He took the step and reached out a hand, and I stared at his nails, long and sharp.

A deep voice said, "Don't touch her, Allcock!" breaking the vampire's hold on me.

"DeAtley," Blaise said. "This is no concern of yours!"

He slashed his hand toward my arm and ripped right through my jacket sleeve. If I hadn't moved fast, he would have cut deep into my arm. I glanced down at the blood oozing from the inside of my elbow over the jacket sleeve, then back at Jake. My eyes widened as he locked gazes with me, his eyes glowing the same way Thora's and LaTonya's and Desiree's had.

The same way Blaise's did now as he turned to meet his foe. "Go now. Leave the woman to me and I'll spare you."

"Now that I've found you," Jake said, "I'm going to send you to hell where you belong before you corrupt someone else I care about."

My heart thudded at the last. Jake cared about me?

My arm was pulsing where Blaise had cut me, and blood was oozing from the wound. I ripped the torn sleeve and used it to press on the cut, then bent my elbow the way I did after having blood drawn.

"It's two against one," I said, taking a quick look to see how Silke was doing. Both hands and one foot free.

Blaise laughed. "Two mortals."

"One mortal," Jake corrected. "And one son of a vampire that you made."

"I'm not your sire."

"No, you're not. You turned my mother while I was in her womb. I'm sure you remember her."

"Which one was she?" Blaise asked, as if he'd turned many pregnant women into his blood-and-sex slaves.

"Vampire!"

Jake spit the word like the curse that it was and then moved so fast he was in the chamber opening one second and standing mere feet before Blaise the next. Vampire and half-breed sized each other up like two gunfighters in the Old West preparing for a duel. Jake had the advantage of size, but I feared Blaise was far more deadly. Suddenly, Jake flew at Blaise, and Blaise likewise leaped at him. The men locked bodies and whirled up to the ceiling, making ferocious, high-pitched sounds that threatened not only my ears but also my nerves.

I gaped. What could I do?

I gave Silke a quick look. She was working on the last of the bindings, which secured her left ankle.

She would be free in a minute.

It was Jake who needed my help if only I could figure out how.

For a moment, all I could do was stare as Jake and Blaise fought blindingly fast and hard, their bodies settling back to the floor as they tore into each other at close range with everything they had. Then Blaise threw Jake across the room and went after him again.

What if Jake couldn't take Blaise?

Still nursing my cut arm, I used the other hand to grab the throwing stars from my pocket. I sent them sailing at Blaise. One, two, three. The sharp weapons embedded themselves in the vampire's neck and head, and droplets of blood rolled down his pale skin, but he barely gave me a glance. As if they were pesky mosquitoes, he ignored the pointy weapons and struck out with clawlike nails that left gashes in the side of Jake's face.

The scar—was that how he'd gotten it, I wondered, from fighting another vampire? I went over in my mind the ways to destroy one. No more holy water or crucifixes available, but I had one other weapon of vampire destruction.

Hands shaking, ignoring the pain throbbing from the cut, I slid the weapon out of the duffel bag.

Silke nearly fell from the bed as she attempted to stand. She wobbled and clung to the post.

"Get out of here," I told her. "Go now, while you can!"

"Not without you."

Silke couldn't defend herself. She was a liability. Part of me wanted to take her hand and run for it.

No. I couldn't. Not while Blaise was still walking.

I couldn't abandon Jake.

This time it was Blaise who went flying. He crashed onto his back and seemed stunned from the force of his landing. Jake was right after him.

Holding the tool firmly on the ground, the dangerous end pointing away from me, I tugged the cord with a quick, sharp motion. No luck. I tried again, then cursed the thing. Maybe three times would be the charm.

Suddenly, Blaise flew from the floor and pinned Jake against the wall, and in his hand I saw one of the throwing stars slashing toward Jake's jugular.

This time, the motor started up with a racket and a kick that almost knocked me on my butt. I recovered fast and grabbed on with both hands. It took all my strength to lift the damn thing. I had to act before Blaise realized what I was up to. He started to turn and I lunged forward, putting the entire force of my body as I swung the chain saw toward him. His gaze connected with mine one last time, wide-eyed and disbelieving.

The bar of the chain saw connected with his neck. Blood splattered me as it ripped Blaise's head off.

Another evil dead.

Jake and I linked disbelieving gazes over the headless body that was still standing. Jake was spattered with blood and I guessed I was, too. Then I realized Blaise had gotten him—the throwing star was embedded in his neck.

I killed the motor and dropped the chain saw. "Jake!" I toppled Blaise's headless body and stepped on it to get to him.

Calmly, he pulled the throwing star free of his flesh and staggered against me. I held his weight and tried not to panic when I heard a gurgling sound. I pressed my hand to his flesh hard to stop the bleeding, but my stomach sank and suddenly my heart felt as if a block of ice encased it.

Then Silke screamed, "Shell, watch it!"

Hanging on to Jake, keeping my hand pressed hard to the bleeder, I glanced over my shoulder to see what was left of LaTonya staggering toward me. I hadn't destroyed her after all, and now she was out for revenge.

There was nothing I could do without letting Jake die.

Behind her, Silke stretched toward one of the torches but couldn't quite reach it. With a screech of impatience, she called, "Fire!" and flattened her hand, palm up. "By my hand and heart, cleanse this room of evil!"

The fire jumped from the torch to skim her hand before continuing on to its target. I gaped as flames engulfed the monster, who went berserk, blindly thrashing into the velvet draperies. The cloth went up like a torch, and I realized the fire would spread quickly.

"Come on," I said, half-dragging Jake toward the tunnel without letting go of his neck. I would get Silke to talk later. "We have to get you to a hospital."

"I'll be okay," he promised weakly. "I heal fast."

He had to be okay. "How fast?" I asked, holding my arm out to Silke, who, with a glance back at the spreading fire, got to Jake's other side.

Jake didn't answer.

Which meant he didn't know if it would heal fast enough. The three of us limped out of there as rapidly as we could while the room went up in flames behind us. I was thinking ahead, wondering if I could call for paramedics with my cell phone down here.

Without thinking about it, I stopped and shoved my cut arm at Jake. "Drink!" I rasped, feeling sick at the thought of his doing so.

Silke gasped and I knew she was freaked.

I wouldn't let him die. I shoved my arm at him harder.

Jake's eyes glowed again as he looked at me and I could see he was tempted.

Then he shook his head. "No. That's not who I am."

I would have argued, but the fire rumbled as if threatening to follow us. "Let's get out now!"

We'd made the turn when the fire must have penetrated a gas line somewhere. The explosion that followed shook the tunnel floor beneath our feet, and I knew I was hearing the ceiling and walls crashing down.

"What was that?" I heard a familiar voice call from somewhere ahead.

Walker.

"Sounded like an explosion. But who the hell knows. I don't even know where I'm at."

Norelli.

Backup had finally arrived.

Chapter 19

By the time we got up to the street, everyone had turned out for the party. Uniforms. Detectives. SWAT team. Mom must have gotten my message.

"An ambulance!" I said, trying to drag Jake toward one that just arrived on the scene.

"I told you I would be okay," he said, taking my hand from the wound that was no longer bleeding.

Why wasn't I shocked? And the slashes across his face weren't looking so bad, either.

"Still, you could use help," I said.

He shook his head. "Too much explaining. I'll be okay."

We'd found Norelli and Walker and they were dragging Hung Chung, who was babbling, answering voices in his head, into a police car.

As a uniformed officer pushed Chung's head down to get him into the squad car, Norelli muttered to me, "You're a dangerous woman to cross, Caldwell."

"Just remember that," I said.

"Silke…Shelley…"

"Mom!" Silke cried.

I turned to see Mom get out of her vehicle and come toward us. Her expression relieved, she held her arms out to us both. I glanced over my shoulder at Jake as I stepped toward her. Then I was enfolded in an emotion-filled embrace.

"We're okay, Mom," I assured her, hugging her back. "We're okay."

"Shelley is a real hero," Silke said. "And Jake."

"We might not have made it out if not for Jake," I stated, hoping Mom would factor that against the issue that Jake DeAtley didn't really exist.

I didn't care what his name was; I was simply happy that he was alive. I was equally happy that he'd heeded my call to watch my back, and I wouldn't mind his sticking around to continue to do so.

As a medical tech cleaned up my arm and bandaged the cut, I quickly told Mom and Norelli and Walker the edited version of what had gone down. No mention of vampires or of stabbing one with a crucifix or of decapitating the master. I figured by the time they dug out the remains, the M.E. wouldn't be able to tell what was what. And the chain saw would be in a million pieces. If forensics could put it together and should ask me why it was there, I would shrug my shoulders and say that Blaise Allcock was a whack job and could have been planning on hacking apart the girls he'd murdered.

Under the circumstances, I might have to tell any number of lies and I would do so in good conscience.

But what about Jake?

"What am I going to do about you?" I asked him quietly when we had a moment alone. "If you disappear now, that would raise suspicions, and an overly zealous Norelli might make it official to bring you in for questioning. But if you stay…we know Jake DeAtley isn't your real name. What are you going to tell them?"

"The truth. It's Jake Kinsella, and I didn't want the man responsible for my mother's death figuring out who I was before I figured out who he was. Don't worry, I'm going to stick as close to the truth as I can."

"What if Norelli asks you details about how your mother died?"

"She burned to death. It was labeled suicide but I knew better. Don't worry, my story will check out."

No sooner had he said it than Norelli appeared. "Time to play Question and Answer."

I took a deep breath and nodded.

We left the scene to the firemen and headed for the Area 4 office where Jake and Silke and I would all be interviewed separately. I knew Silke could psychically eavesdrop and Jake…well, with his vamp-type hearing, he could probably hear me a block away. I was certain they would take their cues to verify my story.

I rode to the area office in Mom's official vehicle. "So what are we going to find when we get down there?" she asked.

"A lot of debris, I suppose."

"Bodies?"

"What's left of them. Allcock, LaTonya, Thora."

"I hope there's something to recover for Mrs. Sanford's sake."

I didn't, but I didn't say so. "I think it'll be enough that I can tell her LaTonya can rest in peace at last."

That was my story and I was sticking to it.

Anytime an officer is involved in a homicide, a review board decides whether or not the officer's actions were justifiable. I went into the meeting fighting trepidation. I hadn't done anything wrong. I hadn't killed anyone. Blaise Allcock had murdered those girls. And Blaise Allcock had been undead himself.

Who in their right mind would buy into a tale of a vampire running amok?

Until tonight, *I* hadn't. And even now, I wanted to deny it, to find another explanation, one that appealed to reason.

I must have told a convincing tale to the board, which included an Assistant Deputy Superintendent, an Assistant State's Attorney, and someone from the Office of Professional Standards, because they believed me. Even so, it was a long process that lasted until dawn.

As per department policy, I would get three days administrative duty and another visit with a department-approved shrink.

I was confident that I could handle it this time.

Mom and Silke were waiting for me when I came out into the hall, exhausted but feeling better about myself than I had in a long time. I knew who I was now. A good detective who didn't belong at the academy teaching a gym class. A sister who was starting to appreciate her special connection with her twin. A daughter who was no longer going to be hostile to the mother who, when all was said and done, loved both of her daughters and stood by them.

I was going to stop being angry.

I was going to learn how to accept being wrong. Well, occasionally.

I said, "You didn't have to wait for me."

"We wanted to," Silke said. "Everything okay?"

"It seems so."

"I'm proud of you, Shelley." Mom looked at me and made like she wanted to smooth down my hair or something. "You did everything right."

I wasn't so sure about that, but I accepted Mom's compliment graciously and gave her a hug that she returned.

Silke said, "We thought we could all go out to breakfast."

"Sorry, I can't. I still have a report to write up."

"I understand, Detective," Mom, the commander, said. "Another time, then."

"It's a date."

"I need to speak to Silke for a minute. Alone."

Mom nodded and told my twin, "I'll wait for you outside."

Once Mom was out of earshot, I asked, "The fire…how did you do that?"

"Do what?" Silke asked innocently.

So that's how we were going to play it for now. Okay. I could wait.

Writing up the report was my pleasure, even though my accounting of what had happened was riddled with half truths. In the end, I got LaTonya Sanford's murder book and closed her case with a veil of sadness cloaking me.

At least she had her justice, and that gave me a huge amount of satisfaction. And I was confident I wouldn't have those nightly talks with her anymore.

By the time I was ready to leave, Norelli was back at his desk. "Is this the way you dress for work now, Caldwell?"

I looked down at my clothes, filthy and ripped, and figured the rest of me looked worse. "I'm working undercover, pretending to be a down-and-out-CPD-detective."

Norelli barked a laugh as I walked out of the office, exhausted. I could think of nothing more appealing than showering and sleeping.

Until I heard a deep voice say, "Need a ride home?"

Turning, I smiled. "Jake." He was still here. "Whose home?"

"You name it."

"I guess it had better be my place. If I miss giving the cats breakfast, they won't speak to me all day."

"Cats speak to you?" he asked, sounding disbelieving. As we headed for the doors, Jake looked around as if what we were saying was highly confidential. "Careful, someone might think you're…you know…strange."

Laughing, I realized we were about to leave the building and it was broad daylight. I stopped short. "Um, can you…?"

Jake put on a pair of sunglasses. "I can do anything you can do." He opened the door for me. "I told you, I'm not a vampire. Does it really matter to you that I'm…well, different?"

Different could be good, I decided. If I hadn't been, I never would have found Silke in time.

I shrugged. "You know, I'm a little odd, too. I'd say we make quite a pair."

Jake grinned at me and together we walked into the sun.

Books by Patricia Rosemoor

Silhouette Bombshell

Hot Case #24

Harlequin Intrigue

*The McKenna Legacy
†Sons of Silver Springs
‡Club Undercover